PRAY FOR TEXAS

PRAY FOR TEXAS

COTTON SMITH

Published by AmazonEncore
P.O. Box 400818
Las Vegas, NV 89140

ISBN-13: 9781477842294
ISBN-10: 1477842292

To my mother,
Margaret Freeburg Smith,
and my father,
Harold Frederick Smith,
who gave me life and love.

This title was previously published by Dorchester Publishing; this version has been reproduced from the Dorchester book archive files.

Chapter One

His cold cheek felt the Yankee bullet humming a death song past him just as his half-dozing brain realized what it meant. The lead spat venom into a grizzled tree trunk next to his gray cavalry hat and rattled loose a string of icicles resting on a forlorn branch. There was no time to curse the frigid weather for numbing him into carelessness, only time to react. Confederate cavalryman Rule Cordell dropped alongside his horse and pulled the .44 Colt pistol free from the flapped saddle holster.

Cordell's first shot, from under his horse's neck, missed as he spurred toward the foreboding figure, framed by breath frost and tardy gunsmoke. A hundred feet behind Cordell's left shoulder was the cutaway edge of a murky Virginia forest. The Union rider had evidently been following the same frozen dirt road through the thickly timbered region, only from the opposite direction. His blue winter cape was barely visible against the dusk-laden dark green of congregated pine, willow oak, and buckthorn. Only the tiny white glimmers of widened eyes—and brass uniform buttons—defined the target.

Lieutenant Cordell had been riding almost asleep in the saddle, instead of paying attention to what was ahead of him. The Union rider probably could have waited another minute, had a much better shot, and Cordell still wouldn't have seen him. But that advantage was gone now. Cordell's big-shouldered roan thundered toward the blue silhouette like a huge, snorting bullet.

The Yankee scout frantically recocked his Spencer rifle as Cordell charged toward him. The Yank's second shot was wild, tearing into an overhanging branch closer to where Cordell had been than where he was now, and dislodging long icicles that had taken up residence. Cordell's second shot was deadly, slamming into the man's chest. His third shot followed so quickly, there was no distinction between gun blasts, and it hit the Yankee in the stomach as he flew from his horse.

Suddenly all was quiet again. Fading echoes of the gunfire were dragged away for later devouring by the immutable, black world of trees. Even the noises of approaching nightfall that should have been in the hilly forest were absent, as if everything was holding its breath to see what would happen next. Only a stream, somewhere off the trail, kept whispering its tale of hardiness. Feeble pink streaks of the dying January sun in early 1865 highlighted a frozen sky, barely seen above the endless treetops. A mountain ridge hinted its presence in the horizon.

Cordell eased his nervous horse toward the fallen soldier lying among brown undergrowth; its hooves clattered eerily in the numbing silence of the wooded pathway. It would soon be fully dark and he was a long way from camp. But that wasn't bothering him. What troubled him was getting caught like this out in the open. He should have been watching for enemies close to the tree line. No, he should have been riding in the forest, not on the only road through it. A greenhorn mistake, one he was lucky to recover from.

And he was curious. Why was a Union cavalryman in this part of the forest? There weren't supposed to be any Union forces near. And usually where you found a Union cavalry scout, Union armies weren't too far behind. Cordell's cavalry company was assigned the task of looking for just those kinds of signs. Not waiting for the traditional spring resumption of battle, Grant was using his tremendous numerical superiority for all it was worth to end the War of Northern Aggression. He had pushed his men forward during the worst winter since the conflict began. Rain and mud took turns dancing with ice and snow.

Lee's Army of Northern Virginia was now nearly surrounded; Union troops occupied miles of entrenched lines from Petersburg to Richmond. Sherman had marched all the way to the sea. Thomas had ripped apart the gallant John Bell Hood in Tennessee; the loss of Hood's leg in battle was an awful, but apt, symbol of his army's defeat. Sheridan had left most of the Shenandoah Valley in flames. And J. E. B. Stuart, the reckless and cheery cavalry general, had been killed months before near Yellow Tavern, leaving men like Cordell leaderless in spirit, if not fact.

If Grant could keep Lee occupied, the wily general wouldn't be able to slip through to the western mountains to fight on. There was no way Lee would be allowed to sacrifice Richmond to connect with Johnson under siege in South Carolina. Still, Lee was always looking for a way to take the offensive. But for the moment, he must sacrifice that tactic to protect the Confederates' last supply connection to the rest of the country, the Southside Railroad. Supplies were already few and far between for his harried army. The South's overall condition was fast growing intolerable. Starvation was taking more lives than Yankee bullets. Their economy was collapsing; it took $45 in Confederate money to buy a pound of coffee in Richmond these days, another $25 to get a pound of butter.

Yesterday, a Rebel division, from Major General John Gordon's undermanned II Corps, had vacated a breastworks five miles west of here, moving to reinforce the two divisions of Lieutenant General James Longstreet's I Corps. Under Lee's direction, Longstreet's challenge was to keep that fragile railroad intact. A second Gordon division was already headed toward Hill's operation to give added support. The ailing Lieutenant General A. P. Hill held the Confederate right with his III Corps strung out west, all the way to where the Boydton Plank Road crossed Hatcher's Run.

Other Rebel units were on the move to the same area, with orders to engage Union soldiers wherever they found them. Lee expected a direct Federal attack somewhere along this desperate Confederate line. Always the realist, he knew his forces were in no shape to take on any extended challenge but also knew they had no choice. Losing the railroad would leave the South with no means of transporting men or supplies. Not even Lee could overcome that.

Assigned to Longstreet's I Corps, Cordell was a part of the cavalry company ordered to determine Union movement. The horsemen were split into patrols scouring the land for information the beleaguered Army of Northern Virginia desperately needed if they were to have any chance of survival. Two days before, Cordell's patrol, under the direction of Captain Thomas Wilson, had confirmed Federal reinforcement on the far side of the Boydton Plank Road, nearly eight miles west of the torn-up Weldon Railroad and ten miles southwest of Petersburg.

Cordell hadn't seen any of his fellow cavalry scouts since then. He had eaten only once and couldn't remember feeling so weary. A piece of hard corn bread, a raw potato, and the last of his jerky. Still, a hunch—no, more like a nagging worry—had forced him to ride through this forest instead of returning to the relative comfort of camp.

His long brown hair brushed against broad shoulders as he slipped from the saddle to examine the dead soldier. Cordell's wide-brimmed cavalry hat, barely holding a scruffy eagle feather instead of a cavalry plume, was pulled down hard on his forehead. His butternut uniform was dirty; an old bullet hole, black and menacing, decorated the upper right sleeve. Half of the original braid and buttons were missing. He looked nearly as wild as he was.

His great gauntlets offered little warmth to his chilled fingers. His dark eyes were rimmed with red and barely visible between the low brim and the pulled-up collar of his long gray coat. His young, chiseled face was reddened by winter exposure, thinned by the South's lack of food, and hardened by the war.

Hanging from his left earlobe was a small stone, a Comanche warrior's earring. Around his neck, on a dirty leather thong, was a tiny buckskin pouch; both were gifts of spirit medicine from an old and dying shaman he had met before leaving Texas for this mad conflict. Cordell remembered the feeble wise man fondly as he pushed the dangling pouch back inside his shirt.

He and Taullery had been welcomed and stayed in a

11

Comanche camp just south of the Red River for three days. The tribe was headed north for the Nations. He remembered the old man wanted to see him and, in broken English, asked Cordell to pray for him. He gave him the gifts along with a prayer of his own. The old shaman had not lived to see the sun go down that day. Cordell was told by grieving tribesmen that the shaman said the young man was close to the white man's Great Spirit and wanted to be ready to meet all of the spirits. Cordell never figured how he knew his father was a minister. That was the winter of 1862, but it seemed like a century ago, not the three years that had passed. Texas seemed like another world, another life.

On his inside collar was pinned the dried stem of a rose, its life and its red petals long gone. The flower was a reminder of Stuart; the dramatic cavalry officer always wore a red rose on his jacket—or a love knot of red ribbons when roses weren't in season. The rose had been given to Cordell, along with several other men, by Stuart's widow, and he had never taken it off. Somewhere in one of his pockets were a few dried petals.

"Easy, Roanie, it's all right," he reassured his horse, who was flinching at the smell of fresh blood. Cordell rubbed its cold ears and patted the hard chest of the tired animal with his gloved hands. "Wish I had me some grain, boy. You've more than earned it, yessir, you have."

He kneeled beside the dead man, holding his reins in his left hand and his pistol in the right, looking first to see if it was someone he knew. A reflex reaction. As if, somehow, it would be. The ruddy face with the thin nose, strawberry-blond mustache, and thick sideburns was a stranger's. Cordell's fingers gently closed still eyelids over unseeing eyes. He took a deep breath and wondered if the man had a wife and children, then shook away the thought.

It still shocked him to see a man in death, a stranger whose life he had ripped away, taking all of his tomorrows. His dreams. Taking him away from those that loved him. Forever. War was a mite easier when it was long range, when a man didn't have to see close up what he'd done to another man. But this was what war was really like, and he had seen too many of his friends the same way. That thought didn't help much, but it was something.

It didn't help much, either, to realize that he should have been the one lying there, unseeing, with a Yankee examining his still body. If the Yankee had been a better shot, or savvy enough to wait...

Cordell's father's stern face floated into his mind. A short, portly, and bespectacled minister who saw himself as a singular force of righteousness and intelligence, Reverend Aaron Cordell expected his every word to be acclaimed, and everyone in his small Waco, Texas, parish to seek his divinely inspired guidance—in all things of the flesh and commerce.

"Who gave you this right to take a life? Only God has that right. Those who take another's life will be plunged into almighty damnation. Yea, verily, I say unto you, it is the word of the righteous God Almighty.," For an instant, Cordell was a little boy again, looking up at his self-righteous father. That would be what Aaron Cordell would be saying if he were here. Young Rule Cordell grimaced as his father slapped him across the face with a leather strap. The Rebel cavalryman squeezed shut his eyes and tried to drive his father's image back into its closed door in his memory.

Forcing himself to concentrate, he examined the uniform. A lieutenant. Same as Cordell, only this was

13

an infantry lieutenant. That would explain why he wasn't wearing the customary long boots of a Yankee cavalryman. This wasn't a cavalryman at all, this was a mounted officer riding advance for the troops. Had to be. Pulling back the dead man's overcape far enough to see the insignia on his upper sleeve, Cordell hissed through clinched teeth. It was the blue cloverleaf patch of Major General Andrew Humphrey's II Corps. What were they doing around here?

The answer hit him where the nagging concern had been riding. This forest trail ran right through the abandoned Rebel breastworks—where his fellow scouts were camped—and then straight on to Hatcher's Run. If Yankees were coming through this trail, they could slide unseen beyond the entrenched Yankee forces at the Southside Railroad and hit Hill's overextended line where it was completely vulnerable.

"Damn! Somebody's read Lee's mind and plans on making him pay dear for it," Cordell muttered.

In the dead lieutenant's holster was a Dean & Adams .44 double-action revolver. English made. Five shot. Cordell opened the flap and removed the gun. His long butternut-colored coat flickered open, revealing three other revolvers—one in a regulation flapped holster and two more shoved into the wide belt carrying the holster and a small cartridge box. Their only commonality was their .44 caliber.

He shoved the new pistol into the belt at his back. Across his long-skirted waistcoat was a bandolier of small pockets holding paper and copper cartridges, as well as loose powder and balls. From the bullet box on the Union scout's pistol belt, he kept enough new loads for his pistol and shoved the rest into an empty bandolier pocket. In spite of the cold, he smoothly slid new caps on the nipples of the .44's, added charge and ball, and returned the reloaded weapon to the right-hand saddle holster. Strapped in place with leather string, two holsters were in front and two more in back.

Long ago, he quit carrying a saber, favoring saddle pistols instead. It was one of a few military tactics he didn't share with Stuart. The famed general was rarely without his fine French sword, set off by a cavalry sash of golden silk with tasseled ends to match his golden spurs and a horseman's coat lined with scarlet. Cordell preferred a pistol in both hands and the reins in his teeth when they hit a Yankee line—but his devotion to Stuart was in no way lessened by a difference in fighting style.

The dead man's horse stood trembling in the middle of the road where it had skittered and stopped after its rider went off. Cordell rose and walked slowly toward the animal, talking softly, leading his own stout roan. After a scared whinny, the Yankee horse lowered its head and Cordell patted the brown nose and neck.

"Easy, boy. It's all right. You're all right. Not going to hurt you, no, not going to hurt you," he said, grabbing the loose reins. His eyes examined the horse for injuries and saw none.

After leading the animal close to the tree line, he opened the saddlebags hidden beneath a tightly rolled double-wool blanket and a separate rubber sheet tied to the back of the saddle. Photographs he didn't want to see were close to the top. He let them flutter to the ground. Then he felt badly about it and picked them up. There was a testament pen, container of ink, papers. Cards. A second shirt. Socks. No, he wanted none of that. Here! Here, is what he hoped to find. Three days' ration of salt pork, remains of bacon, six strips of jerked beef, a small bag of coffee, another of dried, desiccated vegetables. A fat sack of rice and another of flour, mixed in with a tin cup, fork, knife, spoon, and a tin plate. He devoured a strip of jerky and three dried carrots in large gulps. Then he spotted a small muslin bag of shredded tobacco and a sheath of cigarette papers and shoved them into his coat pocket.

"Man alive, there's enough here for the whole patrol—for a damn week! Even Taullery can't beat this!" he exclaimed, then bit his lower lip as he realized how loud he had spoken.

But the thought continued in his head. No wonder the North was winning: Men fight better on full stomachs. Only the energetic ways of Ian Taullery, his best friend and a tireless collector of things, kept the patrol in food. It was magical the way Taullery always found what the patrol needed. No matter where they were. A packhorse was now assigned to him on each patrol to carry all the stuff he collected.

"Hey, you're going to like this," Cordell said, looking back at his horse as he discovered a wrapped nose bag filled with grain at the bottom of the second saddlebag.

He'd seen enough. Grabbing his knife from his right long boot, he cut the holding strings with practiced ease. Quickly, the Union blanket and saddlebags were retied to the back of his own saddle, over his own flat, empty saddlebags. Before leaving, he slid the photographs inside the dead man's uniform. He swung easily onto the prancing roan and resumed his probe eastward.

A handful of dry rice in his fist was shoved into his mouth. He savored the small pieces, tasting each grain before swallowing. A swig of his canteen washed down the rest of his instant meal. To forget the continued gnawling of his stomach, he squeezed his knees against the horse's belly and the animal responded with a smooth lope toward the road's crest a quarter mile ahead. The dead Yankee's horse watched them go, started to follow, but was attracted to some brown grass at the lip of the forest and decided to graze instead. A smoke would taste real good, but he dared not; the tiniest glow could be seen by a knowing man from a long way off.

He heard them before seeing them. Infantry. A forced march. Little talking but a full orchestra of scuffling shoe leather, clanking canteens, and rustling woolen pants as the day was swiftly turning into night. They showed no signs of stopping to bivouac or even pause for a meal break.

Looking first to his right, then his left, Cordell reined his horse in the second direction and trotted thirty yards off the road, into the security of the black forest. Field glasses from the flapped casing adjoining his left-hand saddle pistol holster were soon in gloved hands. He focused first on a flag, shivering in the cold dusk, carried dutifully by a large soldier with wide cheeks, a narrow mustache, and chewing a huge wad of tobacco. It was Humphrey's II Corps, all right. From the length of the marchers, at least two thousand. A full corps. Apparently, they were undertaking an all-night march to surprise and outflank Hill, just as he had guessed earlier. There could be no other reason for this kind of movement at this time of the day. Not here, anyway.

Without thinking consciously about it, he withdrew the Henry lever-action rifle from its saddle boot and sought the target of the mounted officer at the front of the long line. He had taken the gun from a dead 1st D.C. cavalryman after a skirmish two months before. The 1st D.C. was the only regiment in the Army of the Potomac all armed with Henrys. It was a magnificent weapon, delivering fifteen .44 rounds before reloading. No wonder the North was winning, he had observed to himself, after examining the prize on the quiet battlefield.

His lone firing wouldn't do much to stop them, but it might make the Yanks uneasy, especially after they found their advance rider down. Wham! Wham! Wham! He levered eight split-second shots into the blur of blue. The mounted officer hit an invisible wall and flew backward, leaving only a riderless sorrel that raced into the trees, straight toward Cordell. The snorting animal, with stirrups flapping wildly, skittered past the rapidly firing Confederate scout and raced toward an unknown destination in the thick woods. Three troopers stuttered, twisted, and fell against their marching comrades. Another spun halfway around, grabbing a crimson spot on his dark blue coat. A fifth screamed and doubled over. A sixth tried to say something, but only blood came out of his mouth as he toppled forward. Cordell's eighth shot whined past a trooper who was grabbing his own rifle and bringing it to his shoulder.

Deep within his soul came a sound that began like the faraway rumble of early thunder, growing louder and higher, and louder and higher, as if it had a life of its own separate from his throat. A part scream, part war cry, part triumphant yell that curdled the blood of the entire forest—and the men in blue on its road. The Rebel yell was as wild as the gray warrior who gave it.

"Over there! Over there!" screamed the warning. Rifle shots wildly explored the forest, frantically seeking the unseen wraith that had descended upon them. Cordell levered his rifle to continue the assault, but it jammed on the ninth shell. There was no time to determine the cause. Rule Cordell slapped his roan's withers with his rifle and disappeared deeper into the safety of the dense trees and thick underbrush.

Branches grabbed at his coat and hat, trying to hold him for the Yankees, but he lay against his horse's neck and raced on. The roan's ground-eating gallop was hampered by heavy thicket, stunted pines, and uneven land, as well as the unending clusters of trees. They rammed their way through a thick entanglement of dead vine, cut hard to the left to avoid a sudden ravine, and rode recklessly through the wooded darkness.

Soon the shouting and gunfire were only faint memories. Cordell swung the horse down through a dry stream bed, loped through the rock-lined ravine for a hundred yards, then went up a shallow ridge and past a spitting waterfall. He followed the bank of a shallow, frozen stream linked haphazardly to the dry bed until reaching a bottom growth sunken within thinning timber.

Cordell reined the tiring roan to an easy walk and listened. Only the sounds of undisturbed woodlands. An unseen owl challenged his intrusion. The heavy breath of both man and horse floated like white clouds around them. He could barely see beyond his horse's ears, as night had fully settled upon the forest. Overhead, no stars had dared to enter the winter sky as yet, and only a thin crust of a moon had appeared. In a sheltered half-circle of stunted pine, he dismounted. It was urgent to return to his patrol, but without resting his horse, he would never make it. The proud animal was white-eyed and wheezing.

He dared not unsaddle the roan, but decided loosening the cinch would be safe enough. After the damp leather straps released their pressure on the roan's belly, he ran his hands around each leg down to the hoof, pressing lightly on the tendons as he moved. No reaction from the roan. No tenderness anywhere. He smiled grimly after his inspection proved negative.

"Well, you're a sound hoss, Roanie. I haven't managed to hurt you none yet," Cordell announced, and began checking the animal's hooves, picking away any small stones or frozen turf captured in the iron shoes with his boot knife.

He let the animal stand quietly while he rummaged through the Yankee saddlebags. Hot food would have been wonderful, but he dared not have a fire, and the ground was too hard to dig a "guerrilla fire," a hole lined with stones to hold a small amount of heat and then covered with more stones to mask any light. He chewed ravenously on one dried vegetable after another, and bit into a piece of cold bacon.

"Well, it ain't a helluva lot worse than Whisper's cooking," he said, chuckling to himself.

One of the dead Yank's cigarettes would taste good, but its tiny light would be a beacon in this blackness. Although pipes, cigars and chaw were much more popular, he liked the quick kick from the paper smokes. It seemed to fit wartime better. Faster and cheaper. A lot cheaper when it came from a dead Yank.

Chapter Two

After the roan had quit breathing hard, Cordell fastened the Yankee nose bag over its wet mouth. The strong horse stomped its front hooves in appreciation. Cordell sat down beside the roan and ate silently of both vegetable and bacon. Remembering his friends back at camp might not have much, if any, food either—in spite of Taullery's ingenious ways—Cordell stopped abruptly and returned the rest of his newfound bounty to the saddlebags.

Daily meat rations were down to three, maybe four, ounces—scarcely more than a mouthful—for each Confederate soldier on the front line. Food boxes from home, long a supplement to the meager army issue, rarely got delivered anymore. One of the macabre jokes making the rounds in the trenches was that the Confederate supply system should be assigned to the Yankees and the South would defeat them before spring.

Cordell's patrol had fared better than most of the Rebel army and better than the rest of the company of horsemen. That was due to Ian Taullery's constant lookout for food and supplies. On the first day of this patrol alone, Taullery had found a deserted cooling house left by some Virginia farmer. Within the small stone structure, he had brought back a slab of salted pork and two jars of pickled beets. That, plus fellow cavalryman Billy Ripton's last box from his mother and father, was the only food the patrol had shared for a week.

"Well, Roanie, we've got a long ride ahead of us. Are ya up to it, boy?" he turned and asked the busily munching horse.

He slowly got to his feet. Sleep was caressing his mind, flirting with his logic. Only a half hour of sleep, that's all. Only a half hour. He shook his head to push away the insidious thought. He had rested long enough. Longer would mean many men would die. Friends would die. Maybe the South, just for a few hours of sweet sleep. Maybe he would die, discovered by the oncoming blue sea of soldiers behind him. Yet the seductive logic of resting a little longer would not release him. His vision blurred.

His father spoke from behind him. "Son, your mother has chosen to leave us. How she could do such a wicked thing to me, to embarrass me, God's chosen servant, is unfathomable. Her sinful ways will be punished—I assure you. As God is my witness, she will rue this day."

"What do you mean?!" the boy cried out, disbelieving.

His mother was the only thing that seemed right and good in his small world. Her gentle assurance made his father's frequent self-righteous wrath almost bearable. Naming him "Rule" was her wish, to make her son into a king, something important. His father had hated the name and thought it blasphemous, but his mother had refused to change her mind in spite of the beating that followed her announcement. Rule's name had already been written in the family Bible as such, so even Reverend Cordell wouldn't cross it out. Reverend Cordell wanted his son to be a "junior" so he called young Rule by his middle name, "Aaron," if he called him by name at all.

"Aaron, your mother...rode out last night, with three cows, our bull, and the wagon. She left with... that no-good . . . Henry . . . Johnson," the elder Cordell stated as evenly as his bloated anger would allow. His face was crimson with unsatisfied rage as he removed his wire-framed eyeglasses and wiped them vigorously with a handkerchief.

Young Rule Cordell would never see his mother again. He cried all that long-ago day. It was the last time he would do so.

The rebel warrior, Rule Cordell, staggered, trying to regain his mind and fight off the gloom that sought the last of his courage. Long-forgotten furies inside his mind had been loosened by the lack of sleep, food, and companionship. A bewitching wind suddenly punctuated his weariness, sweeping a light snow ahead of it through the trees. The roan fought the tightening of the cinch, crow-hopped once, twice, but seemed to understand their need to move on. Cordell poured the last of his canteen into his hat for the animal to savor.

Something behind him moved. A faint sound, almost nothing, yet not of the forest's normal music. Staying alive meant sensing such a tiny misplaced chord. Cordell eased his right hand inside his coat and withdrew a pistol, keeping it and his body close to the horse. He took a step to his right, as if to check the horse's left rear leg, and spun around. The cock of the heavy pistol crackled in the night air.

A dog!

A large-boned hound dog, a furry mass of black, gray, and brown, stood at the crest of the small clearing. It made no attempt to bark, and Cordell was grateful for that. He shoved the pistol back into place but replaced it with his knife. If the dog began to howl or yap, he would have to kill the animal with his blade or risk giving away his position.

He should ride on, but the hound, with a white spot covering both its muzzle and right eye, looked starved. The dog's ribs were extended; it's tongue stuck sideways out of its mouth; sad eyes searched for a friend.

"Damn," Cordell muttered, "why me?"

But he knew he couldn't ride on just yet. He cut a long slice of the salt pork and tossed it toward the starving dog. The animal stared first at him, then at the meat, then again at him. Finally hunger overtook fear and he lunged for the food. Cordell chuckled and cut off another slice. After downing the second morsel, the hound came closer, its flattened tail reappearing in a vigorous wag. He cut a third piece from the remaining meat and rebuckled the saddlebag straps. Leaning down, he offered the scrap to the approaching dog. As the hound ate, Cordell scratched its long ears and around its neck. The dog licked his hand in appreciation.

"Well, friend, that's all I can spare. You've just had more meat than a Johnny Reb gets in two days. You'd better find those Yanks back there. They've got all kinds of chow."

With that, he remounted and headed out. Glancing behind, he shook his head at the sight of the hound following him.

"Well, Roanie, looks like we've picked up a companion. That all right with you, boy? Yeah, me too. Long as he keeps quiet."

Their progress back to the road was slow. No trail offered assistance, only the humps and bumps of wooded darkness. Gradually, he returned to the frozen pathway, where they could make faster time and it would be easier on his horse. Again he listened for sounds of Yankee infantry before entering the stark openness of the road. Nothing. He had either slowed them down with his shooting or he was farther ahead than he thought. Either way, though, there was little time. Around him, a light snow was decorating the forest with sparkles of white. He glanced down; the hound was at his roan's flank, looking upward into Cordell's face.

"We're headed for camp, boy," he said to the dog. "You'd better go home. Go on now."

Shrugging his shoulders, Cordell began to wave his hand vigorously to shoo the dog away. Tilting its large ugly head, the hound sat on its haunches as if waiting for Cordell to quit the gyrations and move out.

He chuckled and said, "Well now, so you want to be a Johnny Reb, do yah? I reckon you've already learned the no-food part. Come on, then."

Five hours later, a fierce winter wind slammed against Cordell as he broke through the last protective row of trees and entered a wide clearing. The light snow had ended sometime during the night, but the cold had remained in wait for him. The frigid slap woke him from the sleepy sweetness he had been riding in for the last mile or so. He blinked twice to make certain he wasn't hallucinating again. Earlier, he was certain a pack of wolves encircled him, but it was only his trailing hound. Then he saw his father with a bullwhip, which turned out to be a branch waving in the night breeze. Three times he thought they were nearing the clearing only to realize it wasn't close.

This was real, though. Perched on the rolling incline ahead was an abandoned Rebel breastworks where the scout patrol camped. It looked smaller than he recalled. Melancholy had reentered his tired brain during the return, bringing a stark loneliness. More dark childhood memories simmered within him, memories of his minister father releasing violent frustrations on his only son. But the unquestioning attention of a stray dog had kept him going during the long night. Not anger about his father's evil, bent ways. He had long ago dealt with that the best he could.

In its place was a growing realization that many of his fellow Confederates had decided the war was lost. That was tantamount to treason to him. A man was either fighting on for victory—or he was the enemy, regardless of the uniform he might be wearing. It sickened his stomach every time he thought of the Rebel soldiers he had seen yesterday morning, headed for Union lines to surrender. They had decided to quit and go home.

He couldn't. Couldn't go home. Couldn't quit. He had given his word to a dying Stuart. Cordell and many other men in tattered butternut uniforms would keep on, in spite of what everyone thought, in spite of the insanity of it all. And now, behind him, was Yankee infantry marching nonstop to punish the weary Army of Northern Virginia at their weakest point. For the Federals to come this way, they must have known the breastworks ahead had been abandoned. And he was the only Confederate who knew their strategy.

An idea had been growing within him, struggling with the negative frustration and driving loneliness to the musty corners of his mind. If his friends agreed to the wild plan, it might be a way to slow down the advancing Yankees long enough for Longstreet to move men to support the attack on Hill or even counter it.

His back trail was barely evident as the north wind challenged every hoofprint in the thin snow. The hound's smaller prints at the heels of his roan weren't visible. If the horsemen didn't agree, Cordell had decided he would do what he could. Alone. Without thinking, he jabbed his spurs into his stumbling roan to punctuate his determination. The animal winced and responded with a wild-eyed trot. Cordell realized what he had done and guilt washed across him. He slowed the courageous animal to a walk, then to a complete stop.

Patting its neck, he dismounted and apologized. "Damn, Roanie, I'm sorry. Ol' Billy Rip'd be all over me if he saw me do that. He'll be chewing on me bad enough when he sees how hard I've pushed you, boy."

Billy Ripton—or "Billy Rip," as Cordell liked to call him—was a round-faced cowboy from the same region around Waco, Texas as Cordell and Taullery. That had immediately made him one of them. Only fifteen, he was an example of the depth of the South's shortage in manpower. In spite of his age, the husky man-child was good with horses; Cordell liked his gentle ways with them, compared to most horse wranglers, who used every kind of punishment to break a mount. Such care was vital now, since good horses weren't any more plentiful than any kind of food.

That was a marked difference from the early days when the flamboyant Stuart wore out horses as well as men without a backward glance. Only two of the patrol's horses were now Southern-bred animals: Cordell's roan and Billy Ripton's blue-gray gelding. The rest were captured steeds.

27

Thinking of Billy Rip's reaction to the tired roan, Cordell decided he would walk the rest of the way. Fatigue cut across his chiseled face and wouldn't let go. He nearly fell as his wobbly legs hit the ground. Snow popped up as his boots struck the frozen earth. But he walked on, like a man with wooden legs, leading the exhausted horse. The hound jumped at his elbow until Cordell stopped to pet him.

He entered the silent earthworks, constructed of cut logs and mud, from the northern edge. Patting the neck of his horse, sweaty in spite of the cold, Cordell gathered his thoughts and mentally surveyed the quiet camp. Not even the darkness could completely hide the mosaic pattern of a quickly dispatched army behind the hastily built log walls.

Three blankets were under a tree, folded precisely into large squares. Worn or forgotten homespun cotton shirts, pants, underwear, hats, and butternut wool shell jackets were scattered throughout the tramped-down terrain, all made more forlorn by the pallor of nightfall and the earlier snowfall. Dark shapes on the ground thirty yards away were sleeping comrades. Little more than a black blob was the distant shape of a bloated dead horse. The frigid air kept the stench from denying close occupation. He was surprised there weren't more dead animals, the way the Confederates were treating them.

A misshapen artillery shell, two empty grapeshot canisters, and a tin canteen with a bullet hole lay next to a small pile of firewood, peeking out from under a shallow layer of snow. An empty whiskey bottle was cradled on top. A trail of busted water barrel staves and bent tent poles were strewn off to the north, abruptly ending and leading nowhere, like drowning men in a sea of white and brown. It looked no different than it had when he rode out. He wondered if Taullery had checked out the area and gathered anything of value.

A glowing cheroot had earlier given away the location of the tall man with a neatly trimmed, blond beard. He was singing softly to himself. A good tenor voice it was, Cordell thought. The song was "The Southern Soldier Boy." The tall man, leaning against the timbered wall of the simple fortress, knew only a few words: "Yo! ho! yo! ho! ho! ho! ho! ho! ho! ho! He is my only joy. He is the darling of my heart, my Southern soldier boy." They were continuously repeated after several bars of humming the tune that was actually "The Boy with the Auburn Hair."

It was Cordell's best friend, Ian Taullery. If there were words Cordell wanted to say, the cold had them bottled deep inside him. Nevertheless, his joy at seeing his old friend again was enough to make him forget his weariness for the moment. Taullery was the only one awake and standing guard. That was typical. Cordell didn't know anyone with more nervous energy than his friend. He didn't know anyone more methodical, either.

Even the bite of an apple would produce a detailed assessment of its nourishment value, texture, and color from the tall cavalryman. Taullery said he could actually feel the swallowed morsel slide down his throat and hit his stomach. The description would usually include a ranking of how this apple compared to others he had eaten. Of course, he could tell where the apple had been stored, just by its smell. And smelling something was always the first thing.

Everything Ian Taullery did was carefully done. Cordell had never seen anyone take longer to light a cigar than his friend, carefully trimming the end, turning it around a match flame, and examining the ash until he was satisfied the smoke was ready. It didn't matter what it was; apple, cigar, or battle, Ian Taullery rarely did anything without thinking through all the steps first. That wasn't an excuse for not taking action. He just liked to know what he was doing before he did it.

The tall Confederate cavalryman knew who the incoming rider was when he was merely a silhouette in the sullen blackness. It didn't surprise him that his friend had picked up a stray dog while on patrol. It wasn't the first time. Taullery smiled to himself, thinking how fierce most men saw Rule Cordell—and how gentle he truly could be. Taullery's worry had grown with each hour; every other scout had returned long ago. There was no way he could sleep with his friend not accounted for, so he had volunteered for guard duty.

Overactive and gregarious by the will of the gods, sleep usually occupied only a few hours nightly anyway. There was always something more important to do, or see—or worry about. In that regard, Taullery resembled the vaunted J. E. B. Stuart, but it was Cordell who more closely mirrored the late leader's reckless manner. Taullery loved the dash and glamour of hit-and-run cavalry engagements and the lively rehashing of the day's encounters around the campfire. Not the tedious, lonely—and dangerous—work of scouting. Cordell was probably the only man who did. Or if he didn't like it, he never said. That's what kept chewing on Taullery's mind: no one took chances like Cordell; no one pushed himself harder, as if the very outcome of the war depended on his personal initiative.

"Been getting a little worried, Rule. You've been gone since yesterday morning. I see you're walking. Horse hurt?" Taullery said, the words of concern tumbling out with frost smoke decorating them.

"Well, I used him up, that's for sure. Didn't see any choice," Cordell replied, and shook his head slowly, mostly to clear it of the cobwebs nesting there from the lack of sleep.

"Looks to me you damn near wore 'im into crawlin'," Taullery observed as he took hold of the roan's right front leg and ran his hand along it. "Tender. He's not going to be worth much for a few days. Better have Billy Rip check him out real good. What's up?"

"Humphrey's Two Corps is coming right at us. Headed for the open end of our flank. They're marching all night. I figure they plan to catch our boys all stretched out and busy the other direction," Cordell said slowly as he rolled his neck to relieve the tiredness. "They've already got Longstreet, Gordon—and Hill—pinned everywhere else, trying to keep that damn railroad working."

"Damn! They were thirty miles north of here last night!" Taullery challenged, taking the cheroot from his mouth as he rose from the roan. "Where the hell did you pick 'em up?"

"On the forest road."

"So they're headed right through here."

"Yeah, then, right on to daylight—to the open end of Hill's line."

"Well, maybe they're just reinforcements for Meade."

"Thought about that. Why march all night, if they are? And why come this way? Even if he knows they're coming, Hill doesn't have any troops close to stop 'em. He's gonna need time, Ian, while Longstreet moves in some—from somewhere."

The energetic cavalryman looked at the dark horizon from where his intense friend had come, as if to confirm the Union advance to himself. Of course, it was empty, not yet showing even the virgin hints of dawn. But it wasn't like Cordell to overreact or misread. He was accurate and direct; some would say rude.

Cordell's face was contorted, his concern was back to the horse again, and he said quietly, "Got any grain? I fed him some Yankee stuff real quick back there in the woods—but he deserves a good easy supper. How about water?"

"Do I look like some damn stable boy?" Taullery teased, forgetting his friend's bad news for the moment.

"Ah...matter of fact, you do. Like that fancy one we saw in Richmond. You know, the mansion with that..."

"Rebecca Wadison."

"Yeah, her. Remember that ex-slave caring for her daddy's horses? Dapper fellow. Well, he was always pressed and dressing fine like you. Come to think of it, you look a little like him," Cordell said with a wry smile, enjoying the relief from the worry he had carried alone through the forest.

They both chuckled and pushed each other playfully. Even at this time of night and the bitterness of the winter, Taullery looked as if he had just stepped from a victory parade. His uniform was actually only months old, bartered from a Richmond tailor; his polished high cavalry boots had been yanked from a dead Yankee officer. Big-roweled spurs were a prize found on a different battlefield a year ago.

One side of his soft hat brim was pinned against the crown with an ornate crest. An ostrich plume appeared as fresh as the day they had joined. His gauntlets carried a small decoration on each glove flap, a small embroidered rose—his own reminder of Stuart. Unlike Cordell, his own rose at their leader's burial had long ago been replaced by a small cluster of red ribbons. A bright blue silk scarf tied loosely around Taullery's neck Cordell knew was from a female admirer. He was there when she gave it to his friend as they rode off to join the War. Set against his butternut uniform, it didn't match well, but he wore it constantly.

"Who's your friend? Union deserter? Or you starting to collect things too?" Taullery said casually, pointing to the hound and letting white cigar smoke curl slowly around his face before escaping. The cigars were a treasure he had found on a dead Yankee major last week, along with a trunk filled with other interesting baubles, like the crest that now held his rolled brim in place and a small leather sack containing a hundred dollars in gold coins.

"Yeah, I reckon," Cordell said, embarrassed.

He glanced down at the dog, walking close to his heels, and pulled the dead Yankee's tobacco sack from his pocket. After he rolled a cigarette, Taullery snapped a match to life from his belt buckle and cupped the flame in his hands for his friend to light the smoke.

"Where'd you get the tobacco? Yankee?" Taullery asked as he tossed the dead match aside.

"Yeah."

Taullery's palms pushed restlessly on ivory handles of twin silver-plated .44 Colts carried in nonregulation holsters strapped to a wide belt. They were his favorite possessions, brought with him from Texas prior to the War—along with a silver-mounted saddle, whose source not even Cordell knew. Cordell couldn't remember a night when Taullery didn't clean the pistols thoroughly.

Taullery called to the dog, lifting his hands from his guns and clapping them together, "Come here, boy. Come here." The dog glanced at Cordell for approval before responding, and both men laughed. Taullery kneeled and scratched the dog's ears and neck as a welcome.

"Looks like the Wilkersons' ol' hound," Taullery observed.

"A little. The Wilkersons' was bigger."

"What are you going to do with him?" Taullery asked.

"B-r-r-r-r. Colder'n ol' Ulysses S. Grant's heart out here. Got any coffee?" Cordell avoided the question with another.

"Hell, I thought maybe you were running back here with some Yankee beef stew, or some thick maple syrup on a pile of hotcakes. Or, better, some pretty Virginia maiden in need of a hero," Taullery said. His constant smile always made it seem as if he had a private joke oh the world.

To him, making fun of the Confederates' starvation was the only way to deal with it. Cordell's was to ignore the pain and move on. It was one of many contrasts between the two childhood friends who had grown up together in rural Texas. Taullery would talk about anything with anyone; Cordell's conversation was lean and direct, except around Taullery.

"Come on, I'll walk with you to the picket line," Taullery said, standing and letting the dog return to Cordell. "You'll never find the damn thing in the dark."

Their friendship went back a long way. It was nine-year-old Ian Taullery who got his father's shotgun and came running back to the Cordell house after he found his seven-year-old friend, Rule Cordell, beaten from another of Reverend Cordell's Bible-quoting tirades. It was a bloodied Rule Cordell who kept a determined Ian Taullery from using the weapon. A secret, shared-blood ceremony afterward, styled after an Indian blood-brother ritual Taullery had heard about, sealed their friendship for life.

Later, it was Cordell who comforted a distraut Taullery through the loss of his parents to influenza and pneumonia. Then it was Taullery who introduced Cordell to the wonders of the pistol—and to girls— and to tabacco. To this day, Taullery had seen no one as good with a handgun as his friend. Around women, however, Cordell was still shy.

"See any of our boys today?" Taullery asked, and wished he hadn't.

"Yeah, ran into six of them. Yesterday morning, I think it was. They were going to find some Yanks and surrender. Asked me to join them. Gave me this," Cordell said without emotion, pulling a folded-up piece of paper from his coat. "It's a notice from Grant. Says deserters will be welcomed, give you eight dollars apiece for your guns."

"Eight Yankee dollars, huh? That'd make you a rich man," Taullery said, staring first at the flyer, then grinning at his friend. Taullery wadded the flyer into a ball and threw it into the night.

"Yeah, almost as rich as finding sacks of gold in chests that belong to Yankee majors," Cordell responded.

Taullery chuckled at the comeback. Cordell's kidding on the subject of Rebel surrender surprised Taullery. But surely his friend had noticed the Rebel ranks getting smaller, he thought to himself. Since 1861, a force of 750,000 Confederate soldiers had taken up arms; now, in the winter of 1865, fewer than 160,000 remained to fight. The rest were either killed, dying, had gone home to their loved ones, or just surrendered. Taullery himself had known since Gettysburg—if he was honest with himself—that the War was lost.

Every day there was evidence of Confederate soldiers deserting, even whole units. If Cordell saw them, he didn't say. Deep down, Taullery worried for his friend when the inevitable destiny struck. He had seen him inconsolable after Stuart's death, wanting to ride out and find a fight, anywhere with anyone. Taullery could ride away from the awfulness of losing—but could Rule Cordell? He had seen Cordell's fighting skills ratchet ever higher as the likelihood of winning the war diminished—and wondered if they were related. Taullery hadn't dared to put his worry into words.

A long three years ago, the two friends had joined the war effort together: Taullery for grand adventure, Cordell to fight for what he called "our right to do whatever we think is best." They had immediately joined the Confederate cavalry and both been taken with its legendary leader. Cordell because of Stuart's intensity; Taullery because of Stuart's flair; both because he knew how to win.

The taller cavalryman started to tell what his latest scavaging had produced when Captain Wilson's patronizing yell cut through the late night's haze.

"Lieutenant Cordell!"

Chapter Three

Captain Thomas Wilson was a lushly whiskered, polit-
ical appointee, said to be a friend of Jefferson Davis
himself. This kind of assignment was not his idea of
winning honor and glory; it should be left to lesser
men. Cordell's arrival had managed to awaken him as
it did the two other sleeping scouts, Billy Ripton and
Whisper Jenson.

The pair, along with Taullery, had themselves been
out of the saddle only since nightfall, weary from
heavy riding. Captain Wilson had remained behind in
camp, due to a disturbing bout with diarrhea. None of
the scouts cared what he did as long as it didn't get in
their way.

"Lieutenant Cordell, you are to report first to your
commanding officer," he bellowed again as he shook
out his caped overcoat and swung it over his shoulders.

Peering down at his rumpled uniform, he brushed
away a leaf still cuddling against him from the night's

shortened sleep. The tiny shape fluttered toward the ground as Captain Wilson straightened the gold sash around his waist. He wasn't certain, but it felt as if the stomach ailment had finally left him. He wondered if Longstreet or Lee had ever had to deal with such an embarrassing situation. The two other scouts were busy re-creating a small fire that had disappeared during their rest. Cordell and Taullery ignored the officer's command and continued talking.

Cordell said offhandedly, "Be with you in a minute, Thomas."

His saddle weariness barely hid his contempt as he glanced in the direction of the struggling campfire and the obnoxious captain. His eyes caught one low-heeled brogan sitting upright in untrampled grass, as if a soldier had stepped out of it and kept on walking. A wide hole was evident in the sole. He started to point to it when Taullery noticed his Union blanket and saddlebags.

"Where'd you get these, boy? Sunday social?" Taullery asked as he put his hand on the Yankee gear.

"Yeah. There's some salt pork. A little bacon. Beef jerky. Dried vegetables. Rice. Flour. Coffee. We got anything else to eat?"

"Sure, you're with me, remember? I found a farmer who gave us a sack of dried carrots and potatoes. Some onions, too. And some cornmeal. Had a beautiful daughter too. Oh, Rule, you should have seen her. Eyes like a morning stream. Hair like...Asked me to stay...for supper. Anyway, Billy Rip shot us a grouse yesterday. So, ol' Whisper, he cooked us up some stew. Made corn bread, too. I reckon there's some of both left. The stew's a little chewy and the potatoes were overcooked. Maybe a bit too much salt, but..."

"Hey, I found a new pistol too," Rule remembered

and drew again on the cigarette, ignoring his friend's assessment of the stew. Food was pretty much food to Cordell. A white litany of smoke walked alongside his cheeks.

Taullery's eyes brightened at mention of the gun, and he asked eagerly, "Hell, you've been around me too damn long. Let's see it."

Cordell unbuttoned his long coat and revealed his four revolvers, all different makes and barrel lengths, one holstered and three in his belt. He had learned this trick from the guerrilla raiders. There was no time to reload in a cavalry fight. Each gun had been acquired in as many different running battles. He yanked the Dean & Adams revolver from his belt in the back and handed it to Taullery.

"Hey, that's a fine-lookin' piece, Rule. Doesn't quite match that other bunch of iron you've picked up. Lordy, you have a collection! Where'd you get this?" Taullery asked with appreciation as he ran his fingers over the cold steel.

"Oh, it was laying on the road."

Taullery looked up from his examination of the gun and asked dryly, "Was there a Yank attached?"

"Yeah."

"Bluebelly scout?"

"Well, sorta. Infantry officer. Riding point. He didn't have much to say. Just took to firing."

"That where you got the saddlebags?"

"Yeah."

Taullery handed back the gun as Captain Wilson yelled again, "Lieutenant Cordell! Report!"

Cordell's eyes flashed hot, but Taullery put a hand on his shoulder and calmed him. "Easy now. The dumb ass is just trying to do his job."

Taullery turned his head and yelled back, "We'll be down as soon as we picket Rule's horse. You-all put on the coffee—and heat up that stew. Better make that breakfast—for all of us. This here's one hungry Reb—and we've got a long day starin' at us!"

Cordell and Taullery walked to the picket line with the taller man leading the way. Broken, elevated terrain provided a good firing platform to the open meadow stretching out below them. Uneven rock outcroppings, as well as frozen Riptons and holes in the earth, made walking more like trying to move across the deck of a ship rolling in a sea. Left-behind gear made it more like a maze.

They stepped around a left-behind roundsheet and a torn shelter-half, parts of mess kits and empty cotton haversacks, all of which seemed to have constructed their own life pattern on the hard ground. More evidence that an army had once lived behind the temporary walls of log and mud. Taullery moved easily through them, anticipating each piece before he stepped. He made only a passing comment about already checking out the left-behind supplies and concentrated, instead, on telling about the farm girl.

Cordell turned his head away as they passed a chunk of overcooked, wormy corn bread splattered across the bottom of a big tree, along with either some kind of frozen stew—or vomit, luminescent in the pale moonlight. It was enough to make him forget about eating. His roan sniffed the remains, shook its tired head, and trotted to keep up with Cordell, who was loosely carrying the reins. Only the hound lingered at the tree until Cordell called out for him to follow.

Lying beside the spilled food were the remains of a field artillery caisson, like the deteriorating skeleton of a dead animal. A broken stock and split axle were sitting upright in a cluster of bent wheels, chains, hand spikes, and caisson rings. The howitzer itself had evidently been carried off in a wagon for later rebuilding.

Across the plain, they could see the outline of an over-turned wagon and another dead horse in harness.

Taullery stubbed his toe on an unexpected lock chain, cursed, and laughed at his clumsiness. "That's why all the ladies like to dance with me. Nimble footed I be. Watch your step. Thought I'd shoved all this old artillery crap out of the way when I made a path through here today."

"You're just getting old and careless," Cordell teased.

Taullery picked up the chain, studied it for a moment, and tossed it into the darkness. Cordell kicked aside a discarded hand spike, but saw no other discarded metal. His eyes searched the path to make certain his roan wouldn't step on something sharp. He touched one of the bent wheels as they passed, pushed away from the pathway to the horses, and looked back to check on the dog. Trotting only a few feet behind, it was interested in every new thing they encountered. Cordell smiled and whistled for the dog to keep up.

"Hope we don't have to get to our horses fast," he said dryly.

"You can thank Billy Rip for that. He wanted them on the best grass around," Taullery said. "Here we are. Looks like a quiet lot."

A picket line was strung between two sturdy willow oak trees—two mounts for each man, plus a pack-horse. Only the closest sorrel moved its head to observe their advance; the other mounts stood sleeping with heads down. After unsaddling his grateful horse, Cordell wiped down the roan with the Yankee blanket. A fury was whirling inside his tired brain over Captain Wilson's insistent clamoring. Cordell tried to make it go away; why did he resent any attempt to tell him what to do? The poor man was just doing his job, Cordell reminded himself.

Taullery grabbed a bucket from the assembled horse supplies under one of the picket trees. An outlaw wind brought a soft shower of white from the oak's branches just as he leaned over to scoop grain from the large patrol bag into an empty bucket. He jumped back, holding the partially filled bucket and shivering.

"Damn! Damn! Yikes, that is cold! Cold!" he yelled, stomped his boots, and rolled his shoulders to remove the frozen intrusion. The hound ran around him, barking and jumping playfully.

"Well, Ian, you been talking yourself down. Haven't seen prancing like that since Billy Rip tied the cinch too tight on his blue. I can see what the ladies like. Real high-stepping style there," Cordell observed, and broke out laughing. The first time in days. He quieted the dog and rubbed its ears.

"Here, Lieutenant Cordell, don't say I never gave you nothin'," Taullery said, handing him the bucket. "Damn, that crap is still back there!" he exclaimed, and patted his upper back with both hands until the frost had melted.

"And the water, suh?" Cordell asked in a voice imitating a grand Southern gentleman.

"Crick's all. Mostly, it's frozen over, but there's a right good trickle still. But you'd better let him cool down some first. Fact is, I reckon he's too hot to eat too. Better let him settle, Rule. That's one worn-out horse. After you get a bite in you, better have Billy Rip walk 'im around some."

"Yeah, you're right. Forgot how nice 'n' slow things can be," Cordell agreed, and returned the bucket to its position under the tree. "You got any of that ointment you rank so high—from that bald-headed doctor, or whatever he was?"

"Yeah, it's there. Right there. See it?" Taullery said in mock exasperation, finally pointing his finger only inches from the tin container, "Damn, man, how the hell did you see any bluebellies when you can't see a damn jug? Here, I'll see if I can get it to shoot at you. Seems like that's the only way you can spot something these days."

Cordell chuckled, shook his head, and picked up the small container. He tossed the used cigarette to the ground and stepped on it. As he began to rub the soft, yellow mixture on his horse's leg, Ian Taullery watched him for a minute and kneeled beside him. "Here, let me do it. You won't get it on right."

Cordell handed him the jug and stepped back. Taullery proceeded to carefully rub in the medicine. As he worked, he said, "One of us better get to goin' to warn Longstreet—and Hill."

"We've got to do more than that, Ian. We've got to slow them up—or they'll run through our weak side, even if he is warned. Longstreet's got to have some time to move men over. Hill can't do it alone. He doesn't have the men—anywhere."

"Yeah, I reckon you're right. But..."

"I say we send Billy Rip to warn Longstreet. Now. Then the rest of us will see if we can't bust up this little Yankee surprise party—for...for at least two hours, anyway. Half a day would be better. Long enough so our boys can slip into position and dust 'em real proper-like when they come to call."

"Well, I know how to do the first part. Don't know about the second. Soon as I finish here, I'll saddle his blue. That long-legged thing will get him to Longstreet before dawn."

"Cordell! Now!" came the harsh command from Captain Wilson, doubly unhappy because the newly lit fire wouldn't yet yield any hot coffee or sufficient warmth to cut the early morning's discomfort. He was also certain the men were chuckling about his diarrhea yesterday. He stomped his boots to drive heat into his toes, sending off small whirls of snow, getting more frustrated at Cordell's lack of response or respect. At the horses, Cordell and Taullery continued to assess the situation, without regard to the captain's concerns.

An idea popped into Taullery's mind. "Say, you don't think they'll change their plans, knowing you've spotted 'em, do you?"

"Well, I suppose they might, but I doubt it," Cordell answered. "You've got to figure they've got a pretty good idea of where our boys are—and how long it'll take to shove more guns into the end of the line. If anything, I think my shooting'll make 'em move even faster. It would me."

"Yeah, but you're wound up tighter'n a tick on that dog's butt."

"Oh, an' I suppose you'd take off for a walk with that farm girl instead," Cordell bantered.

"Hey, that would be tempting. Mighty tempting. Why don't you go on down to the fire, Rule. I'll be with you as soon as I throw the leather on Billy Rip's piece of lightning."

Cordell turned to go, and Taullery added, "Go easy on Captain Wilson, now. He can't help it, he's an asshole."

Lieutenant Rule Cordell nodded and began walking toward the petulant officer, studying the mostly deserted camp as he moved. The dog took its position at his heels. It seemed wrong for so few men to be in a place that once held so many, almost sacrilegious somehow. His face was unreadable except for the dark circles under his eyes. Something in him curled when a demand was made. Any demand. But he would heed his friend's advice; he would report without any hint of anger.

Ahead twenty yards was the struggling fire and

three figures coaxing it into a fuller life. Wrinkled pages of *Vidette,* the booklet satirizing the Yankees, lay to the side of his pathway. Cordell kicked it with his boot and saw it disappear, shivering in the night. The dog raced after the pamphlet, quickly retrieving it in his mouth. Cordell smiled, thanked the dog, and took the booklet. Shrugging his shoulders, he shoved the unwanted pages into his coat pocket and continued walking.

Two empty bottles of laudanum lay in a narrow gulch, guarded by a flanking row of stunted pine trees. He straddled both, knowing well the sign of hurting men. The dog sniffed the strange items before returning to his new master's side. The medicine triggered a murky picture of Cordell's red-faced minister father yelling at ten-year-old Rule. The child was sobbing about the unexpected death of a young colt.

"Why has God taken Blackie?" young Rule asked.

"Blasphemy from the issue of my own loin!" Reverend Cordell screamed, and slapped the boy's face so hard he spun sideways into the stall.

The red-faced minister stood over the cowering boy and roared one of his favorite verses from Proverbs 1. "'The path of the just is as the shining light, that shineth more and more unto the perfect day.'" With that, the elder Cordell turned and left, leaving his son crouched beside the unmoving body of the young horse, sobbing and wondering what he had done wrong.

More than anything in the world, Cordell desired a Southern victory—to prove his father wrong. The bitter wisp of yesterday disappeared into his soul as he accepted the greetings of Whisper Jenson and Billy Ripton at the struggling fire.

"I like yur dawg. Mighty fine-lookin' pooch. Yessuh, Rulesey," Billy Ripton advised. The young man was the only one who called him that—or could.

"We'll have ye some right fine stew in a few minutes—and some hot coffee to boot." Whisper's words were difficult to catch over the crackling of the small fire. "Where have ye been, Rule?"

Whisper Jenson was a stocky, wide-faced horseman with a thick, bristly mustache covering most of his mouth even when it was open, and a flat nose that appeared to have been ironed over. Before the conflict, he was a prosperous lawyer, and his style was to probe any statement for softness, usually with tough questions.

His nickname was due to a soft, raspy voice, the result of a Yankee rifle bullet four years ago. His real name, Franklin David, was almost forgotten, even by him. And with the voice injury, his dreams of politics after the war were likely ended too; people usually took to a loud orator. A zest for chewing tobacco was quite evident, with streaks of brown already edging his mouth. Whisper's aim had become a source of wonderment. Taullery compared Whisper's spitting with Cordell's pistol shooting and joked if tobacco juice were gunpowder his friend might have a problem.

Before speaking, Lieutenant Cordell warmed his hands over the fire. He couldn't remember ever feeling warm all over. The dog, timid at first, finally joined him, leaning against his legs. Cordell wondered if it was for warmth or courage. His hard face, with its prominent chin, dark eyes, and Roman nose, was warpainted with glowing streaks from the fire. His Comanche earring and long hair completed the appearance of a warrior readied for battle. No one ever remarked about the strangeness of wearing a dried rose stem on his lapel; they knew what it meant. Even Captain Thomas had enough sense not to make fun of the symbol.

Concisely, Cordell repeated his story for the three men in a handful of terse sentences. Silence took command of the campfire and no one spoke, as if the young flames were sucking in all of their intended words. As usual, Whisper was the first to speak. And, as usual, it was to question.

"Are you sure it was the Humphrey's Two Corps? Maybe it was just a big company scavaging the country. Looking for firewood. Food. Whadda ya think?"

"Wish it were, Whisper. No, it's two thousand Yanks pushing through that damn black forest." Cordell respected Whisper's questions, but sometimes they became a bit wearing in their search for detail that didn't matter.

"How far behind do you think they are?" Whisper continued.

"No more'n three hours now, I reckon. Maybe a fat two."

"Any artillery?"

"Couldn't see any. Infantry's all I spotted."

"You're sure they're coming through here?" Whisper's voice was clearly agitated.

"Where else would they be going?" Cordell said, his eyes locked onto Whisper's face.

Unlike Cordell or Taullery, Whisper wore little that was an official uniform. Under a woolen overcoat was a dirty dark blue suit coat. Only his buttermilk pants—with a rip in the right knee that was widening each day—were regulation. A stringed tie was more or less in place on a filthy, collarless, once-white shirt.

He had taken to wearing a beaver top hat once the property of a Manassas gentleman. A woolen scarf was held in place by the hat and tied under his chin. Only one ear was covered, though; the other was sprung outward, glowing crimson. Around his neck were long thongs tied to the trigger guards of two pistols shoved into his waistband. Extra ammunition and tobacco plugs could be seen bulging from his coat pockets, along with a leather-bound diary that he wrote in daily. Letters to his wife and children were dutifully tended to, almost as often.

"What do you think we should do, Rule?" Whisper asked, his forehead layered in frowns, his mind out of more questions for the moment.

Taking a deep breath, Cordell turned to the voice-impaired scout, now a good friend through two years of riding and fighting together, and replied, "Ian and I think—"

"You think! You think!" Captain Wilson snapped.

The words rolled out of his mouth easily. The sharp edge on them was evident. The officer looked at the weary Rule Cordell to rebuff him further. The young man's eyes made him think better of it. Captain Wilson glanced at the dog, saw its homely head contorted into a toothy snarl, and tried not to look startled. He should have expected a savage like Cordell would drag along some wild beast from the woods. The dog continued to snarl until Cordell touched him with his hand and told him to be quiet.

Cordell himself broke the uncomfortable silence that followed, ignoring the officer's comment. "Thomas, send Billy Rip to warn Longstreet. He's the best rider and has the best horse. The rest of us can go to work and, maybe, surprise 'em into stopping. Our boys are going to need time. We're the only ones that can give it to them."

Whisper sighed softly through his mustache as the dimension of their challenge became real to him. His face was half dark, half gold from the close fire. It was a face that couldn't quite hide the fear that blossomed with the realization of what Cordell was describing.

For once, he didn't want to ask the question, because he already knew the answer.

Was this what his nightmare about a huge snake was all about? That same awful dream had come back every night for at least a week: A huge snake came up out of the ground next to him and started eating his arm before he would awaken each time. He spat a long stream of tobacco juice toward a flat rock. Striking in its middle, the ricocheting spit made a light circle of brown in the snow.

"But I wanna stay with yo-all, Rule-sey! Pul-eese, I wanna stay h'yar. I kin fi't—better'n..." Billy Ripton exclaimed loudly, looking at Captain Wilson before finishing his thought, "...better'n most. Yo-all knows it, too. Cain't I stay, Rule-sey?"

What remained of Ripton's butternut uniform was too small, making him look bigger than he was. But his long arms and big hands would have stuck out of any shirt that wasn't homespun. A hand-knit, woolen hood—a balaclava—covered most of his head and face, leaving exposed only his eyes, nose, and mouth. The ham-handed young man didn't look like the kind of person that savvy horsemen would trust with the care of their horses. But he was. Whatever Billy Ripton said about their mounts was the way it was. He might have been the youngest and least experienced in war, but he could read a horse like Taullery could attract women and Cordell could use a pistol.

Cordell put a hand on the husky young man's shoulder. "I know you would, Billy Rip. But none of us can match that blue of yours. We need you to go. It'll be as scary as staying. You'll have to ride smart to stay away from the bluebellies already around there. Ian is saddling him for you. He'll be here in a minute—and you'll need to get at it."

"Am I to assume that you and Trooper Taullery took action prior to my orders, Lieutenant?" Captain Wilson's question rattled in the cold night air.

Cordell took a deep breath, trying to hold back his frustration, and spoke between gritted teeth. "Thomas, you can assume any damn thing you want—but go play officer some place else. I haven't got time for it now. Some of us didn't get into this damn war to lose. I'm going to assume you didn't either. We've got one thin chance to save Hill from getting overrun. So you listen."

Taullery walked up to the fire just as Cordell finished. His eyes went from his intense friend to the foppish officer. Captain Wilson looked like a man who had been slapped across the face with a leather glove. His eyes were wide and white; the edge of his mouth twitched as a touch of saliva reached it and peered over the edge. Any response was caught in his throat, lodged there next to his courage.

Turning back to the assembled scouts as if nothing had occured, Cordell's eyes sparkled as he said, "Boys, I've got an idea that might stop those Yankees. For a sweet piece anyway. Oh yeah, Billy Rip, leave your pistols. Well, keep your saddle pistol—but give us the rest. An' your rifle. Any lead and powder you can spare, too. Any extra shirts. An' that old coat you found last week. Your hat, your regular one, if you can get along without it. We'll need everything we can put our hands on to make an army. What looks like one, anyway."

Billy's face was plastered with confusion. His mouth opened to say something, but Cordell wasn't waiting for a response. The fiery young man outlined his plan with a coiled intensity.

"Before the first bluebellies come into that clearing," Cordell continued, "we're going to set up the extra guns—all along the firing line—so we can fire them all at once. Make it look like they're facing a lot of dug-in Johnny Rebs. Then we'll take all the clothes, knapsacks, hats, whatever...and make it look like our boys are hunched behind the walls. Like our boys didn't leave after all and there's, maybe, a whole division just waiting for the bastards."

Taullery interrupted. "I've been chewing on it, Rule—and I get it. We get those Yanks to figure they got bad reading from their scouts—and dig in themselves, back in the trees. For a piece, anyway. Until they figure us out."

The last part of his assessment faded as he realized its significance.

Chapter Four

Rule Cordell's face showed his appreciation for his friend's understanding. That was much faster than Taullery usually worked through things in his mind.

"Yeah, we'll have to hit 'em hard right off, make it look like a real force when they first come through those trees. I figure we've got at least twenty extra guns between us—and they'll seem like two hundred because they won't be expecting it. Hell, they'll be looking for an excuse to stop. Almost look forward to it, they will, after marching all night."

Cordell scratched the hound's head and shoulders before going on. His eyes checked each man's face as he explained, "It's farther away than we would start shooting, that's for sure. But we can't let 'em get too close—and get a good look. If we can make 'em do some serious thinking before getting around to charging us, that'll give Longstreet and Hill enough time.

Maybe. At least all we can give them. What do ya think?"

Whisper observed, "Yesterday evening, Taullery reported Major General Warren and his Five Corps were digging in a few miles east of Dinwiddie. Two divisions of Major General Humphrey's Two Corps were headed east of there. Don't you think that's where they'll attack? Somewhere on Hatcher's Road. Not through this miserable...wilderness."

Cordell glanced at Taullery, barely hiding his contempt. "I don't doubt my friend's report, Whisper. My guess is that's the Yankees' whole idea. Hill gets pushed hard up and down his line, then bang! They pop through at the corner with a force he never knew was there."

Taullery was pouring himself some coffee, but stopped and quickly added, "Well, this is the only way to get through quick. That's why these damn fighting walls were built here in the first place."

"Rule-sey! I wanna stay! With you-all. Somebody else kin go," Billy Ripton pleaded. "I be a Texan, like you-all. Texans don' run."

Captain Wilson shrugged his shoulders and, in an attempted fatherly voice, said, "That's perfectly fine, son. But don't fear, I'll ride for you. Generals Longstreet and Hill should hear this news from me personally. Lieutenant Cordell, I will leave you in charge of the detail."

Sitting beside the fire, Whisper spit out a mouthful of reheated coffee he was tasting for warmth. He tried hard to hold back a guffaw, but it came out anyway, a mix between a cough and a loud chuckle. Taullery and Cordell looked at each other. A smile passed. Apparently not noticing the reaction of his men, Captain Wilson asked for, and received, a cup of the coarse chicory brew. The bitter taste triggered a spit of the mouthful he took in. Tossing the rest aside, he turned without another word to head for their picket line. The hound growled deep in its chest.

"Thomas, you're staying," Cordell said bluntly. "Billy Rip's going."

"What?!" Captain Thomas Wilson said, his anger outrunning his fear of staying. He hated having his subordinates call him by his first name anyway. One day he would have them court-martialed for this insubordination. General Longstreet wouldn't put up with something like this. When he got the chance, he would wire Adjutant General Cooper in Richmond; he'd show these men what real leadership was all about.

Smoothly, Cordell drew one of his pistols. The cock of the trigger stopped everyone. "Today, you're going to act like a leader, Thomas. You're staying," growled Cordell. "The kid is going."

Captain Wilson studied the black barrel of the shiny gun as if he had never seen one before. A shiver went through him, and wetness grew at his groin. For a moment, he didn't care if anyone saw it or not. Another moment passed and he twisted his body to the side, away from the assembled men, to keep the damp circle on his pants from being seen. He could feel his face reddening.

Taullery stepped up to his friend. "Easy, Rule. He'll stay. Besides, he wouldn't want to see the General in those pants."

Billy Ripton chuckled, and so did Cordell.

"Blue is waiting for you, Billy Rip," Taullery said gently, "We're counting on you, son. Ride with your head now. There's plenty of Yanks about between here 'n' there."

"Yessuh," Billy Ripton responded, and gave his best salute.

Taullery returned it as Cordell walked over to the younger man and talked quietly with him, explaining what he must tell General Longstreet about the Yankee surprise and how the patrol planned to slow it down so entrenched men could be realigned. Billy Ripton's eyes blossomed into wide surprise as Cordell spoke.

He emphasized that Billy Ripton must deliver the report to Longstreet and no one else. "Tell the General we will hold them here—if we can—for at least two hours by fooling them into thinking a full brigade is here, waiting for them. It may not work, Billy Rip, so tell him that too."

Cordell watched the young man's eyes to check for comprehension, and explained his plan again to make certain. Taullery came over and explained the situation as if Billy Ripton had never heard it before. Cordell listened patiently, telling himself it made sense for the boy to hear the story again—and from a different angle. But giving him an overview of the military situation was unnecessary. Finally Cordell interrupted and asked Billy to repeat what he was to do. Satisfied, Cordell urged him to get going. A few minutes later, the young rider galloped away, spurring his horse vigorously and waving. The boy's rifle, four extra pistols, a bag of ammunition, hat, two old shirts, and an old tattered coat were left behind in a hurried pile.

Handing Cordell a bowl of stew and a cup of hot coffee, Whistler spat at the fire and growled hoarsely, "Why don't we just ride out...an' nip at 'em? We've done it before, Rule." With a small stick, he emphasized his point in the ashes of the fire. The same stick was then used to stir the rest of the stew in a blackened pot atop the flames.

"Yeah, but we can't stop 'em long enough that way, Whisper. They'd use a hundred bluebelly sharpshooters to pin us down while the rest kept moving," Cordell explained, more gently than Taullery expected. "We've got to scare the hell out of them. Make them dig in, start jawing about what to do. Send back a courier for new orders and wait until they get them. At least, that's how I'd like to see it go."

Sniffing the air for more of the stew, the hound sat on its heels looking at Cordell as the tired scout ate a spoonful of the stew. It tasted good, but it was too hot. Quickly, he swallowed twice to cool the heat in his throat. He looked down at the waiting dog, then at Whisper. Without being asked, the lawyer-cavalryman spooned a small portion of stew onto a tin plate for the dog.

As he started to place it in the dog's direction, Cordell said, "Let it cool first a little, Whisper. Might be hard on 'im."

Whisper grinned and blew on the stew, stuck his finger in it, and blew again. A nearby canteen provided additional cooling. Finally, he laid the plate in front of the eager animal. Surprising Cordell, the dog looked at the food, then at Cordell for approval.

Smiling, Cordell said, "That's fine, boy. Go ahead."

The dog began eating immediately.

"Well, why don't we cut down some trees along that trail? Make 'em stop and go around. Really slow them down," Whisper asked tentatively, his eyes focused on the dog.

"Thought about that, Whisper. How many do you think we can cut before they hear us—and come a'smokin'?" Cordell asked between bites.

"We won't get out of here, will we?" Whistler said without looking up. His voice was reedy and tense.

Cordell glanced at his gallant friend, Ian Taullery, before answering. "Well, I...we're sure gonna give it a helluva shot. Come on, we've got work to do, boys. We need all the uniform stuff we can find. Especially hats!"

Accepting the fact that they were staying, if not the wisdom of the plan itself, Whisper suggested they select a fallback position, putting the horses there with four saddled and ready for a quick getaway. Their current picket line was good for grazing but not for fast access. Agreement was immediate and Whisper began moving their mounts to a second, much smaller, line of earth-packed logs twenty-five yards behind them on the top of the sloping hillside.

A small dry stream bed running down the hillside would give them a degree of cover—if they crawled—while retreating from the primary position to the hilltop. Quietly, Cordell asked Whisper to make certain his roan was rope-haltered so Cordell could lead him out easily on the fresh horse. He couldn't bear the thought of leaving the roan behind for the Yankees.

Taullery and Wilson gathered stray clothing and suitable poles from around the campground and work began on the construction of a gun line. After some experimenting, it was decided only pistols would be used for the simultaneous firing. Rifles were too awkward to keep in place. Revolvers, though, could be jammed into firing positions along the breastworks, just as Cordell imagined. Each man could fire a set of five pistols at the same time, with a long, straight stick, through all of the trigger guards, acting as a common triggering device.

Cut pieces of rope and thin strips of clothing tied each weapon snugly in place. Three long poles and one straight tree branch were carefully pushed through the trigger guards. After that task was completed, they reexamined the gun placements and reinforced their lodging where needed with propped sticks or more tying to hold them steady when fired. Taullery wanted to test-fire the pistol rigging, but Cordell thought it would be a gamble they couldn't afford. The Yankees might hear the shots and send scouts ahead. After a few minutes of discussion, it was also decided to leave the pistols uncocked until later so there would be no risk of premature firing.

Gathered hats were set on stakes and tent poles jammed into the hardened dirt of the breastworks, so they could be seen above it. Each man donated his own hat, even Taullery. Cordell was amused, but not surprised, when his friend brought six different hats from his pack horse. At first, Captain Wilson resisted giving his plumed officer's hat, but a glance at Cordell, with his hands resting on his pistols, was enough to change his mind.

Left-behind tunics, shirts, coats, plus clothing patrol members could spare and any other pieces of cloth were torn into large shreds to make as many dummy "soldiers" as possible, resting on poles and branches hammered into the frozen ground or propped against the breastworks wall. The few hats were spaced out among the ninety or so other stakes. An hour later, more than three hundred shapes could be glimpsed above the front wall, like Confederate soldiers waiting in the shadows. From the distance of the last tree line, it created a surprisingly realistic look of readied men. Cordell reasoned the advancing army wouldn't be expecting any resistance and would overreact. At least, that's what he hoped. It was not discussed anymore, but if this didn't fool the Yanks, the four horse-men knew they would likely be dead before they could get away.

Taullery couldn't resist, and with an exaggerated wave of his hand, he bellowed, "Stick that one with the captain's hat out there where the Yanks can get theirselves a good view."

"Yeah, he's a mite braver than usual this morning," came the soft reply from Whisper.

Captain Wilson glanced at the discussed stake, breathed deeply, and pretended to be working on another dummy. His hands were shaking; his mouth was so dry he couldn't swallow. Occasionally, he glanced at the waiting horses. This was insane, he told himself. No one in his right mind would be trying to stop a brigade with four men. He was going to be killed—and for what? Letting Longstreet have time to support Hill. Big deal.

That kind of sacrifice was for others. A plan of his own was taking shape. When he had the opportunity, he would grab one of the horses and escape. He would report to Hill that the others had been killed, as they would be. His courage would be appropriately recog-nized, probably resulting in a promotion to major. Now, that was smart thinking. He wiped a tiny bubble of sweat from his forehead, as if it was as scarce as food, and glanced around to see if anyone had observed his daydreaming.

After giving it careful consideration, Taullery came to Cordell with a brand-new uniform that had been neatly put away in his gear. It was a fancy presenta-tion, with extra brass buttons and gold trim setting off the butternut cloth. "Here, we'll put this one where they can see it good."

"I appreciate that, Ian. They'll see that pretty thing and really stop to think things over."

"Yah, I figure I can make it look like a general's outfit with a few doodads I've got around somewhere."

"Good. But hurry, we've got a lot more to do." Then Cordell announced, "I've got another idea."

Taullery grinned, knowing this was typical of his friend. Thinking, adapting, moving. This dynamic style of leadership was hard on Taullery, but he tried to hide it. He preferred careful processing, but this wasn't the time or the place. He had already decided to trust his friend's instincts and just be as thorough at creating the illusion as possible. He looked over at Whisper and knew the hoarse cavalryman badly wanted to ask questions he didn't dare mouth.

"We're going to give them some artillery fire," Cordell said with a lopsided grin.

Biting on the end of his mustache whiskers, Whisper couldn't hold back any longer and asked, "What do you mean?"

"Just watch," Cordell said. "It's magic."

Whisper glanced at Taullery, and the tall cavalryman winked and said offhandedly, "No snakes, Whisper." Taullery was the only one Whisper had told about his terrible nightmares.

Taullery finished placing his "general" at a high point on the wall as the others began work on Cordell's fake artillery. Four long logs were propped along the front wall, in regular Confederate artillery configuration, pointed outward as if they were howitzers. Bark was quickly skinned off and ashes from the campfire rubbed in to cast a gray look to the exposed wood. A singe of fire turned the cut-wood ends into black barrels. Cordell asked Taullery to pack together two sacks of powder.

"They don't look much like howitzers to me," Whisper said.

"They do if that's what you think they are, Whisper,

and the bluebellies won't have any reason to figure otherwise," Cordell said confidently.

Captain Wilson swallowed and looked up again at the waiting horses. Whisper wasn't convinced, but decided against pressing the point.

Taullery returned with three horses. Two were saddled; the third was the packhorse, holding two sacks more than half filled with gunpowder. A third knapsack contained a hexagonal-shaped, Whitworth twelve-pound howitzer shell.

"Hey, Rule, found us a real artillery shell. Kinda banged up. Reckon that's why they left it. Think we can use it?"

Cordell thought for a moment and asked, "If we set it on a branch in the trees, can we knock it loose with bullets?"

"Only if we do it right."

"Let's try." Cordell stared again at the powder sacks. "Damn, Ian, did you leave any powder for us to shoot with?"

"Hell yes, Rule. But we've got to have enough to really blow up—or it won't work, man."

"Yeah, you're right."

"I put some bolts, balls, and other little stuff in there too. It'll feel like a real cannister shell when she blows."

"Good idea. Let's get it done."

Taullery mounted, and Cordell quickly followed with the hound happily at his horse's heels. The fiery scout was light-headed and knew the lack of sleep was rapidly closing in on him, but he pushed his body on.

As they rode out, he turned to the oldest cavalry scout and said, "Whisper, you keep watch. I don't want some damn scout wandering out of the forest while we're finishing up."

"Got it. Do I take 'im out? I can't shout much," the nervous Whisper asked.

"Only if you see him," Cordell joked.

"Yeah, don't shoot anybody you don't see," Taullery added with a thin smile, and then said to Cordell, "You worried about the dog barking?"

"If he barks, the bluebellies are coming."

"Yeah, reckon so. Hope he doesn't bark."

"Me too."

Cordell and Taullery decide to place the two sacks of powder and iron pieces in front of the last cluster of trees along the edge of the clearing. The frozen ground would not yield to digging, and time was growing short, so they flattened the sacks as best they could. Downed branches and scattered leaves were laid over each sack, making them less obvious. But the area itself now looked disturbed against the surrounding thin-white blanket. After a few handfuls of snow were sprinkled over the leaves, both men decided it would have to do. They also decided to fire at the hidden powder sacks when the Yankees first appeared and not risk their discovery.

Staring at the hound as it sniffed the entrance to the empty road through the forest, Taullery was surprised when he realized his friend was climbing the pine tree to the right of the hidden sacks. The knapsack with the heavy shell was on his back.

"Hey, let me do that. It was my idea," Taullery said, rushing over to the tree.

"Hell, you'd take forever getting up here, Ian—or have you forgotten about being afraid of heights?" Cordell said, his words bursting through short, heavy gasps as he worked his way to the top of the mostly accommodating tree.

"Well, don't forget to take a look-see while you're wanderin' around up there," Taullery said with a grin. "We don't need no bluebellies shootin' up your ass."

Within minutes, Cordell had straddled one of the

upper arms of branches and taken the knapsack from his shoulders. He removed the shell and placed it gingerly into the cradle of two smaller branches to his right.

"Don't drop it! Your hound dog is right below you, tryin' to figure out what the hell his master is doin'," Taullery hollered.

Cordell withdrew his hands from the weight, watching the branches sway tentatively as they accepted the shell. He thought they would be strong enough. Looking back at their breastworks, he made certain there would be a clear shot at the supporting branches from there.

"If you hit right here, Ian, she'll come flying down," Cordell advised, his face surrounded by breath frost.

"I can do that in my sleep," Taullery responded, "and it looks like that's what you'll be doing—shooting in your sleep. Maybe you can get a nap before them blue boys come a'callin'."

"I'm fine."

As they rode back to the breastworks, Taullery came up with the idea of adding a dab of powder on the top edge of each "cannon." When lit, it would snap and smoke, looking from a distance like the barrel of a just-fired howitzer. They decided Whisper could set off the powder piles right after the hidden powder sacks were blown up and the shell was freed from its tree branch support.

While Cordell and Taullery were setting up the powder sacks and artillery shell, Whisper had created a battalion flag out of a gray shirt, tearing off the sleeves and tying it to a four-foot stick. A huge *I* adorning both sides was done with a charred piece of wood. He jammed his creation into the top of the log-and-dirt wall as they wheeled their horses into the protected area. The faded cloth wouldn't wave, collapsed by the frigid stillness.

"Looks great," Cordell hollered as he and Taullery reined in their mounts.

Taullery added, "Better kiss that rascal for luck."

Frost smoke covered their reddened faces as they spoke. Whisper hesitated a moment, then planted a whiskery kiss on his flag.

"Where's Thomas?" Cordell asked as he dismounted. The hound came to him for attention and received an ear scratching.

"Well, he's...well, I don't know. He was over by the wall a minute ago."

"Ian, ride up to our horses and take a look, will you? Got a hunch our brave leader has left," Cordell said. "Take my horse too, will you? And the packhorse."

"Damn, man, you want me to iron your shirt while I'm at it?" Taullery kidded.

Whisper paled, spat a weak stream of tobacco juice, and muttered, "God save us."

From the ridge, Taullery reported what Cordell had already guessed. "Thomas is gone. Took his bay. The other horses are here."

Whisper stared at Cordell, expecting him to say they wouldn't stay either, that they wouldn't risk their lives in this wild charade. Instead, Cordell said, "We'd better eat while we can. I've got a Yankee saddlebag with some food in it. Do we have anything else?"

"Ah...ah...only a last bit of that stew like you had...Let's see," a surprised Whisper tried to recall what few supplies were left, "got some corn bread. Coffee, yeah, got some coffee. Handful of potatoes. That's it, I think, maybe."

Cordell turned and yelled into the darkness, "Hey, Ian, bring those Yankee saddlebags when you come! And any other food you got hidden away."

With not a word more about the cowardly captain leaving them, they gathered the small amount of food-stuffs remaining. Whisper fried Yankee salt pork and sliced potatoes in a skillet with the coal-laden fire and warmed the rest of the corn bread and another pot of coffee. Smoke from the coals had taken to wrapping itself within the nearest tree and disappearing, so there was no concern about the fire giving away their position too early.

While the food was cooking, they decided on the shooting pattern when the Yankees entered the clearing: The three men would each fire a set of guns at the same time; Whisper would move over and set off Thomas's set; Taullery and Cordell would begin shooting for accuracy with their own guns, especially at any officers out front. After that, Cordell would go for the powder sacks and Taullery would shoot at the shell's branches to dislodge it. Whisper would set off the powder atop the log cannons. As quickly as they could, the pistol sets would be recocked and fired again.

Quietly, the three scouts took a plateful of the hastily prepared breakfast and a cup of coffee, then readied the pistols in the multiple firing sets, spread out, ate silently, and waited. Suddenly it hit each man that all the preparation was done, and the magnitude of their task began to settle in. Cordell laid the Henry against the wall, cocked and ready. Three pistols, his ammunition bandolier, field glasses, and a canteen were positioned for rapid handling.

After several bites, he tossed a piece of pork toward the hound, lying close beside him, who devoured it immediately. Taullery was arranging his personal weapons and Whisper was writing something.

"If they've got scouts out, don't let 'em wander in close," Cordell advised loudly. "But don't miss, either.

Shooting a scout will warn 'em, but I'd rather have him dead than looking and talking."

His eyes were leaden and his mind was dull. The new day hadn't brought any new warmth. Methodically, he removed a cigarette paper from the small sheath, folded it, and sprinkled tobacco from the muslin bag along the crease. His hands were shaking, forcing tobacco strips to spin onto his coat and the ground.

He shoved the bag back into his pocket and stared at the unrolled cigarette. It registered on his tired mind what he was supposed to be doing. He tightly rolled the paper, capturing the tobacco, licked the loose flap, and sealed the newly made cigarette. It took a few seconds to find a match in his other pocket. He shivered slightly, lit up, and allowed a cloud of smoke to surround his face. He inhaled deeply, then remembered his piece of hardtack and chewed on it in between sips of harsh coffee and drags on the cigarette. He was too weary to worry about whether or not they had forgotten something. Or even if the idea made any sense. All he really wanted to do was sleep. Heaviness in his eyes was eased by their closing. He tossed the barely smoked cigarette aside and took a long breath, letting the cold air turn the exhalation into soft swirls of white.

Chapter Five

Suddenly Cordell realized the tall horseman was standing beside him in silence. He tilted his head upward to meet his friend's solemn gaze. Cordell caught himself smiling at the neat appearance of Taullery's uniform and the silliness of wondering, at a time like this, how he managed to keep it so clean and neatly pressed.

Matter-of-factly, Taullery asked him for a favor. "Rule, I don't want them bluebellies gettin' my guns. If…you take 'em with you. Promise?"

"Ian, you'll be firing 'em with both hands when we ride out of here."

"I know, but…promise."

"You know I will."

"An…an'…there's a lady. In Waco. You don't know her. Works in the Bonner Tavern there. Name of Jessica Roget. Find her an' tell her…I was thinkin' of her when…"

Rule Cordell nodded. For an instant, he thought about teasing Taullery about the time their friendship had nearly ended due to their simultaneous infatuation with auburn-haired Maribeth Yancey. That trouble was solved soon enough when she discarded both friends and walked out with the town banker's son.

"Ride my horse out, will you? Use my saddle. It's a nice one, you know. Take him and your roan. Mine's faster'n your second horse anyway." Taullery grinned, trying to make his continuing requests seem like casual conversation.

"All right."

Glancing up at the trees to make certain nothing was coming—and to gain courage for his question— Taullery asked, "Anybody I should...ah, if...How about your father?"

The smaller horseman hesitated, drank from his cup, and said quietly, "No. Thanks. Nobody. Doesn't matter."

Taullery's shoulders rose and fell as he looked at his friend and asked soberly, "Rule, what if the Yanks charge us right off instead of hunkerin' down? What then?"

"That's a good question, Ian. Figured you'd have that part all worked out by now," Cordell teased as he picked up his closest pistol and spun the cylinder.

"I'm serious now, Rule. They might come pouring out of those woods, instead of stoppin'. We'll have four, five minutes to get out. That's all."

"I know that, Ian," Cordell replied with a bite to his words, "but they won't. They're not expecting us, and they're going to be tired. Real tired. Most of them will be looking at that open field down there as a great place to rest and eat. And then, boom, we hit 'em. No, they aren't going to rush us. Not right off, anyway. Not with any real force, just skirmishers."

"If you're wrong, we're dead."

"Yeah, you might be right about that, Ian. You can ride out now if you want."

"Come on, Rule, I didn't deserve that. It's just that we need to think ahead."

"Thinking ahead is your job. I'm going to take a nap."

Taullery swallowed his next words and returned to his position, mumbling to himself. From his own position to the right, Whisper saw the exchange and stood, his mouth a thin line of red, his face taut. He walked the fifty yards to the strange warrior he admired and sometimes feared. Whisper handed Cordell a thick envelope. Cordell took the offering, already guessing what it contained.

"Will you see this gets to my...my wife, my family."

Cordell didn't know what to say. He stared at the letter in his hand. Blinking his eyes to clear his mind, he raised his head, smiled warmly, and said, "Whisper, I'll take it—an' I'll give it back when this is over."

Whisper returned the smile as best he could, tried to spit but couldn't, and went back to his post. Cordell saw wetness in the corners of the man's eyes as he left. As he pushed the envelope inside his uniform jacket, Cordell's weary mind went again to his last parting with his father.

It was a Saturday evening. The minister was readying himself for Sunday-morning services, sitting as he always did at the kitchen table studying his Bible, ever pushing his eyeglasses back on a thick, short nose that didn't want to hold them. Reverend Aaron Cordell seemed to grow violent with his words and actions after reading certain verses. His former wife had lived in daily fear of her husband until finally running off with another man.

69

Young Rule had missed her every night since she left two years earlier. She was the only thing that made life good, even encouraging his apparent skill with firearms. Before leaving, she had secretly arranged for him to receive additional guidance in defending himself—with gun, knife, and fist—from a known renegade in Waco. Rule Cordell was never certain what she paid the man for the lessons, but he kept his word and was a thorough tutor, if uncouth and alcoholic.

With trepidation, young Rule advised his father that he was riding out to join the Confederacy that night. The stiff-faced minister rose from his studies like a water pump being pushed, was silent a moment, and said, "Aaron, war is not the way of God. You know I wish you to follow my footsteps into the ministry. I have prayed over it many nights. The godly life is the one to follow."

It was the first, and only, time Rule could remember his father saying anything positive to him. But the minister's lamp-lit face seemed more satanic than saintly.

"If the way you live is godly, I'm not interested. I'm going. Just like my mother did. God can do anything he wants," Rule said evenly.

With a rage, the minister grabbed his chair and shoved it across the room.

"What did you say?!" Aaron Cordell screamed, his face dark, his temples pulsing like a flooded creek.

"You heard me. I'm leaving and I'm not coming back."

Reverend Cordell stepped toward his son and swung his hand to slap his face. Rule caught the onrushing arm in an iron grasp; his eyes tore into his father's face.

"Sit down," Rule said. The older man saw the

authority in his son's eyes, felt the power in his grasp, and quickly his anger subsided.

"If you want to pray for something, pray for the South to win. Pray for Texas. And my name is Rule, not Aaron. It'll never be Aaron," Rule said as he walked toward the front door.

A low growl of words stalked after him. "May you rot in hell." That was the last thing he heard his father say.

"Here they come!" rasped Whisper, fear high in his words; his voice cracking as he strained to make the words louder.

The alarm broke into Cordell's daydream. Entering the clearing were Union infantrymen, sleepy and weary, marching in a loose four-by-four string past the last sentinel of trees. Above them, dawn was staining the sky pink and yellow. Yawns reached up to greet the coming day. They weren't expecting any enemy force at this point; their officers had told them the Confederates had cleared out days before. Instead, they were looking forward to a hot breakfast and a few minutes of rest before moving on. No advance riders led the division—only a solitary officer with his head down, dozing in the saddle of a brown horse.

"Don't let 'em get too close. When the first fifty clear those trees, we pull the poles. Ian, you got the officer. Sting 'em hard before they wake up!"

At Cordell's command, the three cavalrymen pulled the poles triggering their lines of pistols. The supposedly abandoned Confederate breastworks roared to life with deep-throated orange flames. Taullery emptied the officer's horse and dropped six soldiers, firing so rapidly it was one long uninterrupted sound of death.

One soldier raced toward the breastworks, his face erased by a fountain of red. He gagged, staggered, and fell. Whisper ran to the remaining pistol line, the one created for Captain Wilson, and pulled back on its pole, unleasing five shots in unison. His eyes were wide and full as he methodically recocked each pistol in a pole set, fired them, and went on to the next pistol grouping, looking like an old woman lost in washday details, instead of a soldier in the battle of his life.

Meanwhile, Cordell's lever-action Henry spit lead into the confused sea of blue-coated troops. Union soldiers were spinning and collapsing under his unrelenting fire. The all-night march had left them in a fatigued stupor; now they were struggling to understand what was happening at the base of this peaceful meadow. Dropping the emptied rifle, Cordell grabbed two pistols and continued his assault, firing with both hands. His own weariness was gone, like the gentleness of the meadow. In its place was thunder, death, and the eyes of a killer.

Acrid gunsmoke danced along the breastworks. Above the roar of the guns came the unmistakable, high-pitched Rebel yell from the three scouts. Joining the distinctive war cry was the howl of the hound, with its head back and its mouth opened to the sky. Waves of panicked bluecoats, still in the forest, took cover within the trees. The three Rebels could hear yelling and cursing. Scattered Yankee bullets searched the breastworks for targets; eight dummy soldiers crumpled under accurate fire.

Cordell shouted down the line, "All right, let's give 'em one of the cannons. Ian, you got the sack. Whisper, you've got the cannon fire. I'll fire the pistol lines again. Let 'er rip, boys!"

Taullery's shot exploded the farthest sack, bringing forth an exploding ball of dirt, leaves, metal, and smoke for a terrifying instant. Grabbing for air and flesh, the mass erupted a few feet in front of crouching soldiers. Cordell raced along the wall, cocking the pistols and pulling the poles to unleash their patterned fire once again. A ripple of painful responses trailed the blasts. Loud yelling led the confused movement away from the front trees, although their own heavy gunsmoke made it hard for the three Confederates to see much of anything.- Whisper added the final touch by lighting the powder tip on the first "cannon" to let it smoke, as Taullery and Cordell resumed their individual firing. Their targets were shadows as the Federals dropped back farther and farther into the forest.

"Hey, we scared 'em off, how about that!" Whisper said, his raspy voice straining with the excitement that was lying on top of his fear.

Cordell responded firmly, "Get reloaded fast. Everything. Keep spread out. They'll charge in a few minutes to try to get a read on our size. If we can stop this probe, that should make 'em think for a while, maybe."

Taullery caught the slight hesitancy in his friend's voice and glanced at Whisper. The older man was biting his lip as he shoved new loads into his weapons. Why couldn't he get the image of that huge snake out of his mind? He wiped away sweat lurking on his forehead in spite of the cold. Keeping an eye on the clearing, Cordell added new caps, charges, and balls from the bandolier. He saw the hound standing quietly near him, reached out to pet it, and sensed more than saw the Union movement. His command to fire was unnecessary.

With one hand, Taullery and Cordell yanked the poles of their pistol rigs and fired their rifles with the other. Whisper fired his pistol set but forgot the fourth pole as two hundred Yankee soldiers scrambled forward in an ordered advance on the Confederate earthworks. The three scouts poured lead into the halfhearted attack.

A solitary Yankee soldier outran the others, dodging and weaving toward the entrenched enemy. He reached the wall, looked back to see where his fellow comrades were, and saw none close. His eyes brightened in discovery just before Whisper's bullet split his forehead. Across the ragged blue line, soldiers were turning and scrambling back for cover in spite of their officers' urgent orders.

"Now the artillery!" Cordell commanded.

His first shot missed the remaining powder sack, but his second didn't. An already dead Yankee soldier was actually lying on top of the hidden powder when it blew up, adding to the frightening effect on the scattering soldiers. Taullery's rapid shots with his rifle clipped the branches and down came the hurtling weight, crashing through the tree. A scream was proof of someone being hit. Whisper smoked the remaining two log cannons and remembered the fourth pistol rig. Running bent over, he reached the pole and triggered the five simultaneous shots as the last of the blue uniforms evaporated into the forest.

Eerie quiet came abruptly. The three men held their fire, reloading weapons while watching the grove. Time was flirting with their nerves. What would the Federals do next? An hour passed with no sign of any movement. Then another. And another, Blackbirds began to sing in the thickets to their left. A red-tailed hawk came to rest on the closest tree behind them. A light wind was gaining the courage to bring more cold.

Taullery walked over to Cordell. "Rule, they may be skirting outside us, to hit our flank."

"Well, they can't do it very fast. We'll hear 'em in that damn thicket. No, I think they're getting ready to send some lines straight at us. Or waiting for artillery to get here."

Taullery came to his real reason for talking. "It's

time to get out. Before they come with a load of men. We can't handle something like that. Rule. If they hadn't stopped, we wouldn't have turned that first bunch—and you know it. They've had glass on us. Soon they'll figure we ain't for real, if they haven't already."

"If they had, they'd have come a lot harder a lot earlier, Ian. Let's give 'em one more. Then we'll go," Cordell said, his eyes squinting in determination.

"We can't stop 'em, Rule. We've done our job. It's been more'n three hours now since they hit the clearing. Nearly four. If Longstreet and Hill don't have men repositioned by now, there's nothing we can do about it."

Cordell hesitated. Clearly, the Yankee command was uncertain about what they were facing. Their own intelligence had been wrong so often; the lack of sureness was evident. He had guessed right; the Yankee division was waiting on orders from somewhere else. Maybe Meade himself. Or Grant. That would take time. Precious time the Rebels needed.

"Now, Rule. We go now. There's nothin' to be gained in our dying here."

Cordell didn't answer for what seemed like minutes.

"You're right, Ian. One at a time. Whisper first, then you right behind him. I'll follow."

As he spoke, a line of blue spread across the open meadow in front of the trees as if formed out of the brown grass itself. Taullery, Whisper, and Cordell opened up on the first wave of Yankee soldiers. Three blue uniforms dropped as if by one shot. Another set staggered and fell. But the rest kept marching toward the Confederate entrenchment as if nothing had occurred. Behind the first line of Union soldiers came a second. A third was in position to charge, barely seen back in the blackness of the trees. Yankee sniper fire ripped at the logs and mud, sending splinters and dirt flying. Thirty dummy stands were blown away like the ticking of an unseen clock, leaving only shredded stakes shivering in the cold midday gray. Taullery's "general" dummy spun sideways and collapsed.

"Whisper! To the horses! Now!" yelled Taullery. "We'll be right behind you. Go!"

As if anticipating the command, Whisper stuffed his pistols in his belt, picked up his rifle, and began running crouched as low as he could. Instinctively grabbing his top hat to make certain it was on tight, Whisper turned to cry out to his friends below. Neither of the rapid-firing Rebel scouts heard his hoarse pleas to hurry.

"Ian! Now! I'll follow!" Cordell yelled without looking away from the rapidly advancing line of blue.

The tall cavalryman scrambled toward the horses along the same route Whisper had followed minutes earlier. Bullets tracked his climb, spitting clumps of frozen dirt. An embedded rock gave way under the weight of his boot. Losing his balance, he grabbed for a stand of dead grass, but it pulled loose in his hand and he slid out of control down the hillside.

Whisper started down to give him a hand, but Taullery shook it off. As the hoarse-voiced Confederate turned toward the nervous horses, a rifle bullet blasted into his left arm. He screamed and grabbed at the spurting blood above his elbow. He staggered and fell.

"Come on, Rule! Come on!" Taullery shouted back at Cordell. "We don't have much time!

A scarlet line across Cordell's head slammed away his response. He struggled to recover from the bullet that had skimmed across his forehead, jolting his mind. The intense cavalryman dropped his chin for an instant, made a cross in the dirt with his finger, and

mumbled, "I love you, Mother...Father." He vomited as the dizziness shook his entire being. The hound
waited for him to do something. Cordell waved at the
animal to seek Taullery, but it stood, waiting on the
man who cared.

Mortar explosions ripped into the hillside and
breastworks. Federal gunfire was without end. Rule
Cordell looked up at Taullery helping the bloodied
Whisper onto an agitated horse, took a deep breath,
regained his balance, and lumbered toward them.

"C-c-come on, dog!" he cried. The hound nearly
knocked him down as it jumped around the staggering
scout, barking gleefully.

"I've got your roan!" Taullery screamed from his
saddle, as if the words would hasten his best friend to
safety. He had tied the tired horse's lead rope around
his silver-topped saddle horn.

As Cordell scrambled up the hillside, Taullery levered his rifle at the heads of Yankee soldiers cresting
the top of the breastworks. Gasping for breath, Cordell
reached his horse but could not find the strength to
climb into the saddle. His face was white with shock.
Blood stung his eyes and blurred his vision.

"G-g-go on, I—I—I can't make it," he muttered, letting go of a handful of horse's mane and staggering
backward.

Before the words were out of his mouth, Taullery
was down from his horse, holding the reins of both
horses and pushing the weakened Cordell into his saddle. The animal seemed to understand, and was quiet
while bullets whined around them and ate at the
ground. Whisper was delirious, his dangling arm dark
with blood. The horses were snorting, stomping their
hooves and nervously churning in place.

"Hold on, Rule," Taullery cautioned, and swung up
onto his horse, using his good leg for leverage. "Whis-

per, you have to grab the mane with your good hand. You have to. Can you do it, man?"

Whisper nodded his head and spat a thin line of tobacco juice toward the north.

"W-w-where's the d-d-dog?" Cordell asked.

"Right here. He's fine," Taullery answered, and then yelled, "Go! Go! Go!"

They broke as one toward the west: three riders, four horses, and one dog. Gunfire sought their bodies as they escaped. A mile from the breastworks, they met up with a thousand Confederate soldiers being redeployed to meet the Yankee flanking division. The Rebel force was supported by a battery of real twelve-pounders; three were already in position and a fourth was being unloaded from its artillery wagon.

A Rebel yell, lifted into the cold air by swirls of breath frost, went up through the entire line as the trio galloped into camp, trailed closely by a dog. They reined to a stop at a wide-bellied major, smoking a pipe and directing the placement of fresh-cut logs for firing posts.

More falling than dismounting, Cordell started to speak, then remembered he needed to salute. It was more like someone brushing dust from his hat. The major returned it crisply, staring at the long-haired cavalryman with two holstered pistols and another shoved into his belt, then saw the small stone earring. A dark crease across his forehead and dried blood fingers down his face could easily have been warpaint. If the uniform hadn't been there, he would have sworn he was looking at a wild Indian warrior.

Between grasps for breath, Cordell reported, "Major, sir, we are cavalry patrol, assigned to General Longstreet. We just slowed down a Union division headed this way. Humphrey's Two Corps. Mile back, at the clearing where the old stand is. Fooled their collective asses, I reckon."

"We were warned by your courier. Good work, Lieutenant. We're as ready as we're going to be. Longstreet can't shift more support than this," the major confirmed. "It may not be enough. All our lines are thin. Too thin. Are you all right, Lieutenant? Let my doctors have a look at you."

The hound, like its master, was panting deeply for left-behind breath and came quickly to his side. Cordell petted the dog's head before answering. The exchange brought clarity to his mind.

"I'm fine. Just a crease—and a headache. But my friend there is hurt real bad. We need to get him to the doctors quick. Ol' Whisper's a tough one, but he's lost a lot of blood. I don't know how he stayed in the saddle."

"I don't know how you did either, Lieutenant."

Taullery dismounted slowly from Whisper's horse, where he had ridden for most of the way, after realizing his friend couldn't stay on by himself. Whisper was slumped over in the saddle, his head now lying against the horse's neck. Taullery's voice was urgent. "We need to get our friend to a doc, Major. Real quick. Where can we go?"

The major's eyes moved from Cordell to Taullery to Whisper. He turned to three soldiers and ordered, "Men, take this man to the field hospital. Now! Tell them I want him looked at right away. He's a goddamn hero. Saved a bunch of Reb lives today, he did."

The soldiers saluted, spun on their heels, and eased the limp Whisper from his horse. Cordell and Taullery walked over to help, but the three infantrymen insisted on taking care of the unconscious cavalryman.

As the two friends watched the soldiers carry Whisper away, Cordell shook his head to clear it of the sickening ache. He remembered the military situation and said, "Major, after we get fresh horses, we'll backtrack and see what's happening, if that sounds good to you. I reckon those Yanks are going to be angry as all hell."

"That won't be necessary. Hill sent scouts out an hour ago, shortly after your courier came in. Surprised you didn't pass them coming in."

Cocking his head to the side, Cordell asked tautly, "When did they leave? Where were they headed?"

"I don't know. They went directly from Hill's headquarters, so they would be riding northwest. I was advised not to send out scouts of our own. You think they ran into trouble?"

"Depends on the men."

"Ever think about counterattacking the bastards, instead of waiting?" Cordell asked, his reddened eyes searching the major's face for courage.

"My orders were to stand and engage. Yours are to stay here, Lieutenant."

"'We have made a covenant with death and with, with hell are…at agreement,'" Cordell recited dully.

"What? What's that mean?!"

Taullery said, "His paw's a minister. That's one of those proverbs or psalms. Which is it, Rule? I can never keep them straight."

"Isiah 28, verse 15."

Appearing at first puzzled by the religious response from such a wild-looking man, the major gave another order: "Bring these two men a plateful of whatever we've got for food—and coffee. Looks like they could use it. Take their horses. Curry them."

He paused, looked at Cordell and Taullery, and said, "Sorry, but we've got no grain for horses here. The boys can water them and take them over to a patch of long grass. It's dead, but it's something."

"Thank ye gladly, Major, that does sound good," Taullery responded, turning toward the officer with a broad smile. Cordell continued to watch the three soldiers carry Whisper toward a stone farmhouse two hundred yards from the entrenchment lines. The major glanced at him and returned his attention to Taullery as the tall man began to embellish Cordell's report.

"Glad to see you boys got the news. Rigged us up a few dummy soldiers—an' a fake firing line made out of poles an' pistols so we could fire a bunch at once," Taullery said loudly. "Damnedest thing I've ever seen. Even had us a few howitzers—made outta tree trunks. Can you believe that? Made 'em think we was a whole Reb army, we did. At least for four hours. Can you believe that, three men stopping two thousand?"

The major removed his pipe and laughed deeply, as if it was welcome relief. A dozen soldiers moved closer to hear the story. Taullery's enthusiasm grew as he added details with a flourish. In conclusion, he pointed at his weary friend and credited him with the idea and his leadership. "You-all have that man—Rule Cordell—to thank for not getting run over by a bunch of bluebellies. It was all the lieutenant's idea. You ought to be damn glad that boy's on our side."

Cordell wasn't paying any attention, talking instead to the soldier who had been assigned their horses; Cordell wanted reassurance about the man's capability. Satisfied, he released the reins and felt the ache in his head for the first time. He was dizzy and took a step sideways to regain his balance. But no one noticed his disorientation. Two soldiers brought tin plates containing a small portion of cornmeal and three bites of beef, along with mugs of hot coffee. Taullery and Cordell accepted them with thanks as the major headed toward an advancing artillery sergeant seeking orders.

"Say, you haven't seen our young rider lately, have you?" Cordell asked the two men who served the food.

One soldier, who had a long, scraggly beard, shrugged his shoulders. "Not since this mornin', I reckon. Last I laid sight o' him, he was a-gittin' in line fer some chow."

Cordell chuckled, and Taullery asked, "How about a Captain Thomas Wilson? Rode in earlier, but I don't know where he checked in. Too damn scared to stay. Ran out on us before the Yanks even showed."

"Naw, ain't seed nary 'nother rider. We all been a mite busy, though. Mighta missed 'im, I reckon."

The other man, a rail-thin sergeant, barefoot in spite of the cold, said, "Heard tell o' a Reb horse without no rider came a-wanderin' into our'n lines this mornin'. Reckon it was a piece after your boy come a-smokin'."

Cordell and Taullery exchanged glances, cleaned their plates in a few swallows, and began savoring the hot coffee, which was little more than boiled water over some old grounds. The two soldiers stayed to ask a few questions about the "masquerade battalion," as it was being spun through the waiting Rebel lines. Taullery answered them with relish; Cordell was quiet, smoking a cigarette. Finally, the two soldiers left for their assigned posts.

Taullery said as he turned his head toward his quiet friend, "Well, I didn't think those boys would—"

He stopped. Cordell was asleep, lying on his back with his hat atop his face. The ugly dog was curled beside him, its head across Cordell's lower legs. Taullery chuckled and said softly, "You deserve a nap, my friend. Look at you. God was sure with us today."

Stepping gingerly to keep his large-roweled spurs from waking Cordell, Taullery eased away from his sleeping friend and headed for a campfire and someone to talk to. He reached inside his coat for a cheroot and realized his cigars had been left behind.

"Damn it!" he muttered, saw the major, and hollered, "Say, Major, you wouldn't know where there's an extra cigar, would you?"

Chapter Six

A push on Cordell's shoulder jarred him from syrupy sleep. It was Taullery. Sundown was gathering in the remaining daylight.

"Are the bluebellies attacking? What time is it?" Cordell asked, stretching his arms to pull his body fully awake and not really caring about the answer. The bullet crease across his forehead throbbed with pain, and he touched it before remembering what it was. He winced as his fingers drew along the scab.

His sleep had been marred by a nightmare that kept returning: his father was leading a Yankee army, spouting obscenities from a Bible. In the dream, Reverend Cordell ordered his son and his mother, the minister's wife, to be hanged for treason. He pushed the unresolved images back into the hole in his mind from which they had crawled and picked up his cavalry hat with its weathered eagle feather.

The wide brim clicked against his Comanche stone

earring as he put it on his head. Tugging on the brim made his head wobble with pain. He looked more bedraggled than wild: his long brown hair stringy; his long coat wrinkled; his hard face lacquered with dried blood and the need for more sleep. One of his pistols had fallen from his belt during the rest. He reached over to retrieve the weapon, wiped it clean, and shoved the short gun into place.

He straightened the bandolier of ammunition lying across his waistcoat. Instinctively he touched the medicine pouch hanging around his neck and whispered a Comanche prayer the shaman who gave him the pouch had taught him. It always seemed more comforting than any his father ever recited.

"Here, wipe your face, Rule," Taullery said, handing him a handkerchief damp with water from his canteen. "You look a sight."

"Yeah, probably so." Cordell accepted the cloth and gingerly wiped his face. "I don't suppose you have a mirror for your friend."

"Do I look like a man who'd carry a mirror? Don't answer that."

They both laughed. Cordell returned the handkerchief and said, "Thanks."

"Our boys turned Humphrey's Two Corps back," Taullery said with pride. "Been watching it most of the afternoon. Thought maybe we ought to be checking on Billy and Whisper."

Taullery withdrew a cigar from inside his coat, then asked Cordell if he wanted one. He declined. Cordell watched his friend methodically rub the cigar, cut one end carefully, and twirl it slowly in his mouth with his fingers as he held the match.

"You going to smoke that—or play with it?" Cordell teased. It hurt to laugh, but he chuckled anyway.

"Better than foolin' with those little paper smokes of yours."

"Man, it's almost sundown," Cordell groaned. "We should've helped. You should've waked me. I shouldn't have slept!"

"Most folks do. Every now 'n' then," Taullery said. "You were all in. Still don't look worth a damn. Oh-h-h-h, it sure didn't get any warmer today. Let's find us a fire someplace."

Cordell grinned at Taullery's remark and answered, "Let's get the horses instead. We've got to find Billy Rip—and check in on Whisper."

Taullery smiled; he had just suggested that. But his words turned to the subject his mind had been spading up and turning over for several hours.

"What do you think will happen next, Rule? With the war, I mean," Taullery asked, his voice thin and tentative.

He looked down at his uniform, then over at Cordell, and brushed away some imagined dirt on his butternut waistcoat. His preening continued with an adjustment of the blue silk scarf around his neck, straightening his rose-embroidered gauntlets and repositioning his plumed hat. He assessed his cavalry boots and was disappointed to see they were now badly scuffed. Quickly he rubbed each one on the back of his leg as they walked.

"Depends—on us," Cordell observed, ignoring his friend's cosmetic antics and moving swiftly toward the picket line. "Grant's going to hit us again. Like a big pincer. Two ends at the same time. Hell, he's got enough troops to smash through anyplace—if he can catch us, and we're standing still right now."

"What can we do?"

"Well, if it were me, I'd send cavalry smashing into one of their pincers, leave a small holding force to slow down the other—and pull my boys out fast. If we stay here, it's just a matter of time."

"It's over, isn't it?"

Cordell's eyes flashed anger at the statement. "Hell no, it's not over. We've just got to find a way to flank 'em hard. Put them on their heels, then race for Washington. That'll end this thing once 'n' for all." Anger brought a sharp pain, and he pushed his fingertips against his forehead to relieve it.

"If you did that, they'd take Richmond."

They reached the picket line, found their horses, and began saddling them.

"Richmond's a town," Cordell said as he yanked the cinch. "If I have to choose between a town and my army, I'd take my army."

Taullery thought a moment, pushing the bit into place in his horse's mouth before responding. "But... that's our capital. That's where Davis is—and his... his cabinet. You just said taking Washington would end it—for them."

Cordell swung into the saddle and said with finality, "You asked what I would do, Ian. That's what I would do. I'd rather run these sons of bitches all the way back to Canada—but I think a run at Washington would end it. The trick is not to get hung up on the importance of a town. Let *them* do that. Make them worry about *their* special place. Richmond ain't Texas, Ian."

That satisfied Taullery, and they rode in quiet, keeping alert for their young companion, Billy Ripton. Suddenly, Cordell saw him among a group of tired troops pulled back from the front lines; the teenager was watching three soldiers sing some sad song while another played an old banjo. The young man spotted the riders at the same time and sprung from a squatting position like a June bullfrog. He ran toward them, laughing and crying at the same time. Both men swung down from their horses. Cordell gave Billy Ripton a hug, followed by an enthusiastic handshake; Taullery repeated the greeting.

"Ohmygod! Ohmygod! I reckoned ya was dead! Ohmygod!" Billy hollered into the bitter-cold dusk. "I tol' 'em ye were the best that ever was. I tol' 'em what ya was up ta—an' they all didn't believe me. Nossiree."

The long-armed teenager pulled off his woolen hood in excitement at seeing his friends again. He stomped first one boot and then the other on the hard ground to express his joy in an awkward-looking dance.

"Ohmygod, Rule-sey, ya bin hit! Damn, them Yanks came 'bout as close as a feller could to puttin' yur lights out. Is ya all right, Rule-sey?"

Cordell assured him that he was fine; the teenager looked to Taullery for assurance, and he shrugged his shoulders. Not certain what to do or say next, Billy told them about seeing Captain Wilson's horse come across the line earlier in the day—without a rider. He had feared the worst. Taullery told him about the leader sneaking out and proceeded to explain in grand detail how their surprise had worked.

Impatient, Cordell told the young man to swing up onto his horse and go with them to visit Whisper in the hospital. Billy looked at the big roan, patted its withers, and said he would rather walk along with him and not put the horse to the extra load. So they rode on, with Taullery elaborating about the day and Billy Ripton walking and listening with a goofy smile on his face.

Rule Cordell was the first to enter the stone-walled farmhouse doing its best to be a field hospital. He told the stray dog to stay outside; it melted obediently next to the front steps. Ian Taullery and Billy Ripton followed, two strides behind. The three cavalrymen stopped inside the doorway and surveyed the medical operation. Death moans, murmured prayers, and soul-splitting screams of agony greeted their ears. Stomach-twisting smells of dying flesh, dried blood, and sweat, mixed with medicinal aromas and stale air, rushed at their noses and spat at their eyes.

Every space, from litters to carts, from makeshift bunks to the floor itself, was layered with wounded, sick, and dying men. Many were so weak from malnutrition and disease that any wound was likely to be fatal. Typhoid, dysentery, and pneumonia were worse killers than bullets, with no clue as to their cause. Some doctors thought certain odors might set off the diseases; others suggested changes in the air were the culprit. No one considered the lack of cleanliness as a possible place to start, much less the placement of latrines in relation to the water supply.

Yet the entire hospital was in a slow waltz, waiting for the next battle to yield a new harvest of bloodied warriors. Throughout the honeycomb of rooms, doctors and their assistants ceremonially checked their patients, moving in a measured dance of anticipation, without apparent energy or focus. At least the brittle cold had been turned away at the door. A humid warmth greeted them, created more from too many men occupying the space than from the efficiency of a woodstove in the corner. The laboring cast-iron unit was adding as much raspy smoke as heat.

Around the stove, four bloodstain-jacketed men and two women stood, talking about a party they had attended in Richmond the previous Christmas. Six men, coughing and wheezing, lay on a harvest wagon with no wheels; Billy Ripton wondered aloud how the vehicle had been brought inside, but neither of his older companions answered. The youngest rider held his nose briefly to remove the smell of death seeking his brain and looked at his older friends for agreement, but neither was paying any attention to him.

Taullery's interest was a young woman with long reddish curls and a band of freckles across her pert nose. She was gently washing the face of a wounded soldier. Cordell, too, was distracted, watching a gray-haired minister kneel beside a bed in solemn prayer. The soldier he was praying for was obviously dead. Though he still held his nose, Billy Ripton's vision left the flattened wagon and was immediately drawn to a soldier, younger than himself, lying in a blood-soaked litter; the boy's face was a mangle of red and black. Billy Ripton swallowed, blinked, and tried to look away, but couldn't.

"I don't see Whisper, do you?" Cordell finally asked, and turned his head toward the young rider, struggling with his emotions.

"Ah, no," Billy answered, embarrassed to be holding his nose, so he acted as if he were wiping it.

"Let's get him out of here. I don't like this place," Cordell grunted. "We can take care of him ourselves. What do you think?"

"Ah, yeah," Billy answered, his hand now at his side but his eyes continually returning to the dying boy.

"Ian? What do you think?" Cordell said, but got no answer. "Ian? Hey man, let's get Whisper out of here. What do you think?"

Taullery slowly realized that Cordell was talking to him. He turned his head away from his blossoming flirtation and asked, "What?"

"Oh, hell, Taullery, leave her alone. Let's find Whisper and get him outta this goddamn place."

"Oh, it's not so bad, Rule. Hell, it's a hospital. What did you expect it to be like?" Taullery said.

In the far corner, tending to an unmoving soldier

with his face completely wrapped, was the closest surgeon. He was a huge man with a numb expression over
which were wild eyebrows enjoying a life of their
own. His long hospital coat was heavily splattered
with blood; his eyes carried the stare of a man who had
done too much, too often. It didn't appear he had seen
them come in. He took a cursory look at the soldier's
leg wound and was pleased to see that pus was forming within it.

"Hey, Doc! We're looking for a friend. Came in two
hours ago. Whisper Jenson's his name. Got hit in the
arm," Cordell called out, ignoring his friend's
response.

The surgeon turned slowly toward the door, his
movements like those of a much older man with
aching joints. Before speaking, he stared down at his
hands and seemed surprised they were stained a weird
reddish color. A long sigh disconnected his mind from
the visual reminder of his responsibilities.

With a rhythmic accent and spiked eyebrows bob-
bing up and down like strands of buffalo grass in a
high wind, he responded, "Yo-all stand easy. I saw ya
a-comin' hither. We'll git to ya in a spell, ya hear? Got
some folks to be a-tendin' to, ya know."

As if he had already forgotten his own statement, he
strolled over to the three men. His breath was laced
with whiskey; his eyes were reddened with the tension
of his activity. He stood at least eight inches taller than
Cordell, and forty pounds heavier.

"We're not staying. Just came for our friend—and
maybe some bandages and whatever. We'll take care
of him ourselves," Cordell answered tautly, looking up
at the surgeon. The difference in height was apparently lost on Cordell, who stepped aggressively
toward the man as he spoke.

Young Billy Ripton loudly uh-huhed agreement.

Cordell glanced at Taullery, but he was silently evaluating the doctor's size, bothered by his being three inches taller than the lanky cavalryman. The surgeon hunched his shoulders to push away the frustration growing within him and said with a slur, "Yo-all don't like the look o' this hyar place, I take it. Yo'all see any bandages? Any medicine? Hell, boys, we dun run outta things like that thar a long piece back. Bin a-usin' ladies' dresses mostly—and corn liquor, if we kin find it."

Taullery started to speak, but Cordell's growl beat him to it. "Looks like you found some, Doc. If there's any left, give us some of that—for our friend. And how about that bedsheet, or whatever it is, on the camp chest...there. We'll take that. I'll ask again, where is Whisper Jenson?"

"Yo-all a doctor?" the surgeon asked, the corner of his mouth pulled upward by the sarcasm of his question but pushed slightly off line by the whiskey's growing effect.

"Well, now, that's an interesting question," Cordell said, his eyes flashing. "If you're asking me if I have a piece of paper stating so, the answer is no. If you're asking me if I know how to heal wounds, the answer is I'm as good as anything I've seen in here so far. Now, where's our friend?"

The surgeon visibly recoiled from Cordell's harsh response; he rubbed his palm against his mouth to wipe the liquor away. Taullery frowned.

Hands resting on his holstered pistols, Cordell continued, "We aren't leaving him here to have one of you cut off his arm—or God knows what else—and fling it into a pile of other pieces of men in some godforsaken corner. If you don't know where he is, step aside and we'll find him."

Without moving closer, the surgeon cocked his

head, saw the line of dried blood along the side of Cordell's forehead, and grimaced at the sight. He'd seen that too many times before on dead men. He was growing fascinated by this heavily armed cavalryman.

"Yo-all think yah kin jes' come in hyar and take yur fill o' bandages and whiskey, son? Shoot, yo-all looks like yah could use some doctorin' yurse'f. That's a mighty mean crease. They didn't miss ya by much. Reckon ya got yurse'f a heap of a headache, don't ya?" the surgeon said with a tired whine. His eyebrows stood alert; his eyes betrayed a friendliness not heard in his words or seen in his expression.

"I'm just fine, Doc. We're here to get our friend." Cordell's voice was edged with impatience.

Taullery put a hand on Cordell's shoulder and said, "Easy, Rule. He doesn't mean any harm." Taullery smiled at the nurse he had seen earlier. She was standing and watching their exchange. Her pale face reddened in response to his attention. Her own smile was hesitant but definitely inviting.

"Just point us toward our friend and we'll be out of here quick," Taullery said without much conviction while enjoying his visual inspection of the young woman.

"Your friend...well, if'n he be the one I recollect, he jes' came off the table—not more'n, oh, ten or fifteen minutes, I reckon. Lucky for him, it were kinda quiet when he arrived. Got him ri't on thar. Took that mess o' an arm off," the surgeon said, his eyes betraying no surprise or concern, only the dullness of the whiskey taking over.

Cordell's entire body burned, turning his eyes into flames of anger. His mouth opened but nothing came out. He hadn't expected this. Not at all. His mind searched wildly for an explanation, an understanding. How could this have happened? Why did they leave

Whisper alone? Was this a nightmare? Let him wake up—now! Taullery's head spun toward the drunken surgeon, and his eyes sought verification of this statement.

Only Billy Ripton found words. "You dun what?!"

Cordell's bewilderment finally found expression. "You son of a bitch! You goddamn drunk sonuvabitch! How dare you cut off Whisper's arm! I'll k—"

Around the corner came a second surgeon, a short, stout man with an equally bloody hospital coat. In his hands was a double-barreled shotgun.

"Soldier boy, we'all don't take kindly to such as you bargin' in here a-tellin' us how to do things. You get the hell outta here. Do it now before I add to the blood in this place."

Through gritted teeth, Cordell motioned toward the armed man and spat, "Is this the bastard that sawed on our friend, Doc—or was it you?"

The first surgeon muttered, "Yeah, he done the sawin'. Good work it were. It had to come off, son—or it'd turned all infected an' kilt him, yessir."

Taullery whispered, "It's all right, Rule. It's all right. They're doctors. They know what they're doing."

Billy Ripton stared at the doctor as if not comprehending how a shotgun and a physician could be together, especially one who had just severed their friend's arm.

It was Taullery who spoke to the shotgun-waving doctor first. "Easy now, we just came in to see our friend. Didn't mean to cause any ruckus. We're just worried about him. Didn't expect to hear he was operated on. We thought—"

The doctor with the shotgun ordered, "He's in good hands. You-all git. They'll be needing you at the fightin'." He paused and said with a half-grin, "Maybe I'll be seem' you back here then—on my table, like your friend."

The big surgeon pursed his lips as his magnificent eyebrows rose in response to his associate's performance. "Dr. Harrison. Yo-all jes' take that thar belly gun back whar you found it—an' git back to the table. Thar be a fine soldier boy a-waitin fer yah."

Hesitating at first, the stocky doctor let the barrel of the shotgun dip toward the ground, started to leave, but stopped, unable to resist the urge to take another verbal jab at Cordell.

"Anybody tell you that damn flower on your lapel is dead?" Dr. Harrison snapped, his eyes matching the sassiness of his words.

Taullery's gasp could be heard over the hospital's sounds of death. Cordell said nothing in response. Dr. Harrison looked at Cordell with a sneering anticipation, but the stocky doctor's face withered against the intensity of Cordell's stare. Shaking his shoulders to relieve the tremor within him, the doctor turned and went back to the operating table in the next room. A nervous laugh was more relief than satisfaction.

"Yo-all come 'n' see yur friend now, ya hear. He's back hyar," the first doctor said, filling the hard silence with as friendly an invitation as his own whiskey-sluggish mind could create.

Whisper lay unconscious or asleep on a bunk. A fat log was tied in place where one of the bed's legs should have been. The stump of Whisper's arm was wrapped tightly with a blue calico cloth trimmed with white lace. Purple bloodstains added their own pattern to the former dress. Billy Ripton gagged and fell away.

Taullery put his hand on Cordell's shoulder and said, "Rule, you know they had no choice. I looked at

Whisper's arm when we rode in, man, and it was pure mangle. Rule..."

For a moment Cordell said nothing, and Taullery thought his friend was going to listen to him. But without a word, the intense cavalryman spun away from his friend's light restraint and headed for the second doctor, who was preparing for surgery. A moaning soldier with two bloody legs was stretched out on a table in front of him. Dr. Harrison sensed Cordell coming before he saw him. His eyes darted for the shotgun propped against a walnut cabinet across the room. It was too far away.

In a dozen furious steps, Cordell was standing inches away from the frightened surgeon. Cordell's hard eyes caught the doctor's fearful face and he slapped it. Dr. Harrison took a step backward, his trembling hands awkwardly held away from his side. Cordell spoke slowly, the menace in his words like the cocking of a pistol hammer, his arms folded. Anyone farther than a few feet away might think he was simply chatting, or possibly apologizing for his earlier outburst.

Taullery had no illusions about what his friend was doing, but he remained next to Whisper. When the big doctor started to move toward the exchange, Taullery touched the man's arm and whispered, "No." The word was a saber to the doctor's intent; he jerked to a stop and straightened his back. Billy Ripton vomited on two soldiers lying on the floor.

"You shouldn't have cut off his arm." Cordell's words rolled out like the distant first sounds of a thunderstorm. But the pain in his head became the lightning as he grimaced to keep it from controlling him.

"I—I—I h-h-had no choice. E-e-everyone a-a-agreed," Dr. Harrison said.

"Did you ask him if he wanted his arm cut off?"

"N-n-n-o-o, he—he w-w-was unconscious, ya k-k-know. U-u-unconscious-s-s. I—I—I . . . we c-c-couldn't w..."

His voice trailed off as he watched Cordell lift surgical instruments one at a time from an open wood box. Cordell came upon a surgical saw, held it up, and ran his fingers along the serrated edge. He looked up and said, "I'll be back. If my friend dies, I'm going to saw off your arm and ram it up your ass. Then I'll follow it with that scattergun of yours over there. Do you understand?"

The doctor's mouth sagged, and drool ran down the right corner of his trembling lower lip. He said nothing. His eyes ran toward the huge doctor and pleaded for assistance. The first doctor deliberately looked down at Whisper Jenkins and ignored the second doctor' s plight. Cordell laid the saw down, turned, and walked away. He took two steps, wheeled around, and swiftly returned to the doctor. Cordell's face was red; his forehead was furrowed; his mouth was a slash of intensity; a trickle of fresh blood from the bullet crease was searching the right side of his face.

Dr. Harrison took a deep breath and bit his lower lip to stop the shaking. His eyes could see only the many pistols in this frightening man's belt.

"Do you have any chewing tobacco?" Cordell asked.

The question stunned the doctor, who could only manage to shake his head.

"Damn, he's partial to it," Cordell said, and turned his head. "Ian, Billy Rip—got any chew?"

Billy said he did, and Cordell waved him over. As Cordell took the tobacco square from the young rider, Billy was wiping vomit from his mouth with the back of his other hand. Cordell stared at him but didn't say anything, then turned back to the fearful doctor.

"How about whiskey? The big doc said you had some corn juice," Cordell said as he gave the tobacco plug to Dr. Harrison. "Our friend will want some whiskey when he wakes up."

"W-w-we've g-g-got some," the doctor stammered, watching the plug quiver in his outstretched hand. He pointed toward the cabinet with the shotgun leaning against it. "G-g-got a bottle of T-T-Tennessee w-w-whiskey. G-g-good stuff."

Cordell hurried to the cabinet, ignoring the shotgun resting against it. He opened the thick walnut door and saw three full bottles of whiskey. Grabbing one, he kicked the door shut with his boot and returned to Dr. Harrison, who stood unmoving, waiting for instructions and hoping this strange Rebel warrior would not erupt again.

"Put a bottle by his bed, so it's close when he wants it," Cordell said.

"Y-y-yessir," Dr. Harrison answered as he accepted the bottle from Cordell.

"When he wakes up, I expect that nurse over there to read to him. As long as he wants. We'll be back with a book. If he's unhappy, I'll be looking for you. Got that?"

Cordell's answer was a rapidly repeating nod.

Chapter Seven

"By the way, asshole, General Stuart wore a rose. We rode with him. This one came from his funeral. I shot the sonuvabitch doctor that let him die," Cordell said flatly, then he turned around and walked toward the door. Billy Ripton was right with him.

Taullery had already left Whisper Jenson's bed and was talking to the freckle-faced woman. He saw Cordell leaving, quickly kissed the lady's hand, and caught up with his two friends. Out of the corner of his eye, Taullery saw the big doctor take a bottle of whiskey from a drawer and put it to his lips. The gray-haired minister was standing near the doorway, obviously waiting for the exiting cavalrymen.

With his jaw thrust forward, the watery-eyed minister advised Cordell in a syrupy voice, "My son, have no worry. I will pray for your friend."

Cordell stared at the officious minister and saw, instead, his father. He started to speak, but Taullery recognized the torment in his friend's eyes for what it was, and cautioned, "Don't, Rule. He means well."

Taullery immediately took Cordell's arm to guide him past the encounter, saying as he moved, "Thanks, Reverend, we would appreciate that."

Cordell started to resist his friend's pushing but didn't. Billy opened the door and the three cavalrymen went outside. Cold air rushed to greet them before the tail-wagging dog could. Their horses, tied to the hitching rail, were hunched together for warmth. Billy Ripton knelt to scratch the animal's ears; Taullery shivered away the first reaction to the cold; Cordell was somewhere else, untouched by the winter's grasp or the dog's eagerness for attention. No one spoke for a moment. The winter's dusk was maturing into a dark, starless void.

In a raw voice pushed by his feelings, Cordell said, "Pray with me, Ian...Billy. Pray that Whisper will live."

Billy Ripton looked up from petting the dog as if he had been hit with a rock in the face. Taullery said simply, "I will." The tall man's face was a lamp of relief; he had expected Cordell to be angry at him. Both friends bowed their heads, with Billy first watching, then standing and bowing his.

"God...our friend, Whisper, n-n-needs you. P-please watch over him, will you, God? Make him w-well...please," Cordell stuttered softly, his eyes squeezed tight.

"Amen," Taullery said, and patted Cordell on the shoulder. He noticed fresh bleeding from Cordell's head wound but decided not to say anything about it. He knew Rule Cordell well, and mentioning it would only anger him.

"Uh, yeah, amen, too," Billy added, still puzzled by

Cordell's sudden spiritual expression and his obvious distress over Whisper's condition.

He had never seen Cordell this way before. At least, not that he could remember. Cordell was like a fierce prairie fire, always hungry for new things to attack, unable to be stopped. No one was like him in battle. Unmerciful. Daring. Flaunting Yankee gun and sword. Billy Ripton wanted to ask him if he was all right but didn't dare to do so.

The silence was broken by the sound of a horse galloping toward them. The rider reined in the horse, jumped down, and nearly disappeared behind the thick frost smoke from the horse's nostrils even in the heavy dusk. The ears of their mounts were immediately alert. Cordell's roan stomped the ground in anger at having his solitude broken.

"One of you Lieutenant Cordell?" the rider asked. His thin, light mustache matched his youngish, pimpled face.

"I am."

"With General Longstreet's compliments, sir," the courier stated with a newfound crispness, saluted, and handed Cordell a folded paper.

"What's this?" Cordell asked dully.

"I believe, sir, you've been promoted to captain," the young rider reported with a wide smile. "The general wants you to bring your patrol and report to his headquarters immediately. A regiment of cavalry are forming there now—for you to lead. Counterattack, I believe, sir."

Taullery and Billy Ripton crowded around Cordell as he unfolded and read the orders silently. The dog pushed against Cordell's leg, and he handed the document to Taullery and squatted to pet the animal.

"All two of us will be joining him, son," Taullery

said to the courier with a sour grin. Cordell hadn't responded, and it was obvious he hadn't.

"General Longstreet wants you now...Captain Cordell, sir," the courier advised. "Are you hurt bad, sir? Your wound, it's..."

"What if I don't want to be captain?" Cordell asked with eyes that drove the courier's eyesight to the ground. Sensing the blood trickle for the first time, he dabbed at it with his hand, examined the redness on his fingers, and rubbed it away on his long coat.

"We'll be there," Taullery answered for his friend. "Just don't make it sound like an order, boy. Captain Cordell doesn't respond real well to orders. You ride on back to the general and say he'll be along shortly—with his patrol."

The courier appeared relieved, but he kept his gaze from recatching Cordell's as the cavalryman reached inside his coat for the bag of tobacco, then rolled and lit a cigarette. His duty completed, the young soldier remounted and kicked his horse into anew gallop, trailing bits of hard ground and frost smoke.

"There goes another good night's sleep," Taullery remarked.

"Since when did you take up sleeping?" Cordell growled. "And what makes you think I want to be a damn captain?"

Taullery laughed, shook his head, and said, "I don't give a damn if you do. But if you don't, I'm betting Lee will find another fool like Wilson to lead us around. So—you don't have any choice, Rule. You're it, by God."

Billy Ripton wasn't certain whether he should laugh or not, so he coughed. As he leaned forward, he saw the dog again and blurted, "What about the dog, Rule? Is he coming with us?"

"Why not. Give him a gun."

All three men burst into laughter. The ugly hound's ears perked and its tailed slapped the air. Cordell squatted on one knee, and the animal came instantly to him.

"What are we going to call you, boy?" Cordell said with a cigarette in one hand and his other running along its furry back.

"How about Sam? For good old Sam Houston," Taullery suggested.

"Sam's a good name for a dog," Cordell observed.

Billy Ripton was quiet, then finally stuttered, "Ah-h-h...my'b-big brother's name was Sam. Sam Houston Ripple. He...d-done died at Bull Run, the fust un, an'—"

"Sam's not a good name for a dog. How about Texas?" Cordell said.

"Texas! That's the right one," Taullery agreed.

Cordell turned his head toward his friend, and the dog took advantage of the distraction and licked him on the cheek.

"Hey! I guess he likes Texas too!" Cordell exclaimed, and flipped the smoke toward the ground.

"Texas it is, then," Taullery pronounced, noticing that Billy Ripton's eyes had become glazed and distant. "Hello, Texas. We're glad to have you with us."

Cordell stood, looked from Billy Ripton to Taullery, and said, "We've got to find a book for Whisper before we leave. You still got that sack of gold?"

Taullery smiled and said, "You take Billy Rip and get him something good to ride. I'll rustle up a couple of books and something to eat. An' some captain's bars while I'm at it. But I'm saving that money for us to celebrate with—after this is all over."

Cordell stared at him, touched the crease on his head, and looked away. He would will the new pain to go away; this was no time to be slowed down.

The rest of the day and night was a whirl of preparation mixed with catnaps. Under a bitter dawn, the frigid ground blossomed with mounted soldiers struggling with horses as anxious as their riders. A chilling wind created a colorful dance of the swallow-tailed company guidon, the squared regimental flag, and swirling snowflakes left from yesterday. A rabbit watched from the edge of a scraggly line of pine trees, uncaring of the intense Rebel cavalry officer or his men, but wary of the large dog loping beside them.

Behind Captain Rule Cordell was the familiar song of rattling canteens and jingling bit-chains, mixed with the dry scuffle of saddle leather and the fretting and snorting of horses. The raw bite of Taullery—now Lieutenant Taullery—and his counterpart, Sergeant Hale, could be heard giving orders. Mixed in was the low muttering of men who wished for more sleep, a good cup of coffee, and something to eat.

Breakfast had been a cup of hot water and a pone. That would be the only meal of their day unless they scrounged something from the Yanks. It had been a long time since any of them had enjoyed the simple comfort of a real bed, or savored a home-cooked meal, or felt safe from ambush, or felt warm, or enjoyed a woman's smile. Taullery had managed to find some honey and another cigar. He shared the honey with Cordell and Billy Ripton.

As he readied the cigar, the memory of the nurse's perky face burned into his mind. He could still smell the closeness of her, savor her firm bosom moving gently in rhythm as she walked, and take in her bright eyes seeking his in a silent embrace. He could hardly wait to see her again. Of course, she probably had forgotten all about him, if she ever thought of him at all. He would probably never see her again. He would probably die in this godforsaken cold for a cause that was long past saving. Sometimes he wished he could share that thought with Cordell. But he was afraid his friend wouldn't take it well. Or understand.

Cordell led the regathered horsemen in a controlled gallop toward the last known position of Meade's nearest flank. Lee hoped an unexpected thrust would cause the Union leaders enough worry to move some of their force toward the new problem and give his army an opportunity to strike elsewhere. The general dared not use his already-spread-thin infantry for a flanking move.

At the same time Lee was alerting two of Gordon's divisions to reinforce A. P. Hill's force for a push at the Federal forces near Dalney's Mill in late afternoon. Artillery would support the thrust. If the attack broke open the Federal line, Lee wanted to pour another division into the breach. First the Rebels needed a distraction at their flank, where inexperienced soldiers, according to the report, were lined up alongside battle-fatigued veterans.

Squinting into the gray, the newly appointed Captain Rule Cordell couldn't remember feeling so weary. He had slept some while the cavalry assembled, but it seemed like an eternity had passed when he first saw Humphrey's II Corps in the woods. He shivered and wondered if the clattering hooves on the frozen ground were as loud as they seemed to him.

The silhouette of a rider appeared on the raw hillside ahead. Man, horse, and earth were black, as the yellow rays of morning washed the closest ridge, one of a series separated by mostly frozen marshes, an area jointly populated by heavy stands of pine trees or scrub hardwood trees choked into stunted growth by thick brush. Cordell thought it wasn't the best place to have to fight. In the distance, gunfire greeted the new day. The rhythm of the shooting meant it was entrenched rifle fire. Now the boom of artillery from both sides accented the day's dance of killing.

Captain Cordell held up his gauntleted hand to halt the sixty-eight gray troopers riding behind him. The collected breath of man and horse formed a small cloud within the force. The oncoming rider was Billy Ripton, at full gallop over a long roll of crumbling hills that could hide anything. His return was expected. Urgent spurring could mean good news or bad. The best would be that the ridges ahead were unoccupied and the enemy was fully engaged away from his men. The worst? They were waiting for him. He shifted impatiently in the saddle, watching for the young scout advance.

"Captun Cordell! Captun Cordell!" came the agitated call from Billy Ripton as his horse thundered toward the halted line of gray. The boy thought "Captun Cordell" had a great sound and said it as often as possible.

"Over here, Billy Rip," said Cordell, not trying to guess what the boy had seen and wishing he wouldn't yell.

The winded outrider saluted hurriedly, trying to catch his left-behind breath before reporting, "Goddamn bluebellies ever'whar, Captun Cordell, suh." He liked saying cuss words, which were not allowed in his parents' home.

"Yeah, they grow in this country."

"Huh?"

"Never mind. What did you see?"

"Ol' Marse Robert done guessed right agin, Captun Cordell. We'all's ri't at thar flank. Open door it be into thar whole damn line—but, holy damn, thar be a lot of 'em!"

106

Cordell frowned and asked, "How far away are they?"

"Jes' over that thar ridge. Ya kin see 'em in a meadow, Rulesey—I mean, Captun Cordell, suh. All strung out."

"Are they dug in?"

"Couldn't see real good, Rul—Cap-tun Cordell, but I reckon they's done built theirse'ves some fine log fences an' sech. You know, the regular."

"Are they firing hot 'n' heavy—or is it being controlled?"

Billy Ripton shook his head vigorously before answering, "Captun Cordell, they look ri't serious at it, to me."

Cordell frowned again; Billy Ripton wasn't the best at detail. The young scout went on to explain that the Union force was facing the far east end of Longstreet's line. He said he had gotten close by crawling and that the ridge itself was occupied with a small patrol around a well-placed cannon that was also firing into the Longstreet line. From the boy's description it sounded like a hundred-pounder Parrott rifle mounted on a carriage and firing at the entrenched Rebels.

"That thar's an awful lot of blue," Billy Ripton said, completing his report.

Cordell declared, "Not for us, Billy Rip."

The lad shrugged his shoulders and knew better than to object.

"See any horses?" Cordell asked.

"No, by golly. Nary a one I seed. Mighty hard to git a good eye-set, though, what wi' all the haze 'n' smoke, ya know, Captun Cordell."

"Custer's in there somewhere, I was advised."

Billy Ripton swallowed, and found his courage.

"Onc't we done hit them bluebellies, they's gonna be all over us, ain't they, Captun Cordell?"

"Our job is to make them commit some men from their middle. That's what we're going to do."

"Captun Cor—"

"We're going, Billy Rip," Cordell said with clinched teeth. "If we can take that ridge first—and that long torn—they'll have to support their flank with more men. Our boys will charge the hole they leave. Got it? Now, how many are on that ridge again?"

"No more'n twenty, I put it. Counted 'em real careful-like, figgered ya'd want to know. Wal, reckon I'd say four mo' fer good meausre, suh."

"You're sure, Billy Rip?"

"Wal, damn it all, Captun, that thar's all I dun seed. Counted 'em twice, I did. I kin do that, ya know."

"Good. How close can we get without them seeing us—from the ridge?"

"Don't know 'bout that, Captun Cordell," the boy answered. Then he thought for a moment and said, "Maybe, I reckon, a long smoke away—if'n we's real careful-like."

Cordell asked his young scout to make a picture of the assembled ridge force on the ground with rocks and twigs. After completing the task, Billy Ripton paused as if trying to find the right words and said with a widening grin and refound confidence, "If we'uns go now, I reckon we kin kick 'em hard in the ass. Fer a change."

Cordell turned around to his men and ordered, "Sergeant Hale! Lieutenant Taullery! Front and center, on the double."

Watching the two men swing out of the column and canter toward him, Cordell was struck by how even their riding styles matched their personalities. Taullery sat stiff-backed; his uniform like a winter flower; his arms in perfect equestrian position; his body alert to any change in the horse's movement; his eyes darting about the land seeking answers to questions his brain hadn't yet formed. The ostrich plume in his cocked hat and the bright blue silk scarf around his neck fluttered in rhythm with his canter. His skeptical nature could be frustrating to Cordell, but he appreciated his best friend's thoroughness. Most of the time.

The big sergeant's legs were thickly wrapped around his mount; his free hand dangled close to his flapped holster as his other hamlike fist controlled the reins. Even in the dark, the man's huge feet could be seen extending from each side of his horse. Hale wore rough-hewn, handmade boots—probably because there was no Confederate issue to fit him, Cordell guessed.

A permanent red blotch on Hale's right cheek and an eye patch over his right eye were the result of a Colt .56 revolving rifle, a Union weapon, discharging three chambers at once, one of them exploding in his face a year ago. It was an ironic scar for the lumbering man who had a good reputation with a gun. Better with guns than with men, Cordell had observed. Hale's way of talking was mostly an outgrowth of his shyness tucked within a thick physical frame. He seldom spoke unless spoken to first, and his orders were made in absolute brevity. His troops laughed, to themselves, that the only way to obey a Hale order was to know what it was before he made it. But Cordell had instantly liked this bear of a man.

Reining up in front on him, Cordell quickly apprised his two leaders of the situation. Taullery was the first to respond. His hat brim hid most of his wind-burned face. From the brim's shadow, his reddened eyes blinked rapidly; the rise in his voice gave away his apprehension. Cordell expected as much; it was his friend's normal reaction to anything new.

"Longstreet doesn't expect us to take on Meade by ourselves, Rule...uh, Captain. They'll swallow us like breakfast."

"We're supposed to scare 'em enough to bring reinforcements."

"All right," Sergeant Hale said quietly, as if he hadn't hear Taullery's concern at all. To punctuate his feelings, he moved a piece of horehund candy from one side of his mouth to the other.

"I appreciate your attention to orders, Lieutenant, and will make certain it is noted for the record," Cordell said with a grin. "Your logic is, as usual, sound—and, well, logical. But we're going to split the force into three groups, each of us with twenty or so. Sarge, here, goes afoot as close as he can and opens up on the ridge with rifles. Just as he does that, I'll hit the main line down below and you'll hit the ridge with your riders. Then you and Sarge can cover our retreat back here. That satisfy you?"

It took guts to question Cordell's judgment; the eye-patched sergeant had figured that out just since he rode up at Longstreet's headquarters. Hale silently appreciated Taullery's nerve. Something about this Captain Cordell was singularly daring. Riding behind him was like being swept along by a strong wind. Looking into Cordell's eyes now—before battle—was to see purgatory. The scabbed-over bullet crease across his forehead only added to the perception of Cordell as a warrior from hell.

Hale's candy shifted once again to the other cheek, waiting for Taullery's response. He knew of the friendship between the two men and didn't intend to get caught in the middle. Frowning, Taullery sat astride his horse as he thought through the implications of his friend's plans. Catching the sergeant's

stare, Taullery glanced away as if examining Billy
Ripton's froth-mouthed horse.

"Yeah!" Sergeant Hale mumbled self-consciously,
surprised at his own exuberance but still looking hard
into Taullery's face. He spat candy juice downward
without paying attention to the direction. It zinged past
the chest of Taullery's horse, so close that the animal
stutter-stepped sideways to avoid it. Taullery's pained
expression was lost on the sergeant who was watching
Cordell for additional orders.

"Skirmish formation. Flankers in," Cordell ordered.
"Sergeant, tell the bugler hand signals only. No talking
in the ranks. Leave their canteens and spurs behind
with our rear guard. Leave anything else that makes
noise. Sergeant, you pick the twenty best riflemen.
Your choice. You've got five minutes. Then, forward
at a trot. To gallop on my command. When we stop,
you'll dismount and go forward on foot."

"All right," growled Hale.

Cordell paused to assure himself that they compre-
hended his orders, particularly Hale. Satisfied, he continued, "Billy Rip, you'll take the point. I want to be as
close to that ridge as we can get—without any Yanks
seeing us."

Retracing the young scout's direct route, Cordell's
cavalry covered the first hillside in minutes. Tired men
were suddenly alert but silent. Overhead, a shivering
moon clung to the sky. Dawn was two hours away,
Cordell guessed. The long columns of twos eased
down a short incline, crossed a checkerboard flat of
scrub brush covered with snow, then galloped to a fat
grove of trees where they could see the base of a long
jagged ridge without being seen. On its top was the
ugly shape of an artillery piece spitting hell down on
the beleaguered Rebel position. On the other side, the

land descended gently into a meadow woven with hastily built Union earthworks.

With a hand signal, Captain Cordell halted the company. Billy Ripton pointed to the the top of the ridge. As he turned his horse around, Cordell silently studied the column and waved at Hale to bring his riflemen. The sergeant stared at him for a long instant, then pursed his lips and nodded affirmation.

Satisfied with the silence of his troopers' response, Cordell also dismounted, handing the reins of his horse to a nearby trooper. Cordell's field glasses quickly picked up the Union troopers on the ridge, as Billy had advised. His own count put them at thirty-five.

Hale came foward on foot, in an awkward trot. He held his rifle at his side. Behind him in single file, like puppets on a string, were twenty grim-looking troopers, each carrying a rifle. Two had Henrys; two had Colt .56 Military Revolving Rifles. Seven had Springfields; the others had a mixture of weapons, most of them Union issue.

"Billy Rip, which way should the sergeant and his men go up?"

"Ri't along that shelf. Yeah, that one. That's whar I went. Ya kin git worrisome close—without no Yank a-seeing ya. Leastwise, I done it."

"Good. You got that, Sergeant?"

"Yeah."

"Once you are in position, wait for my signal to start firing."

"What?" Hale said.

"You'll hear us."

"All right."

"Here, take this—along with your own," Cordell said, and yanked his Henry carbine from its saddle scabbard. "I won't be needing a long gun."

As the grinning sergeant eagerly grabbed the big

gun, Cordell reached inside his coat pocket and retrieved a sack of ammunition. "Here's lead for it. See that it's put to good use."

"Thank ye!"

Sergeant Hale bounded past him, up the uneven hill. The dog beside Cordell started to growl at the sudden movement, but Cordell quieted it with a touch and a "No, Texas." Cordell kept his glasses on the rifle team as they scooted on hands and knees up the hillside, past a row of misshaped cedars, past a huge rock shaped like a sleeping bear, and disappeared from his view.

As Cordell watched, he remembered Taullery's last remark to be careful about sun reflections even early in the day. He held the glasses in his right hand and draped his open left palm over the end to keep any stray light from hitting the glass. He told himself the sun couldn't possibly be a problem at this time of day, but he did it anyway. He kneeled and gave the dog a brisk rub with both hands, talking to him quietly.

Standing, he ordered, "Texas, stay here. Stay here, boy. We'll be back."

Taking the reins of his horse from Billy Ripton, he returned the young scout's too-brisk salute, told him everything was going to be all right, and remounted. Behind him, cavalry horses snorted and pranced, sensing the coming of battle. They always did. The nervous energy flowed from their riders. It was the worst time, those moments before the battle. Cordell was quiet; his mind raced to find any holes in his plan. He was glad his oldest friend wasn't next to him, because he would find many. No, it was time to fight, not think.

"Uh, Captun Cordell, should I be a-a-a-prayin'?" Billy asked timidly.

After watching his older friends do so outside the hospital, Billy Ripton was eager to try this new thing.

If Cordell prayed, it couldn't be sissy stuff, that's for sure, he had told himself. He had always thought praying, Bible reading, and the like was something only womenfolk did.

Cordell was surprised at the request. His tired mind shot back to his father yelling out to his mother that she needed to pray for forgiveness because she was weak. That was after she had asked if she could buy some cloth to make a new dress for Sundays. Cordell saw him strike her again in his mind and the small child ran at his father, swinging his fists.

"Captun Cordell, should I, huh?" Billy Ripton's question saved Cordell from seeing the rest of that memory, the one where his father beat him with a fireplace poker.

Sweating in the cold morning air, Cordell swallowed and tried to answer, "That would be fine, Billy Rip. Just fine."

The scout squeezed his eyes and said, "Ah, we be a-headin' ri't into them Yank guns, Lawd. I do be takin' kindly to yur keepin' them from shootin' straight this mornin'. Thank ye. Amen."

Chapter Eight

With a brisk hand signal, Cordell ordered the rest of
his company to follow him in a wide swing north of the
ridge, moving far enough out of sight to avoid detec-
tion. Billy Ripton rode ahead as his point. The dog
immediately took its place at the big roan's heel, in
spite of Cordell's several attempts to wave it away. His
motions only served to make the animal's long tail
wiggle enthusiastically.

After several wipes into the morning air, he gave up
and began to concentrate on the direction of his cavalry. His continual glances to the ridge to his far left
were insurance against discovery. But there was little
chance of being caught on this side of the ridge; the
Union's attention was completely in the other direction and the scattered trees offered a reasonable shield
at this time in the morning. Finally, he reined in, holding up his hand to halt his men.

Satisfied with their position, he pointed to Taullery

and saluted. His friend nodded, then returned the salute and swung in the saddle to direct his men. Taullery's group spun off to attack the ridge from a northern angle. As Cordell watched, his friend turned to face him and mouthed, "Good luck."

Cordell smiled and rode on with the remaining men. They loped on with little sound except the scuffle of horses' hooves on frozen ground and an occasional muffled cough. They curled across a deep creek bed that wandered to the northwest. The pockets of water that remained in its rocky trough were frozen. With a wave of his hand, he commanded Billy Ripton back into formation. There was no need for him to be out front on the attack itself.

Texas the dog stopped to lick the ice in the creek and search further for something it had smelled. Ahead was a smoldering Yankee campfire with three large black pots of coffee and the delicious smell of cooking bacon. Cordell thought momentarily about getting some but that was too reckless, even for him.

Wagons, caissons, delivery carts, and evenly placed rows of tents laced the uneven ground, accented with an occasional campfire, shielding the Rebel advance from the soldiers firing in the other direction from their log-built barricades. Rifle, mortar, and cannon fire was loud now, even though the main battery of artillery was two hundred yards to the west and hunkered down among some tired trees. One continuous sound.

He motioned for this men to spread out. His fingers indicated three lines of skirmishers. Without meaning to, he glanced over to see Texas and was pleased to see the dog occupied in the creek bed. Maybe he'll stay there, Cordell thought. Cordell's right hand moved to one of the two Colts carried in his saddle holsters and yanked it clear. Cordell took a deep breath and spun the cylinder of the big pistol, checking the loads. Inside he was cold. This was what he was made for. Putting the reins in his teeth, he grabbed the second saddle gun. As he did, his eyes caught the sight of a silent ambulance to his right with stretchers propped against it. His mind acknowledged they would be needed before this day was done.

"Follow me! Pistols at the ready! Fire at will!" Cordell screamed as he spurred his roan toward the Union enforcement.

It was the last order he gave until recall as his onrushing force began to give and take the first fire of the surprised Federals. With a fierce, throaty whoop of all men yelling together, the skirmish line broke into a ragged gallop. Somewhere behind him, a man was praying out loud. Another spat a long curse. Cordell's horse's eyes were wide, its ears flat against the back of its head as the powerful animal hurled itself forward. Two strides away and gaining was his dog, adding his bark to the Rebel yell.

A hatless Union soldier stumbling out of his tent, putting a white suspender over his shoulder, was rammed by Cordell's roan as it flew past. The luckless Federal was thrown into the nearby campfire coals. His scream was drowned by the Rebel attack. A cook dropped his kettle and began to run as the horsemen hurled across the meadow. He fell among a cluster of cooking utensils and didn't rise.

Dark shapes hurled themselves against the log walls, never to move again, as the Rebel gunfire tore into their backs. Wild-eyed Yankee soldiers turned from their posts in disbelief; some screamed and waved their arms; more spun and tumbled to the ground; some aimed their rifles at this advancing fury tearing them apart. The ridge to the left was lit with gunfire as the Union artillery there was suddenly silent.

Two dozen Union infantrymen spun to meet Cordell's advance. Another hundred ran stumbling and unseeing toward the west and safety. Vicious pistol fire from Cordell's men ripped open the Union flank. Out of the corner of his eye, Cordell saw a Union colonel running and screaming orders to men who had no thought of listening, much less obeying. That made him think of his own infantry, only a rifle bullet away. They should be coming now to help his horsemen turn this into a rout. This was the time to turn the Yankee advance. At least here. The hell with worrying about whether or not the bluebellies brought men to meet his attack. Give him the soldiers at the flank and he'd run those bastards all the way up their damn line! But he couldn't tell if the Rebels were coming or not. His distraction was momentary.

Gunshots blistered the air around him as his roan entered the whirling melee of Union soldiers. Bullets from several directions whistled their death songs at the same time, like a deadly train passing at full steam. A bullet slammed into the Rebel cavalryman beside him and the trooper was yanked from his saddle by unseen hands. Another nipped the sleeve of Cordell's coat.

Cordell wheeled his roan sideways with a pull of the reins in his teeth reinforced by his right heel kicking hard against the horse's belly. He avoided a swinging sword and fired into the soldier wielding it. Ducking the wide swath of a rifle butt, he fired again and the Yank's face disappeared into a red mass. Without taking time to aim, he shot at orange flames blossoming from blue shadows dancing around him. He jammed the empty saddle guns into their holsters and pulled two fresh weapons from his belt in one motion.

A Union soldier, in his stockinged feet, stood fifteen feet away and aimed his rifle at Cordell. Two shots from the Captain's pistol yanked him backward, his rifle sailing alone into the sky. Cordell fired four more times at three escaping Yankee soldiers, dropping one. Then he clicked the hammer on an spent chamber, realized both guns were empty, and shoved them back into his belt. He drew two Colts and began firing as rapidly as his thumbs and fingers could work them, so fast they sounded like one long, extended explosion.

His mouth gaped as he tried to gather air that wouldn't come fast enough. He felt, more than saw, Rebel soldiers pouring into the opened hole in the Yankee line. Suddenly he was aware the cannon fire from the ridge was blasting away at the distancing Union mass. Taullery and Hale had captured the hill! Blue-clad soldiers were escaping to the south and west; the enemy was in full flight, stopping to return fire only in desperation. Cordell fired at the fleeing shadows. Again and again. A few Rebel soldiers had stopped at the campfires to grab anything they could find to eat. But most were pressing the Yankees' retreat. The valley Union artillery had been abandoned in haste and Rebel soldiers were desparately trying to move the big guns toward the fleeing enemy.

Ten yards ahead of him was a Union colonel, his back to Cordell, pulling a wounded soldier out of the way of the fight. Sensing Cordell's advance, the colonel turned to face him as the bleeding soldier slumped to the ground beside him. Cordell's cocked revolver came into position. The tall colonel stared with no fear and without moving. Cordell froze for a moment, then let his gun drop to his side. He nodded to the Union leader. Only after the fighting was over did he realize that was what he had done. He vaguely remembered the tall man nodding in return. Cordell spun his heaving horse away, leaving the officer with the opportunity to retreat with the rest of his men.

He drew another set of pistols as his horse raced back into the wall of bullets and screams. His eyes searched for fleeing targets, but they were only darting shadows. Cordell knew it was over, shoved one gun back into his belt and took the reins from his teeth with his empty left hand. The wind-broken horse was pulled slowly into a walk, then a complete stop. White froth covered the roan's flanks and chest. Heaving for air that wouldn't come fast enough, the big horse lowered its head in exhaustion.

From somewhere, Cordell's mind suddenly realized a bugler was playing recall. It took a few more moments for him to realize the trumpeted order was coming from his side. Everywhere, there were shouts to hold up. His mind raced for the reason. They had the Yanks on the run for a change; why stop now? Why?! He started to scream at the bugler, then he sensed someone walking toward him. With a swing of his pistol toward the movement, he saw a hump-shouldered Confederate major with exhausted eyes coming toward him. Cordell lowered his gun.

Stepping alongside him, the major laid a hand on Cordell's knee, looked up, and said, "Nice work, Captain. Nice work."

Cordell squeezed his eyes shut to gain control as the pain in his head pounded without relief. "Why...are we pulling back?"

"Orders, man. Yank reinforcements are comin' hard at us. Longstreet wants us dug in when they hit. Right here where we've got that ridge behind us. An' that fine big iron. Hill's gonna hit 'em at the Mill with a big force. Two of Gordon's divisions with him. Hell, man, we're gonna have 'em in a crossfire for a change. How 'bout that! Just like the plan!"

"Crossfire? Plan?" Cordell's throbbing brain tried to remember. He shook his head to clear away the cloudiness of his mind worsened by the whirl of battle. *Who ordered us back?* Fresh blood seeped from the far edge of the scab and sought his left eye. He wiped it away brusquely with his coat sleeve.

His instinct was to challenge the major, but the man had walked on, mumbling about getting his men to move some of the Union breastworks. He felt dizzy. Looking up, he saw the silhouette of a man on horseback at the crest of the ridge. The shadow was waving vigorously. The image blurred and he shook his head to regain clarity. It was Taullery, and he was trying to get Cordell to retreat. Cordell wondered how long his friend had been there.

He had to find his men and bring them together quickly. It was time. He had no real sense of where they were or how many were down. Cordell's eyes caught movement in the grayness to his left, and his gun followed. He heard feet shuffling behind a downed wagon, near a bent-over tree with a sprawling double trunk. Down his tanned face rolled a streak of sweat. He wiped away the wetness with the back of his right hand, cocked the pistol, and looked again.

It was Trooper Theus Webber, a young, red-haired, freckle-faced Alabaman, carrying a bloody dog. Stockton's eyes linked with the solemn cavalryman for an instant before realizing what was in the trooper's arms. The shock hit him like a bullet. He dropped his pistol, jumped from his horse, and rushed to the soldier. With a moan that was more animal than human, Cordell took the dying animal from the stunned man's arms. Texas licked his hand weakly, and tears burst from Cordell's eyes. He turned away, holding the still shape, uncaring of his direction, or the commotion of recall around him, or the war, or his own dead men.

"Oh no, God, no!" Cordell's twisted face was almost beyond recognition. "Not Texas! Not Texas. Please... God, please..." He lifted one hand from the dog's body, and it was red. Quickly he returned it to the same spot as if he could close the life-draining hole.

"I-I'm sorry, sir, I really am," Trooper Webber replied softly, his voice barely audible.

Cordell turned back and asked in a thin voice, "Pray for him, soldier, please. Please. Pray for Texas. God, not Texas. Isn't Whisper's arm enough?" Into his mind shot the leering face of his father, his arms folded in triumph.

From the ridge, Taullery raised his field glasses to see why his friend wasn't gathering his troops and getting back to safety. He watched Cordell fall to his knees and press his head against the lifeless shape in his arms.

"Sergeant Hale!" Taullery barked.

"Yeah," came the reply from the gritty sergeant who was watching his men fire the Union artillery toward the horizon.

"Take charge of the men. I'm going down to help with recall."

"Yeah."

Taullery didn't hear him as he spurred his horse down the slope toward his grieving friend.

Nightfall came with mixed blessings. The fighting was over, at least for the day, but a cold north wind rode in with the shadows, bringing a terrible mixture of sleet and snow. Cordell's cavalry had finally been reassembled and had retreated to the relative safety of the far side of the cannon-topped ridge. He could remember little of the afternoon, a dulled whirl of sound and color. Nothing mattered but the dead dog.

The rest of the day had been confusing on the field as well—and, from the scattered reports, indecisive. No Union advance had come their way, evidently choosing to fight off the attack of Hill's forces instead. It didn't sound as if the Confederates had been successful at day's end. But battle reports were often, at best, little more than hearsay—and, at worst, statements of concerns that had long since changed by the time they arrived. No one really knew; no one really cared. It was too cold to care.

His men had hastily built brush shelters to help protect them from the weather's curse. On the armored ridge and angling across the meadow, Rebel infantry had done the same. Fires were a luxury none of the dug-in Rebels dared afford, with the possibility of an enemy probing their perimeters. Cooks brought each man a small pone of bread, the first taste of food since dawn for most. As usual, Taullery had managed to scrounge up some left-behind Union food, which he shared with the cavalrymen.

Under a bent pine tree, away from his troops, Cordell knelt and dug with his fingers and a knife to penetrate the frozen ground. Around him, wet snow and sleet were an unrelenting splatter. The chilled earth resisted his efforts to create a suitable grave for Texas. A long icicle dropped on his shoulders from a bent-over branch. Two more crackled and fell, and one slid down his shirt collar, making him jump. He slapped his back to rid it of the unwanted ice, paused to catch his breath, and saw that his gloves were torn. His exposed fingers were black with earth and red with his own blood.

From behind him came the grunt of boots on hard

ground, and he looked around. It was Billy Ripton, Trooper Webber, and two other young cavalrymen. Without speaking a word, they knelt in a small circle around him and began digging with knives. Soon, more battle-weary men joined them, also in silence, and the ground begrudgingly gave up its soil. The night sky talked the sleet into a light snow.

Standing beside his own shelter, Taullery watched the growing gathering and smiled grimly. On the other side of the ridge lay the bodies of their friends. But, somehow, this dog's body needed tending. That would be like his friend. Maybe it was a way to make sense of it all. He shook his head and saw Sergeant Hale come from his brush tent, carrying a folded shirt and Cordell's loaned rifle. He was headed for the burial area. Taullery guessed the cloth was to wrap the dog in for burial.

Taullery took off his hat and ran his gloved fingers along the ostrich plume to freshen it and brush off the new snow. Dirt was removed from the ornate crest holding the feather and wet splats of sleet from his hat. He clicked his teeth and realized one of the embroidered roses on his gauntlets was nearly torn off. He felt filthy and chilled to the edge of his courage. The fierce north wind told him the South was defeated. He didn't know if his body was bothered most by the frigid air or by the deep futility that came over him.

He replaced his hat and walked toward the burial, blinking away the falling snowflakes. Most of the cavalry had gathered there in an odd tribute. Cordell patted the replaced mound of dirt and watched as a trooper placed a large, flat rock over it. Trooper Webber laid his hand on the stone for an instant, then three other cavalrymen bent over and repeated the tribute. Ceremonially, each man stepped forward and touched the burial stone.

From the somber group, someone said, "Let us cross the river and rest in the shade," one of the phrases supposedly said by a dying Stonewall Jackson. Someone else muttered what sounded like a prayer.

Another started to sing "Dixie" in a soft, choked voice. "I wish I was in the land of cotton, old times there are not forgotten. Look away, look away..." When no one joined him, his mournful tune gave out. All of the men watched their leader. Slowly, Cordell stood, looked into each man's face as if seeing them for the first time, and spoke in a broken voice.

"Thank you, men. For this. I know we lost friends today. Too many. And we lost more friends yesterday—and the days and weeks before that. Like you, I guess I can accept that, or I'm trying to, but this dog wasn't in this war. He was innocent. Like our wives and families are. Back home. Ol' Texas here was something from home, in a way. Maybe it reminded me of what we're fighting for. Thank you."

Standing at the back of the group, Taullery marveled as he heard the words from his friend. Rarely did Cordell let anyone into his soul. But he was now, and his men—strangers a few hours ago—were pulled to his anguish and made stronger by it. They understood what he was saying and why he was grieving. Taullery watched many of them cry unashamedly. If they only knew what Cordell's home was really like, he thought to himself. But he knew such wouldn't matter; it was their own homes that mattered.

Cordell's head bowed, his eyes closed, and he prayed, "God, this is a hard time for all of us. We lost friends today. Good friends. Take them in, will you? They deserve...your warmth. Take this little dog, too, Lord. He was...my friend....Amen."

Mutters of "amen" followed, and slowly the men

returned to their huts, their bootprints quickly covered by the falling snow. Hale hesitated, then left Cordell's Henry propped against a scrub oak and hurried to catch up with the others. Billy Ripton came over and said he thought the prayer was especially nice. Feeling awkward about the comment, he quickly left, with his face reddening from expressing himself in that way.

Taullery walked over to his friend and placed a hand on his shoulder. Cordell didn't acknowledge the connection.

"Your words were a great comfort to the men, Rule. I've never heard you talk like that before. It was good for them to hear. Come on, I've got some food for us. Yankee food. You'll feel better if you get something in your belly."

"I'll be along, Ian," Cordell said without looking up.

"Let me wrap that wound with some cloth so you won't keep busting it open."

"It's just fine the way it is."

"Rule, it's too damn cold to be out here. Come on," Taullery insisted.

Cordell's eyes flashed, and he stammered, "L-leave me alone. Just leave me alone."

Taullery's shoulders heaved, and he said softly, "Little Texas is with God now, Rule. He's running free and happy—in heav—"

"There's no God, Ian, don't you know that? I know that. People just say prayers to make themselves feel better. God wouldn't let this happen."

"You don't mean that, Rule."

His eyes changing from hot to sullen as he spoke, Rule said, "God wouldn't let a man like my father go around using his name to hurt people—and then let this happen. Or let Whisper get..."

Cordell let his words go and squeezed his eyes tight. The wind swirled falling snow around them, grabbed at their long coats, and sealed off any more words. Taullery walked away without looking at Cordell or speaking. The mournful captain sat beside his newly dug grave all night. Some thought they heard Cordell crying in the darkness; others thought they heard him scream at his father. Others said they had heard wounded men who remained on the battlefield

In the morning, they found him asleep, lying across the rock, covered with a thin blanket of snow. They rode out together, more united than they had been in battle. Later, no one was quite sure who started calling their cavalry unit "the Dogs," but it caught on. Evidently, Cordell liked the description too, because he began to use it as their battle cry: "On, you dogs!"

In the bitter days that followed, the stretched-thin Rebels watched the Federal line extend their entrenchments another three miles to the Vaughan Road crossing of Hatcher's Run. There wasn't much Lee could do about it. His men already stood fifteen to twenty feet apart in places. Worse, he had little food to keep them able to fight—or march.

As if the death of a stray dog had consumed him, Rule Cordell's intensity grew as taut as wet rawhide being pulled. He neither heard nor saw the crumbling army around him. Instead, his "Dogs" slashed at the corners of Meade's ever-pressing advance, trying to protect Longstreet's ground forces as they scrambled to keep from being overrun, buying time for the disintegrating army. His men rode with him, dragged along by the force of his strange leadership. No one dared to speak of letting up, not even Taullery.

A bedraggled spring finally arrived, leaving behind a winter cluster of more battles that cost thousands of Union and Confederate lives as Lee scrambled to keep his force intact. Cordell's cavalry lost thirty-three men, but he was given additional riders from fragments of other torn-apart units, bringing his force to a full company. But even Taullery's skill at finding things couldn't keep them in ammunition or food beyond meager supplies.

During those hard months, Lee managed to escape from Grant's suffocating grasp, leaving Richmond to face savage pillage and burning. But Rebel forces continued to shrink as the weather turned warmer, while Union armies blossomed with men and equipment. Lee could no longer mount a major counterattack without committing every man he had—and that would have brought no assurances of victory, only possible destruction of his remaining army. Only the most ardent believer could think the South would eventually prevail. Defeat was everywhere.

Lieutenant Taullery saw his friend become maniacal in his desire for victory. He didn't sleep; he didn't eat. He only fought or made plans to fight. He wore out horses and men. But it didn't matter. The Confederacy's life span could be measured in days now. Finally, on April 9, outside the sleepy little community of Appomattox Court House, Cordell and his horsemen were ordered to stop fighting and wait for further orders, like the rest of the Army of Northern Virginia. Cordell obeyed, but only after Taullery's insistence. After standing around most of the ominously quiet day, Cordell could wait no longer.

"Ian, I'm going to talk to Longstreet about this crap," Cordell said, grounding out a cigarette butt with his boot heel and pointing toward a tall figure across the field, leaning against a fence with several officers around him.

"What? Are you crazy?!" Taullery snapped. "They'll let us know. This is a damn truce, Rule. Something's happening. We're probably going to surrender. Dammit, Rule, don't you know we're whipped? Everybody else knows."

He regretted the words the instant they came out of his mouth, and clinched his teeth in a belated attempt to hold them in. There was no reaction from Cordell, as if he hadn't heard his friend at all. Cordell's eyes were burning; Taullery had seen him this way before.

"You're in command of the Dogs while I'm gone, Ian."

"Dammit, Rule, you can't...."

Chapter Nine

General Longsteet glanced up to a see a wild-appearing captain of his tattered cavalry striding toward him, four pistols jammed into a wide belt, in addition to two nonregulation, no-flap-holstered guns. From under a battered hat, a stone earning fluttered against long dark hair. Dark tight eyes looked unreachable. A light scar-line angled upward across the right side of his forehead.

Under his breath Longstreet took the long cigar from his mouth and muttered, "Son of a bitch. I'm glad this one's on our side."

A junior officer attempted to step in front of the oncoming Cordell, but Longsteet quietly said, "Don't." As the officer stepped aside, Cordell brushed past him without ever giving the man the slightest recognition of his even being there. Cordell stepped in front of Longstreet, saluted haphazardly, as if he didn't really want to do it, and asked, "General Longstreet, sir, what are we waiting for? My boys can sting those damn bluebellies right now. Give me the say-so and I can—"

"There's an armistice in effect, Captain," Longstreet said, his voice tired yet expectant.

"So what?" Cordell asked.

Longstreet gave a half-grin, nodded, and said, "Captain, I wish I'd had you before."

"General, my men have fresh mounts and a full supply of ammunition. We could make 'em hurt a little. Make 'em a little slower. Give you a chance to—whatever, sir."

The tall, sad-eyed leader looked away for a long moment, then back at Cordell, and said, "Would it be correct to assume those are Yankee horses and Yankee bullets you're talking about?"

Cordell cocked his head to the side, caught the steady gaze of the senior officer, and said, "Yessir, it would. Didn't seem they needed them anymore."

"I'm sure they didn't, Captain Cordell. You're the one that pulled off the 'masquerade battalion,' aren't you?"

"Me and my friends, yessir."

"Wish I'd been there to see it. All of them Texas boys like you? Only bright spot in a long time. A long time." Longstreet shook his head as he took another pull on his cigar.

They both stopped and stared as a young Yankee general galloped toward them, flanked by two Confederate riders. Blond curls bounced on the shoulders of the dramatically attired officer. His gold-buttoned and gold-braided uniform was highlighted with a long red scarf.

One of Longstreet's aides spat and snarled, "That

thar's the biggest damn set o' shoulder straps on a major general I ever done seed. Yessuh, mighty fancy lad a-comin'.''

Reining up in front of Longstreet, the brevet general saluted with his sword in an exaggerated motion and announced loudly, "I am General Custer and bear a message to you from General Sheridan. The general desires me to present you his compliments, and to demand the unconditional surrender of all the troops under your command."

Longstreet's cigar fell from his mouth. His face turned crimson as he fought to control his temper as he declared angrily, "May I remind you, General, that I am not the commander of this army; that you, sir, are within the lines of the enemy without authority; that you are addressing a superior officer, and in disrespect to General Grant, as well as myself, who is conducting a negotiation with General Lee at this very moment."

Custer's face tightened, like a man who had been slapped hard. Finally, he sputtered, "You will be responsible for the bloodshed to follow."

Longstreet growled, "Go ahead and have all the bloodshed you want."

Stepping between Custer and Longstreet, Cordell saw his father's snarling face suddenly take over the countenance of the yellow-haired Custer and challenged, "How about starting it right now, errand boy. Just you 'n' me. The rest will watch, I guarantee it. Pull that iron. I'll wait 'til you do. Come on, Custer— or are you tough only when you've got us outnumbered ten to one?"

General Custer blinked, turned red, and wheeled his horse. He galloped toward the small farmhouse with two Confederate outriders kicking their horses hard to catch up. Cordell watched him go, trembling with the anger that shook his lithe frame.

After a few minutes of silence, Cordell asked, "General Longstreet, sir, what is General Lee meeting with Grant about?"

Longstreet paused, rubbed his whiskered chin with a gloved hand, and said, "Surrender, Captain Cordell. He's in that house over there now."

"Surrender?" Cordell repeated the word as if it had something bad tasting wrapped around it. "General, sir, you're jesting, right? We're not surrendering. We can't—"

"Cordell, that's enough," Longstreet replied softly, stared at the cigar in his hand, and fell silent.

Cordell stood for a few moments and walked away. He didn't hear Longstreet say, almost as an after-thought, "If the General's not offered honorable terms, he'll let us fight it out."

Like a drunk man, Cordell staggered back to Taullery and his men, trying to fight the wildness in his mind. Instead of pausing to report to his best friend, he went directly toward the big roan.

"Where are you going, Rule?" Taullery asked from his position, lounging beneath an oak tree, sipping Billy Ripton's coffee, which wasn't quite strong enough.

"Come on, Ian. Let's go find some Southern boys that aren't ready to quit. Lee's going to give up. Can you believe that? So is Longstreet. Damn!"

Taullery jumped to his feet and ran over to his friend, who was already saddling the big horse. He put his hand on Captain Cordell's shoulder. Pausing with the latigo strap in midpull, the younger cavalry looked at Taullery's hand as if it were a rattlesnake, then up into Taullery's face. The blond-haired Rebel couldn't remember seeing so much rage in his friend's face.

Still, he managed to speak calmly. "No, Rule, this is it. It's over. Everybody says Marse Robert's in there surrendering...us. You know it's time, man, look around. Our boys are so damn weak from hunger, they couldn't charge a schoolhouse. Rule, we did the best we could. All of us. You know that."

"He isn't surrendering me," Cordell spat, his face twisted purple. "Are you going with me—or not?"

"Rule, you have an obligation to these men to stay. You're their leader. They're your Dogs, remember? They've followed you into hell without a question or a waver," Taullery pleaded.

"You stay, then, Ian. You're better at this than I am, anyway," Cordell said, and yanked the cinch in place.

"You'd ride away and leave me here?" Taullery's word stumbled as they came out. "What about the Dogs?"

"Maybe it's best this way, Ian. I'll probably just get us both killed. Tell the Dogs I was proud of them."

"You should tell them yourself."

Cordell didn't answer. He swung into the saddle and saw the sour-faced cavalry sergeant also walking toward them. "How about you, Hale?" he said.

"Nope," the veteran replied in his usual manner. His eyes, though, could not meet Cordell's.

"Fair enough. See you boys in hell," Cordell said, spurred his roan, and galloped away. Taullery watched him disappear against the yellow horizon. The tall cavalryman couldn't remember feeling so alone, so empty. A gnawing feeling said he should have gone with his friend. It had all happened so fast. It seemed like a dream.

"Ya were right," Sergeant Hale said, guessing what

was on the tall man's mind, and giving more words to his feelings than Taullery could remember ever hearing before.

"I don't know about that."

"Yeah, ya did."

Seeing the exchange, Billy Ripton rose from his napping position under a tree, wiped the back of his pants with a swift brush of his hands, and trotted over to Taullery and Hale.

"Whar's Captun Cordell a-headin'?" he asked.

Neither man wanted to speak. Finally Taullery said, "Billy Rip, we're surrendering. The South has lost."

"What's that got itse'f to do with...Captun Cordell?"

Taullery looked at Hale and said softly, "He's... not going to surrender, Billy Rip. He's ridin' off to... find some place to fight on."

"How come us Dawgs ain't wi' him, Ian? I dun—"

"It's over, Billy Rip. We can go home now," Taullery said in a voice barely heard. "We can go home—to Texas."

"But...but I wanna be with Rule. I'm one o' Cordell's Dawgs—like yo-all. Doncha figger we oughta—"

Taullery looked hard into the teenager's face and spat, "If he wanted you along, Billy Rip, he would have come and got you."

Hale glanced at the young cavalryman but turned his eyes away as soon as he realized the teenager was about to cry.

Several hours later, Taullery, Billy Ripton, and the others watched a tall, gray-haired man, astride a white horse, ride into the Confederate lines. General Lee's proud face looked as if it would burst with sadness. He was immediately surrounded by butternut-uniformed soldiers with only one question in their collective faces. One soldier put it into words. "Are we surrendered?"

The grief welling up inside Lee looked for a moment like it was going to take his life. The amazing self-control that had taken him through so much deserted him. His body trembled. He began to weep. Finally, he said, "Men, we have fought through the war together. I have done the best I could for you. My heart is too full to say more."

Silence took command of his forces. He rode away within the stillness to his headquarters in an apple orchard, where he was visited by well-wishers the rest of the day. Almost at the same moment, the Union lines exploded in one long joyous celebration.

"I reckon that makes us prisoners of war, doesn't it?" Taullery asked no one in particular.

He looked across the open field and saw Yankee soldiers advancing with pots of hot coffee and opened haversacks of food. "Hell, this is going to be a damn picnic." He smiled, but his mind was riding with Rule Cordell.

The Rebel cavalry captain rode south. Roads were choked with Confederate soldiers heading home; many were carrying the tale of the surrender of the Army of Northern Virginia. No matter what President Jefferson Davis might attempt, Lee's capitulation would be the bursting of the dam. As fast as the news could spread, the remaining Rebel armies were rendered little more than paper forces as men left for their homes as soon as they heard the word.

No one paid much attention to a report from a Federal division lined up against the waning Rebel Army of Tennesee. The dispatch said Union soldiers had been engaged by a Rebel patrol at night and had been forced to retreat until daylight under blistering fire. Veteran soldiers in the line whispered that the "patrol" had actually been only one man, and officers urged their men to avoid premature celebrating that would bring on such exaggerated reports.

Nearly two months later, crimson rays of a fresh morning sun hit Rule Cordell's shoulders as his roan stepped into the first small channel that introduced the mystical Red River. Ahead was Texas. Soon, he would be among fighting Rebels again with General Kirby Smith Is great army of the Confederate Trans-Mississippi Department. He should feel happy that he was returning to his home state, but he didn't. Only defeat and anger reached him, burning like lit candles in his stomach. He was a far different man than the one who had crossed it four years earlier.

High banks dully imitated the dawn's color due to endless paintings of clay sediment from upstream. Brackish water, shallow land bars, and driftwood matched the morning hue. Even shoreline timber was striped with red passings. Soon his roan was swimming as the main river accepted their crossing without challenge. The Red was deep this morning, but not vicious as it often was.

Trailing behind him, on a lead rope, was a fine Union cavalry horse. The animal had wandered into his camp one night, and Cordell had awakened to discover the saddled bay standing next to his grazing roan. Having a second horse gave his great roan an occasional rest as he tried to find where Rebels were still fighting. Cordell was under the impression Kirby Smith's 36,000-man command stretched across Arkansas, parts of Louisiana, Texas, and Missouri, as well as the Arizona, New Mexico, and Indian territories. It would be good to be among warriors once more, he told himself.

His mind was lodged with hate and frustration. He had been riding for a lifetime, it seemed, trying to find a Rebel army standing against the North's overwhelming sweep to victory. He hated the North for emptying the South of its great will. Without a last great fight. Without a memorable last stand to the bitter end. Without the glory of death in battle.

He hated Lee for what he did at Appomattox Court House. He hated General Johnston and General Taylor for surrendering their armies after hearing of Lee's final collapse. It didn't matter to him that their men had vanished as soon as word about Lee's surrender hit their lines. He hated Bedford Forrest for letting his cavalry be destroyed by a massive Union force. He hated his best friend, Ian Taullery, for giving up.

But the news of Lee's surrender seemed to travel faster than he could ride, especially since he was forced to hide from the increasing Union cavalry patrols roaming the area for unrepentant Rebels like himself. Relief from his bitterness would come only in joining Rebels yet remaining to fight. That was becoming difficult to do. There was only one remaining Confederate force capable of accepting Cordell's tenacity, besides Kirby Smith's, and that was Brigadier General Watie's. Stand Watie, a fierce Cherokee Chief, led an unbroken Rebel battalion of Cherokees, Creeks, Seminoles, and Osages somewhere in Indian Territory.

As Rule Cordell crossed into Texas, the world of the North was jammed with victory and pulsing with hatred for the defeated South at the same time. Many blamed them for the murder of President Lincoln and demanded the Rebels be treated as traitors. In Washington, D.C., Major General George G. Meade's Army of the Potomac paraded with precision and polish through the happy streets. Women and children tossed flowers in their path and sang their praises.

The next day, over the same roads, came Major General William T. Sherman's Army of Georgia and Army of Tennessee. In sharp contrast to Meade's soldiers, they were a wild-looking bunch of ruffians, strutting with gusto and pride. Some sat astride mules, laughing and shouting, while others tied chickens, legs of lamb, and hams to the ends of their muskets and waved them proudly.

Mixed in with the marching celebration of soldiers was a wild collection of dogs, goats, even a few raccoons the men had kept as pets. Some marched with pigs on long leashes. Negro men, women, and children rode mules or sat in wagons filled with military gear. Live turkeys gobbled loudly from atop some of the wagons. An occasional gamecock sat on top of parading artillery, an appropriate symbol of the swaggering army. One soldier even showed off a pet monkey to appreciative crowds. Cordell knew nothing of this victory madness. If he did, it would have served only to make him more determined.

Clearing the muddy far bank, Cordell glanced back at the wide river as if to capture some sense of the past. His roan shook its body to rid the excess water, and the sudden jarring irritated him. Remains of last night's awful dream rode with the lone Rebel cavalryman. A feverish sleep had brought a nightmare of his father pointing at the dead men Cordell had led into battle, laughing at him and urging Cordell's stray dog to go into a huge fire.

This part of Texas wasn't familiar to him, so it felt

even stranger to be in the land that was once his home. He tried to keep thoughts of Ian Taullery and his friends from crowding into his mind. He was riding in search of a war. They would be riding into Texas themselves soon—but not in search of a war. They would be coming home. Twinges of loneliness struck at his courage and yanked at the anger in his heart. He shook his head to rid himself of those feelings and nudged the big roan into a lope. He would probably never see his friends again, and that was as it should be, he decided.

As he rounded a hillside once battered with artillery shells, all remnants of thought left him in an instant. "What the hell is this?!" he roared and the roan's ears snapped back to catch the words. The sight made him want to vomit. A small burial ground from some unknown battle was being torn apart by eight hogs rooting up corpses and tearing at their remains. He gagged and swallowed hard. A harsh "whoa" stopped his horse in midstride. He drew two pistols and killed the animals, releasing some of his frustration in the shooting.

As he reloaded with easy familarity using cap, paper, and ball, a stocky farmer appeared over a small ridge strewn with wild scrub oak and mesquite. He was following the tracks of the hogs. His boots were too big for his feet and made him wobble as he walked. A shotgun was held at his side with his right hand. Cordell sat silently on his horse as the farmer stopped at the edge of the burial ground, studied the dead hogs, looked at Cordell, then back to the lifeless animals. The farmer's fingers squeezed the stock of the shotgun, but he made no attempt to raise it.

"Them's is my hogs yo'all done kilt," he stated in a low, methodical voice. His sprouting eyebrows looked as if they were in a perpetual state of surprise. His work clothes were old, with dirt more a part of the cloth than thread itself. What passed for a hat had once been a derby shoved over curly dark hair. His eyes carried a sadness mixed with a spark of anger that dared not show itself.

Cordell held both pistols at the man as he replied, "They were tearing up a holy place. Good men died here, mister."

"Yeah, reckon so. Goddamn shame, too," he said, and spat a long, brown string of tobacco juice. "Still them thar t'were worth a mite more than bones n' sech."

"Tell you what. Lay that shotgun down on the ground—and I'll pay you for your hogs," Cordell said. His roan stamped its hoof impatiently. Cordell told the animal to stand easy.

"What with? Reb paper ain't worth spit," the farmer responded defiantly. After thinking about it for a moment, he squatted and laid the shotgun on the ground, then stood with his arms crossed.

"How about two Yankee gold pieces? Would that square us?" Cordell said, smiling slightly.

He shoved one pistol into his belt and cocked the other in his left hand. Leaning over, he pulled a small purse from his long boot with his freed right hand and tossed two coins toward the farmer. The short man squatted again to retrieve his reward, tested their worth with his teeth, and stood, gripping the coins tightly in his fist.

"I reckon that'll square it. I thank ye. Reckon not many'd do that, Reb or Yank." The farmer tried to smile, but it was one-sided, revealing yellowed and broken teeth.

Cordell nodded and said, "I'm headed for General

Kirby Smith. Down Houston way, I'm told. Can you tell me the best way to go? Haven't been in this part of Texas before."

"Yo-all a Texican, are ye?"

"Yessir. Been four long years, though. From around Waco."

The farmer was quiet. He shut his eyes.

When he finally spoke, it was like a voice from somewhere else had entered his body. "Lost two sons. Vicksburg. An' Manassas. After that, the missus lost, wal, she kept to her'nse'f. Buried her two months back."

"I'm very sorry," Cordell said quietly.

The farmer went on as if not hearing him. He said Smith was, indeed, around Houston, or was, the last he'd heard. That was months ago. The farmer outlined a different picture than the one Cordell expected. The Union controlled almost everything since they had cut Smith off from the rest of the Confederacy two years earlier. It was after the fall of Vicksburg, the farmer said, pausing to think what that meant to him personally.

He added that something bad had happened in November. According to the rumors, General Sterling Price's cavalry had gone to Missouri with great gusto and been driven back whimpering. Smith's actions since that time had been no more than small guerrilla raids spread out among vast stretches of land.

"He ain't got many boys wi' him no mo', I hear tell. Only a few of the real mean 'uns. Reckon the rest all done left fer home after we got the word about Lee. A real shame, t'were."

Cordell's heavy sigh caught the farmer's attention.

"Yo-all weren't a-headin' home, were ye?" he asked.

Cordell shook his head.

"Neither is ye a-carryin' pardon papers, is ya?"

Cordell's puzzled look was enough of an answer.

"Shoulda figgered, from the looks of ye. No offense, Cap'un."

Satisfied the man wouldn't try to shoot at him when he rode off, Cordell said good-bye and galloped on. A few miles later, his nose rejected an approaching area and he swung wide to avoid the carcasses of dead horses and mules rotting in the sun because no one had the shovels or the will to bury them. Both of his horses pranced nervously past the putrid reminder.

Farther along, he watched a farmer plowing a field two hundred yards from his path. The farmer's head jumped up when he heard the hoofbeats. Realizing it was a Confederate cavalryman, he smiled weakly in Cordell's direction, gave a wave, and returned to his work. To the south of the plowing, a woman was searching the torn-up earth for old bullets and scrap metal to sell. Cordell turned his head away when he realized the farmer had accidentally turned up a corpse. Cordell nudged the roan, and it immediately broke into a smooth run.

In the next several days, he passed streams of slow-walking, discharged Rebel soldiers—headed home, he guessed. A few waved as he rode by, but most didn't raise their heads. From one bunch, Cordell learned what the hog farmer had meant about the "pardon paper." Each soldier was given a signed certificate, after his unit surrendered, to show Federal patrols the bearer was no longer a combatant and had been properly released and pardoned for his actions against the North.

He passed a gang of freed Negro men gathered around an old wagon harnessed to a dead mule. They were yelling at each other and jabbing fingers at the lifeless animal. They stopped arguing and eyed his Union horse as he rode by. A chorus of syrupy invitations begged him to return. He waved and kicked the roan into a gallop. A bullet whined past as he left their angry ravings behind.

Directions to Kirby Smith's entrenchments had been vague from the various people he had stopped to ask. Most seemed nervous about being asked that kind of question. A hard-eyed woman gave him some specific instructions; she told him about Lincoln being murdered and asked if he was the one who did it. He soon realized her advice would have placed him right in the middle of Sheridan's advancing army and wheeled his horses toward the west. Later that same day, he became aware of a faint dust cloud far behind him. Could it be a Union patrol on his trail? Perhaps someone he talked to had summoned them. The next day, he saw no signs of pursuit and decided he was just jumpy from being alone so long.

An old corn farmer angrily told him about Jefferson Davis being captured, disguised as a woman; he and his wife had heard the rumor in town when they went to trade. He also insisted everything would have been different for the South if Stonewall Jackson had only healed from the wounds of his own men at Chancellorsville and Jeb Stuart had been quicker to get to Lee at Gettysburg. Cordell didn't tell that he had been with Stuart; the man didn't seem interested in listening, only in talking. He spoke disparagingly about Longstreet and held his highest praise for Rip Ford, an older Texan volunteer and leader of the so-called "Cavalry of the West."

After a few more minutes of "what ifs," he told the exasperated Rebel captain, in a hushed voice, where he might find information about the Confederate army.

Cordell cut the farmer off in midsentence and rode on, thanking him as he loped away. When he looked back, the man was talking to himself. A week later, he rode into a no-name settlement. Nightfall was spreading around him. Beyond was prairie decorated by scattered hills and thick tree lines. His destination was a ramshackle saloon the farmer had described.

A ribbon of moonlight spun wildly across the wood-planked floor as he stepped inside the lamp-lit building. Eight armed men at the long bar turned, and every eye caught the haggard Confederate cavalryman with the Comanche stone earring, carrying a Henry carbine at his side, a belt full of revolvers and an ammunition bandolier across his shoulder. A nearby wall lamp painted half his face orange. Rule Cordell nodded a greeting, which the eight men returned without emotion, releasing them to their drinking.

He was pleased to see two of them wore butternut pants, although nothing else of a Rebel uniform. One of these former Confederate soldiers had an empty left sleeve, pinned at his shoulder, that wiggled as he talked to the other. The second had a bulldog face with a flat rock for a nose and a droopy mustache attached. His head looked as if it was connected to his shoulders without benefit of a neck.

Cordell couldn't help noticing the bulldog-faced man wore crossed belts holding two holstered revolvers with their handles forward and a homemade shoulder holster carrying a third weapon. The one-armed man wore a belt gun; another pistol, which hung from a lanyard around his neck, was stuck in his pants. Neither made any attempt to recognize their affiliation to the same cause the uniformed cavalry officer had obviously fought for.

A small man in a scruffy buffalo coat and fringed leggings was eating alone at a table near the door. He avoided contact with Cordell's eyes, pretending to be engaged in cutting his steak. But the big-nosed bartender watched him uneasily, slowly putting down the glass he was wiping and letting both hands disappear under the bar. The one-armed ex-Confederate mumbled something to his friend as they drank. The other grinned and swallowed the rest of his whiskey, letting a streak of it run down his flat chin.

Chapter Ten

Weary from weeks of outrunning the Northern sweep of victory, Cordell moved to a solitary table in the corner. When he sat, a halo of dust from his long coat popped around him for an instant. He reached down to assure himself that his small money sack was in his boot, then rubbed his eyes to clear away fatigue. He laid the rifle on the floor beside his chair.

In the far corner, a five-handed poker game was into high stakes from the looks of the stacked coins and paper in the middle of the table. A heavyset man in a dark business suit with a well-groomed mustache and rosy cheeks was winning. At least it appeared that way from his toothy smile.

Cordell glanced again at the card game, drawn to the sudden curse of a loser, and spotted a strange-looking man dressed in Mexican jaguar-skin pants with two matching holsters holding black-handled pistols. Thin as buffalo grass, his narrow frame and face made his large blue eyes appear even more so. His right eye-brow was arched by a wide scar that gave his chiseled face a continuous quizzical expression.

White suspenders, holding the strange trousers, set off a dark red shirt. His wide-brimmed hat was decorated with a matching band of jaguar skin. He noted Cordell's interest with a slight nod and returned his attention to the cards in his hand. Behind the strangely dressed man, with one hand on his shoulder, was a young Mexican woman. Even in the shadows, Cordell could see she was beautiful.

A flat-crowned Spanish hat lay across her shoulders, held by a tie-down thong now resting around her neck. An ammunition bandolier slung across her shoulder accentuated her firm breasts under a light violet blouse with full, pillowy sleeves. He could see the handles of two pistols extending from the waistband of a buckskin skirt separated so it wouldn't bunch up when she rode. Lamplight walked across her long, black hair and stayed to make it shine. Large, dark eyes caught Cordell's evaluation and stayed an instant for her own. Her white-toothed smile that followed was enough to make any man weak. She whispered something in the wildly dressed man's ear. He chuckled.

"Hey, Johnny Cat, ya need whiskey?" yelled the bartender, concern in his uneven voice. The cardplayer with the jaguar-skin attire nodded his head and told the big cattleman on his left, the one cursing, to ante or fold. Cordell made a mental note of the name: "Johnny Cat."

"Hi, honey, what'll you have?"

The bosomy waitress with tired eyes, a thin mouth painted red beyond the lips, and long, yellow hair stood beside him, smiling. Her perfume was syrupy; her red, satiny dress featured much cleavage and long, bony legs; her voice was much younger than her face.

Before he could tell her that he wanted coffee and something to eat, she asked, "Would you like to go in the back? I can make you forget things."

"No, thanks. Just hungry. I'd sure go for some coffee and a big steak. Whatever else the cook is fixing today would be just fine, too."

"Sure, sweetie," she responded with a bemused smile.

His responding smile was a magnet to the saloon whore. Quickly she returned with the coffee, stood close to his chair and leaned over in front of him to place the steaming cup on the table. Her right breast rubbed against the side of his face as she positioned the coffee. Cordell was deep in thought and didn't notice the attempt to get his attention.

Letting the coffee cool, he rolled himself a cigarette, licked the loose flap, sealed it, and brought the smoke to life with the pop of a match. He inhaled and let the smoke drift away as he examined the gray room. It felt good to sit on something besides a saddle. His mind returned him to the time when he and Taullery, barely teenagers, had swaggered into a saloon for the first time. He grimaced, recalling his father's whipping with a razor strap that followed, and sipped the hot coffee.

An older, full-bearded man in faded Confederate pants entered the saloon and staggered toward the bar, breaking Cordell's daydream. He realized the hazard of such carelessness, and his eyes searched the room and briefly caught those of the fat gambler across the open space. He wondered whom he could trust to ask about General Kirby Smith's whereabouts. The farmer hadn't mentioned anyone's name. A heaping plateful of beefsteak, beans, and fried potatoes, topped with two freshly baked biscuits, ended his survey. It was presented in the same way as the coffee by the brazen waitress. This time she paused longer while leaning over, gazing coyly upward to make certain he had received an eyeful of her nearly exposed bosom.

"Now, honey, if these's anything else you want... you just ask," she said with her best smile. "My name is Lacy."

He smiled again and thanked her. She touched his arm in response as she left, letting a veil of thick cheap perfume settle around him. Cordell thought he might start his inquiry by asking her about Confederate forces in the area; she might be able to suggest someone to talk to. But there was surely nothing about the place that made him feel he was among friends. In response to the thought, he drew a Colt from his belt and laid it across his lap under the table. Eyeing the food, he dropped the cigarette to the floor and ended its smoking with his heel.

Halfway through a second plate of beans and beefsteak, Rule Cordell heard horses outside, followed by gruff orders. A Union patrol! Six dust-covered Federal troopers lunged into the saloon with readied carbines. Another man was cloaked in shadow behind them. A bigger man. Cordell was certain additional troops were outside. He glanced down at his rifle but decided against grabbing it. He knew instantly they were looking for him.

A slump-shouldered sergeant, with thick eye spectacles and an overgrown mustache cutting his face in two, spotted him first. The soldier's eyebrows twitched nervously, then he hunched his shoulders to shake off the emotion. He said something to the skinny horseman to his left. In response, the thin man grinned a mouthful of big teeth, bright against his darker skin, but the smile didn't reach his eyes. The young Rebel had seen that look before, and it loosened memories that weren't helpful now. A shiver ran down Cordell's back.

The soldiers separated from each other with quick sidesteps, allowing the man in the shadows to come forward. From behind them strode a copper-haired officer, six feet tall, with a jutting chin and prideful chest. His stiff back and formal stride spoke of a confident leader used to having his way and liking it. He was an impressive-looking man and knew it.

At the bar, a man's whispered conversation to his companions snapped through the forced stillness. "That thar's Colonel Red Fletcher, yo-all. He's the one bin a-hangin' Johnny Rebs when he ketches 'em without a goddamn parole pass."

"Damn! So he's the one."

"Yeah, that's him, all right."

"Whadda they want here?"

"That Reb hossman."

"Damn. Let's get outta here."

Four men slid away from the bar and headed for the back door. The other four sought refuge behind turned-over chairs and tables. Cordell wondered if they would run into more Union soldiers there. His eyes went back to the redheaded officer, who spoke with a haughty authority in his deep voice.

"Those your horses outside, Reb? That's a Union mount."

Rule Cordell sat, silent and unmoving, with his right hand holding his coffee cup and the other in his lap. He took a deep breath to push away the nervousness creeping through him.

"Evening, gentlemen. Obviously, you have me mistaken for someone else," Cordell responded. "I don't take well to questions—from Yankees. I suggest you take your act somewhere else."

His words stung. They had expected him to be afraid, getting caught alone. But showing fear wouldn't help him. His supper was not far down his gullet and inching up. He knew one thing: He wasn't going to let them arrest him. No. He would die here, taking the red-headed colonel and a few of his men with him. Out of the corner of his eye, he noticed the bar was empty, except for the drunken older Confederate.

Oblivious to the saloon's tension, the old Southerner studied the amber liquid in the glass next to him, left by one of the other drinkers. A swift jerk to his mouth and the whiskey disappeared. The room was so quiet the old Confederate's whining stomach could be heard by everyone. He looked down to determine where the sound came from, then resumed his new task of consuming the hastily left drinks along the bar. No one had moved from the poker table; the game continued as if nothing had happened.

"Let's quit this foolishness, Captain Cordell. Yeah, we know who you are. Not many Rebs go around wearing dead roses in their lapels. You want to show me your parole pass? To show you've become a nice, little Southern boy again." Fletcher pulled himself up to his full height and towered over his henchmen.

He paused, waiting for Cordell's answer. The Rebel cavalryman's eyes cut the colonel's so hard that the tall Union officer blinked and looked away.

"I didn't think so," Fletcher said, but kept his gaze on the slump-shouldered sergeant. "Captain Cordell, you're under arrest—for treason."

Cordell was surprised. His answer was more emotional than he wished: "Go to hell."

"Why, you Southern piece of—"

"Shut up, Sergeant," Fletcher ordered.

Without another word, Red Fletcher walked confidently closer to the young Confederate officer, then stopped in the middle of the quiet room as his six henchmen fanned out beside him. Cordell watched the slump-shouldered man's eyebrows twitch again, followed by hunching his shoulders to remove the nervousness.

"Take him—but don't kill him. He's going to hang. Toss your guns toward us, Cordell, and do it slowly," Fletcher snapped wickedly.

As instructed, the Rebel captain left his chair and squatted beside his Henry rifle. With his left hand, he shoved it toward them. All eyes were immediately drawn to the rifle scooting across the floor. The slump-shouldered sergeant ended its travel with a stomp of his boot. Cordell rose, cocking the hammer of the Colt in his right hand.

"Colonel, you'll never know what happens to me." Cordell's words were broken glass.

A second pistol jumped into his left hand; the cocking of its hammer was a click behind the first. Both weapons were aimed at Fletcher's middle. The colonel's eyebrows raised. He understood the Rebel captain's meaning clearly and wasn't certain he liked this scenario at all. His face drained of color as he motioned for his men to stay where they were.

Swallowing his own fear, Fletcher continued with a low, calm voice. "Captain, you're making a big mistake. We've got fifty thousand troops coming into Texas. Where do you think pissants like you are going to hide?"

"Texas ain't a place to be talking like that, Yank," came a voice from behind the Union soldiers. The threat was hard and low. It was from the man in jaguar-skin pants.

Fletcher turned to meet the challenge, and gunfire tore into his chest from pistols jumping into the strange man's hands. The colonel stared down at the blossoming red circle staining his blue uniform and grabbed at it with both hands. His haughty face cracked into utter fear just before another bullet struck him in the head. He flew backward; his head thudded against the far wall, rocking the lamp above him. The jittery wall lamp spewed drops of hot kerosene onto his still face.

Cordell dove to the floor, firing as he moved. Around the colonel, his six henchmen spun to shoot; four got off rounds from their carbines. Three shots blistered the table where Cordell had been a moment before. Orange flames roared from every corner of the room, tearing into the Union soldiers. Five buckled and tumbled in death over each other. Even the whore waitress fired a shotgun into their midst from behind the bar. The thunder of the guns drowned out the cries of dying men. Smoke danced across the oily room in rhythm with the crashing bullets. The acrid smell of gunpowder ran into every corner and stayed there.

As his fellow troopers died around him, the slump-shouldered sergeant dropped his misfired carbine and reached for the pistol stuck in his belt. Cordell's first shot drilled him low in the left shoulder, spinning him sideways. His second and third shots followed so quickly, the two cracks sounded like one long explosion. The bullets punched the sergeant's chest and slammed him against the drunken Confederate at the bar.

The collision splattered his drink across the bar and he stared at the spreading whiskey uncomprehending; then a sad expression slid across his face. The sergeant's pistol exploded harmlessly into the floor before slipping from his hand. Grabbing the drunken Confederate's leg, he tried to stand and couldn't. His groan was throaty and animal-like as his head thumped face first against the floor. He curled his legs into a ball and tried to hold his scarlet shoulder and chest. After three shallow gasps, the man moved no more. His eyes stared up unseeing at the drunken Rebel, who looked down at the lifeless body and spat in the sergeant's frozen face. In the old drunk's hand was an empty Walker Colt.

Just as suddenly as it began, it was over. Cordell stood, searching the unmoving blue bodies for any movement. There was none. Strolling toward him came the man in the jaguar-skin pants. Both hands held smoking pistols. His eyes were bright with killing. He kicked a dead Union cavalryman's leg aside to get through the clutter of bodies and slipped slightly on a pool of blood. He was grinning widely and talking lightheartedly to the others, as if they had just come from a town dance. Cordell thought he even looked like a big cat at that moment. Johnny Cat shoved his guns into their jaguar-skin holsters without reloading.

"The name's John Deane Carlson. My friends call me Johnny Cat," he said, extending his right hand. "Glad to make your acquaintance, Captain Cordell."

Cordell grinned, put one gun into its holster and the other in his belt, took the wild man's hand, and said, "It's Rule."

"Rule?"

"Yeah, my maw wanted me to be a king or something."

"Sounds like a mother."

Cordell nodded and returned the smile. Clearly the leader of this band, Johnny Cat turned toward a fellow who had been standing at the bar when Cordell had entered. He was a long-framed man with a chin that didn't seem to match his thin face and thick runny lips that also looked like they were an afterthought. He was reloading his pistol from behind a turned-over table.

"Harrelson, what about the Yanks outside?"

Wallace Harrelson nodded, licked his mouth, and headed for the back door. Before he reached it, the four who had left earlier burst in with recently fired guns in their hands. They were cheerful and laughing.

"How is it out there?" Johnny Cat asked.

"Four dead Yanks," answered a farmer with a neck disorder that caused his head to constantly twitch.

"Well done," Johnny Cat replied. "How about a drink, Rule—to the Confederacy?"

"I'll drink to that," Cordell said. "I'm on my way to meet up with Kirby Smith. Doesn't seem like there are any Rebels left fighting. Current companions excluded."

Johnny Cat cocked his head to one side and said, "Sorry to have to tell you this, Rule, but Smith surrendered. Handful of days ago. On a Yankee boat outside of Galveston."

Harrelson approached with an asthmatic wheeze to his angry words. "Hell, then that sonuvabitch took off for Mexico. Don't that beat all? Afraid he was going to be arrested. We heard he wasn't wearing stars 'n' bars when he crossed.

"Yeah, speaking of Mexico, there's a bunch of fighters joining Jo Shelby. Ol' Jo didn't surrender. Said he wouldn't—and, by God, he didn't. He's headed for Mexico too, going there to fight for the emperor. Or maybe it's the other side. Not sure. Anyway, I hear there are some generals and politicians with him too."

"Yeah, Jubal Early's with him!" came a confirmation from the back of the room. "An' Slaughter. Heard Terrell done went too."

"Hell, so did Governor Murrah!" a bulldog-faced man with the wide-set nose and stubby neck hollered. He was introduced as Joe Lockhart.

Cordell said, "I want to fight for the Confederacy.

Got no quarrel with anyone in Mexico. Anybody else still standing?"

"Maybe Stand Watie," one of the other men offered. He was another originally standing at the bar, now joining the growing group around Cordell and Johnny Cat. Cordell noticed, for the first time, that the man's right eye was white with a red scar on either side of it. Thick, rimless spectacles accented the loss.

The one-eyed Rebel explained, "You know, that Injun general? Over in the Nations. Ain't heard that he 'n' his bunch o' redskins quit yet. Tough bunch, I reckon."

The fat gambler crossed the room and said, "We must've scared Grant something fierce, though. They're sendin' 'Little Phil' down here—with fifty thousand bluebellies. Can you believe that? Fifty thousand Yanks—to handle us?!"

Hearty laughter followed his remark and he enjoyed the attention, turning his head left and right to soak up the response. With dramatic emphasis, the fat man stepped backward four exaggerated steps, bent his knees, and broke wind over one of the dead Union soldiers. Amid exploding laughter, he bowed deeply.

"Sheridan's here?" Cordell asked, bringing the room back to seriousness.

"Yeah. Brought in all his hossmen, miles of 'em— and a bunch of other hardasses," answered the one-armed Rebel from the bar. Caleb Truitt was his name.

Truitt had a wispy, long mustache and spotty beard covering a pale, skinny face. Johnny Cat stage-whispered that the Rebel had lost his arm at Shiloh and shot the surgeon who removed it when he regained consciousness. Truitt smiled with pride when Cordell nodded his approval of the story. Cordell tried to keep the picture of his old friend, Whisper, out of his mind.

Of course, the only similarity was the removed arm. Yet it was enough, and he fought away the linkage.

Quietly, Johnny Cat added, "I think the main reason Sheridan's here is to send a message to them Frenchies in Mexico. Grant's tellin' them that they shouldn't think about messin' with Texas. But he's here to make sure we don't get the fire going again too."

The daredevil leader explained that Sheridan had brought over Canby's army from Mobile plus two full corps: Ord from City Point, Virginia, and Thomas from Nashville. He said, with an impish grin, that "Little Phil" was angry he hadn't been able to participate in the Grand Review in Washington, D.C., because of Grant's orders to go to Texas.

"So it's really over," Cordell said softly.

"Hell no, it isn't over," said a large, barrel-chested man with a trim, dark mustache, who went by the name Creede Bledsoe. His swagger was that of a brawler used to intimidating other men with just his reputation as a fighter. Cordell noticed that the knuckles of his ham-size hands were covered with scars. He was wearing cross-belted pistols and a large sheathed knife; a third gun hung in a shoulder holster. Bledsoe's wide-brimmed hat looked new, and so did his coat and vest. His trousers were Confederate issue, but his boots were Mexican-styled with large-roweled spurs.

"Not for us, it isn't," Bledsoe continued. He patted the handle of his knife with his right hand and spouted lines from Tennyson: "'My good blade carves the casques of men...My tough lance thrusteth sure... My strength is as the strength of ten...Because my heart is pure.'" With a sour face, Bledsoe waved for the blond waitress to bring him a bottle.

Harrelson shook his head in admiration and said, "Man, that's purty stuff, Creed."

Cordell smiled with one side of his mouth and

responded, "Well, *my* heart's not pure. It's full of hate for Yankees." His eyes asked the next question of Johnny Cat Carlson.

The energetic leader declared, "Creed likes to hear himself spit out that Tennyson fellow's stuff. I don't know about *blades* and *lances,* but he's right about one thing. We're going to hit Yanks every goddamn place they sit—and get away before they know what hit them. We're going to make those bastards rue the day they ever set foot in Texas."

Johnny Cat paused, put his arm around Bledsoe's shoulder, and added, "We rode with Rip Ford. Part of the 'Cavalry of the West.' Yeah, that's what he called us. Has a nice ring to it, don't it. Yanks called us bush-whackers, bastards, bandits—and everything else."

Laughter and Rebel yells followed his declaration. Cordell glanced around the room at the gathering of men who, minutes earlier, had been cold strangers. The jaguar outfit was enough to tell him the man was theatrical at best and, more than likely, maniacal, but Cordell shrugged away his brain's alert. It felt good to find men who weren't ready to bow to the Northern aggression.

"Rip went to Mexico too. So we're what's left of the Confederacy," Johnny Cat pronounced proudly. "Do you want to join us?"

Cordell paused, smiled, and said simply, "Yeah, I do."

His glance caught the advance of the Mexican woman who had smiled at him earlier. She had reloaded the second of her two pistols and was shov-ing it into her skirt band, next to the first, as she strolled toward them. Her face was smooth, and her smile revealed dimples on both cheeks. Shiny black hair with reddish highlights draped across her shoul-ders. Cordell was certain her eyes matched the color of her blouse. He couldn't remember seeing a more beautiful woman; she was a magnet for his eyes.

Johnny Cat also watched her, beamed, and announced, "Captain Rule Cordell, meet my secret weapon, Aleta. She can fight like a wildcat—and make love like one too."

Ignoring the last part of the introduction, Aleta smiled at Cordell and said simply, "You show no fear, Captain Rule Cordell."

"Didn't seem like it would do much good, ma'am."

"*Sí.* I am Aleta. Call me that."

"Yes, ma—Aleta," he replied. Her eyes searched his face and returned the interest in his eyes for an instant.

"That's her brother—over in the corner. Zetto. Doesn't talk much. Can barely understand him when he does. But he's a heller with a gun. The Yanks burned out their family down on the Rio Grande."

Cordell blinked and looked across the room at a young man with a sombrero pushed down on long black hair. His wide shoulders made him appear shorter than his average height. Zetto wore a short Spanish buckskin jacket with matching bell-bottomed breeches. A silver-studded pistol belt carried two holstered guns; two more were shoved into the belt. Cordell nodded hello, but it wasn't returned.

Johnny Cat slapped Cordell on the shoulder and hollered, "Hey, bring us that bottle, Lacy, we're going to celebrate. It's a good night. Eleven more dead Yanks—and one more goddamn Rebel. That's good odds from where I come from. Looks like you 'n' me got a few things in common." He pointed at the scar at his eyebrow. Cordell chuckled and touched his forehead self-consciously. The last time he had had a look in a stream, the scar was barely a pale line.

The fat gambler elbowed, through the crowd and

asked Cordell where he had come from. Cordell told all of them of his journey from Virginia; that his cavalry had surrendered at Appomatox Court House, including close friends. He explained that he had been riding since that awful morning, searching for a Confederate force.

"So ya were thar when Ol' Marse Robert done give it up?" asked the muscular Harrelson. Cordell nodded affirmatively.

"Wal, how come ye didn't stay in Texas—to he'p us hyar?" came a second question, from the former soldier with the white eye and red scar.

Cordell cocked his head and said, "I thought there was a better place to fight back then. I rode with Stuart until he died."

"Damn! If Stuart had just come to Marse Robert at Gettysburg when he was supposed to, we might not be in this hell," the fat gambler announced loudly. Heads bobbed in agreement.

Cordell's face turned dark. Johnny Cat Carlson watched him with a quiet amusement. The fat man hadn't realized the seriousness of what he had just said. Looking first at the floor, then gradually up to the fat man's eyes, Cordell said, "Mister, I wouldn't say that if I were you. You don't know what you're talking about."

The fat gambler continued. "Wal, it's a fact, dammit! Marse Robert didn't know where Stuart was—and he needed—"

Her dark eyes sparkling, Aleta interrupted. "Senor Darryl, *tenga cuidado.* Be careful. I think you are not listening. Captain Cordell *rode* with General Stuart. Do you understand? He *rode* with him. He knows what happened; he is not running with the mouth."

"Hell, Aleta, I'm not..." Jacobson Darryl, the fat gambler, suddenly realized what he had been doing and jabbered a rambling sort of apology. "What I really meant is—if only those damn Brits had recognized us, that would've turned it. I didn't mean that Stuart…"

"Forget it," Cordell said.

Harrelson tried to smooth things over by saying, "It wasn't Stuart that was the problem, it was Longstreet."

Another ex-Confederate clamored, "Oh hell, it was A. P. Hill who done lost the whole thing fer Marse Robert. Ever'body know'd that."

Creed Bledsoe studied the Confederate captain curiously and started to repeat another line from Tennyson: "'But o'er the dark a glory spreads…And gilds the dri—'"

It was cut off by the enthusiastic bump of another small guerrilla fighter passing him to get closer to Cordell. Bledsoe glared at the man, but he was too intent on saying something to the Confederate captain to notice.

Chapter Eleven

Wearing a scruggy buffalo coat and fringed leather leggings, both too warm for the season, the diminutive Rebel stepped close to Cordell and tried to smile, but he was too nervous to make his mouth get there. Cordell remembered the small man was eating alone when he entered. He couldn't recall where the man was during the fight.

As the small man spoke, his face turned bright red from the embarrassment of being in the limelight. "I knew you were one of us, sir. I just knew it. They call me 'Quick'—Quick Miller. My—my real name's Orville. You can call me Quick though—everybody else does."

Cordell said, "Thanks, Quick. I'm glad to meet you."

"Do you wear that…for your lover, Captain Rule?" Aleta asked, noticing the remains of the rose on Cordell's jacket. He looked down at the flower, and his face flushed.

Johnny Cat Carlson spun toward Cordell, spotted the rose and patted him vigorously on the arm, turned to Aleta, and kissed her. She kissed him back. No one heard Cordell say the rose was in memory of J. E. B. Stuart.

The diminutive Miller grew bolder and added, "Did you know them Yanks just caught John Hood—and two of his boys—a-trying to cross the Rio Grande? A pity. Him with one leg 'n' all."

Quick Miller was proud Cordell didn't know about Hood. He looked around the room, shaking his head to verify the statement's truth. Cordell sensed it somehow helped the man deal with his low status among the gang. Quick Miller was a gentle soul, in Cordell's immediate estimation, given to following others just to be a part of something, without much thought of the consequences. He should have been a schoolteacher or a store clerk, Cordell thought. His nickname had nothing to do with his speed in handling a gun, only that he was "quick" to help with cooking, packing, and other chores.

Johnny Cat yelled to the bartender, "Hey, Sam, we'll get this Yankee trash out of here when we go. No one will ever know they were here."

Turning back to his band of guerrillas, he started singing, "Oh, I wish I was in the land of cot-ton…"

Soon every man in the saloon was singing the beloved "Dixie," including Cordell. From deep within him came a defiant Rebel yell that triggered similar cries of defiance from the rest of the band. Cordell looked at Johnny Cat Carlson and they shook hands once more. God, it was great to be among warriors again, Cordell thought. Out of the corner of his eye he caught Bledsoe's gaze. It wasn't friendly.

Aleta's was, though. She turned her head to the side,

smiled at the Confederate captain, and ran her fingers easily down her hair to the tip of her right shoulder, past her breast, then down to the gun at her waist, making certain Cordell's eyes followed. But this was no hang-around whore; this was Johnny Cat's woman, and something inside his mind kept hammering away at that reminder. Still, she could make a man feel alive just looking at her.

The next day Johnny Cat's guerrillas hit a Federal patrol escorting a military payroll wagon. Cordell led the flanking assault. The captured funds were kept in the stolen wagon along with their other things; Johnny Cat had only smiled when Cordell suggested they give the money to needy Rebels. Two days later they attacked a wagon train of military supplies en route to Galveston. A week later, they ambushed a company of Federal cavalry, killing seven troopers and wounding eleven in a three-hour fight that ended with the cavalry fleeing.

In the following week, they joined with returning Confederates and seized wagons, plows, mules, and other property confiscated by the state during the War. Everything was distributed to the Rebel families in greatest need. Cordell had insisted on giving away half of the previously stolen money to the same families, and Johnny Cat had reluctantly agreed. Summer watched their selective warfare ripsaw the soft underbelly of a depressed Texas. They weren't the only ones taking out their frustration on anything deemed Northern and vulnerable to attack.

Other Rebel confrontations passed across Texas like tree shadows in a late afternoon. It was a way for some to deal with their bitterness. It was a way to live for others. Either way, they were fiercely angry. They had left behind politicians who hadn't protected their great state from the destruction of its resources—or who had participated in its systematic looting. Indignant Rebels seized state property and ripped apart stores. The state treasury itself was stolen. Johnny Cat's band hanged a carpetbagger tax collector, held their own against a company of Union regulars, and burned out a turncoat rancher.

The North was determined to quell any fantasies of continuing the Rebel uprising, especially in Texas, which seemed to be a gathering place for unrepentant Confederates. The names of Johnny Cat Carlson and Rule Cordell were whispered fearfully along with those of other Texas hellions like Clay Allison, Bill Longley, Bob Lee, Cullen Baker, and Creed Taylor and his clan. Austin itself became the home of a puppet governor, controlled by General Sheridan.

Civil courts lost to military courts-martial. Local offices, from sheriff to mayor, were cleansed of any possible Confederate leanings and replaced with scalawags or carpetbaggers. Cattlemen found the trails to Missouri blockaded by Union soldiers who confiscated their herds. Farmers sagged deeper into poverty because their crops couldn't be sold or shipped. Freed slaves wandered about the state with little purpose, only desire.

A well-armed, uniformed militia, known as the "Regulators," became the governor's arm of enforcement and added their authorized terror to the statewide woe. Regulators arrested civilians without cause and took their homes. They shot prisoners in the back and hanged the rest. They emptied corrals, smokehouses, and grazing lands as enforcement of Reconstruction twisted into hateful revenge against the South. At the ballot box, they turned away every white male who couldn't pledge the "ironclad oath" that he had never voluntarily raised arms against the Union. Few qualified.

Quickly, Johnny Cat's guerrillas learned Cordell was an intense leader, better in many ways than the fearless and dramatic, but erratic, Johnny Cat himself. Only Creed Bledsoe refuted it, but not to Cordell's face. The others also marveled at Cordell's ability with a handgun. None could match his skill—certainly not Johnny Cat, who actually favored a shotgun in battle, nor Joe Lockhardt, whom most thought of as a pistol fighter.

The powerfully built Bledsoe told anyone who would listen that he could tear Cordell's arms off and shove them down his throat if he wanted to. Jacobson Darryl, the fat gambler, was among those who agreed with Bledsoe's assessment and quietly told him it was a shame Johnny Cat thought so highly of the new Rebel cavalryman. Of course, no one expressed this thought around Cordell, one way or the other.

But Cordell's relentless desire to attack the North was an unquestioned force with no equal among the guerrilla band. Not even Johnny Cat, with his disgust for Northern intruders and Southern turncoats, could match Cordell's intensity. The guerrilla leader avoided dividing the spoils around the former Confederate captain, choosing instead to keep any looted money in their stolen wagon, except as needed occasionally for supplies. The men, including Cordell, replenished their weapons and ammunition any way they could after a battle.

No victory relieved the blackness within Rule Cordell. He drove horses and men—but no one harder than himself. His moody reactions were to be avoided as much as a rattlesnake curled in the sun. Even Bledsoe became subdued when word came around that Cordell was angry about something. Federal dispatches haunted the guerrilla gang's trail, pronouncing them "insurrectionist rebels and wanted outlaws."

While the gang attacked their selected targets, Northern military rule grabbed the throat of Texas life.

Although the other men were always joking and talking with Aleta, Cordell kept his distance. Simple greetings when they happened to pass in camp or on the trail were the extent of their conversations. But he was drawn to her wild beauty and fascinated by her matching fierceness in battle. The men treated her as one of them because she fought as well as they did, never asking for special favors. Johnny Cat had quietly told Cordell that Aleta had complained that the Confederate captain didn't like her. Cordell assured the jaquar-skin-outfitted leader that he did and that where he came from it was polite not to engage in casual conversation with another man's woman. Johnny Cat had enjoyed the response and asked him to try to be nice to Aleta. Cordell said he would try.

Returning from a scouting assignment, Cordell once came upon her bathing in the small stream near their camp. She did not see him due to the thick trees half surrounding this corner of the stream as well as the camp itself. She was leaving the water, her naked body sparkling with water droplets. He couldn't help himself, and watched as she slowly wiped herself dry. Lust for her drove him to take a bath in the same stream later that night. Afterward, he avoided her even more, afraid his eyes would betray his feelings.

But there was little time to express them even if he wanted to. Sheer numbers against the gang began to cut into their manpower and their ability to move easily through the country. Four guerrillas were shot; three more were caught and hanged when their camp was overrun. Fierce determination—personified by both Carlson and Cordell—kept the gang hitting and hiding, running and raiding, causing irritation among military leaders, fear among local politicans—and a strange sense of pride among downtrodden Texans. As the harried guerrillas continued to nip at its heels, Reconstruction fattened on the carcass of Texas.

After a running gunfight with a combined regiment of Regulators and Union troopers, the Johnny Cat guerrillas took refuge in a supportive farmer's barn for the night, eight miles from Waco. Three fresh horses were traded for windblown mounts left to recover. The night was short for the Rebels, for they dared not stay long in one place. Daylight was hours away and the gang was already saddled.

Aleta and Quick Miller tended to the four wounded men, treating their bullet wounds with a cornmeal poultice and wrapping them with torn cloth kept with the cooking supplies. One of the wounded was Rule Cordell, who had an ugly bullet crease along his upper thigh. It had ripped a long hole in his uniform pants. The former Confederate captain's uniform coat was torn at the shoulder, most of the buttons were gone, and the left sleeve drooped across his forearm. The coat's destruction had occurred during a hand-to-hand battle in the saddle with a Union soldier after both had emptied their guns earlier in the battle. He had tried to avoid being treated, but his obvious limping attracted attention.

Aleta walked over to him and said, "Take down your pants, Captain Rule. You need that wound—"

"Take down my pants?!"

"Aleta will not look, I promise."

"Oh, I'm all right."

"Captain Rule, your pant leg is more red than gray. You cannot walk with limping. Please do not be silly," she said without emotion, but her eyes sparkled with interest.

Cordell didn't match her gaze and asked, "What about Quick? Can't he do this?"

"Look for yourself. He is busy with others. You are not the only one who got shot. Leave your pants on, Captain Rule. I will cut them as I need to. Will that satisfy you?"

"That would be fine."

She kneeled in front of him. Deftly, she cut apart the pantleg to reveal the wound, cleaned it of dirt, pieces of cloth, and dried blood, and treated it with the poultice. Fresh blood was oozing from the long, dark crease. Cordell did not dare to look down at himself for what was happening to his manhood due to her closeness. Her face was inches away from his groin; he was glad his Confederate jacket covered it.

"What is the real reason you wear that dead flower stem on your coat, Captain Rule?" she asked, looking up at him. The dead rose had long before become nothing more than a curved stem on his lapel but he refused to remove it.

"General Stuart—Jeb Stuart—was my leader until he got killed. He liked to wear a rose in his lapel. I've worn this one in his honor ever since…that day."

"Are you sure it is not for a woman that you wear this, Captain Rule?" she asked. "An hombre such as you should have a fine woman waiting for him."

"No one waits for me, Aleta. I have no family."

"Why do you wear that earring? It is more like something my people would wear, or a Comanche."

"It is Comanche. A gift from an old man, a wise man whose name was Moon," he answered. "He gave me the earring and this medicine bag. They brought me safely through the war. He said they would." He held up the bag briefly with his fingers and shoved it back into his shirt.

"You are an unusual man, Captain Rule. Aleta does not read you well, I think. Sometime, we must talk more. Aleta needs to know you better."

After wrapping the folded cloth around the wound and knotting it in place, she stood slowly. She arose so close to him that he took a half-step back in response. She searched his face and broke into a wide smile and whispered, "But I am glad to see that you like me." As she spoke, one hand pulled on his coat as if to straighten it and the other slid along the hard mound at his groin.

Spinning away, she paused, looked back into his eyes, and said, "Perhaps next time you will join me in the stream."

She walked toward Johnny Cat, who was talking to the farmer and his wife. Cordell stood red-faced. The farmer tried to ignore Aleta's obvious femininity. His wife was watching Rule Cordell.

"Take this as our thanks," Johnny Cat said as he handed a small sack of coins to the farmer who had agreed to hide the gang in his barn for the night.

The farmer's sun-beaten face tried not to show his fascination at the guerrilla leader's wild dress. He was standing next to a Texas legend, something he would share someday with friends. He stared at the sack, rubbed his tanned fingers over the soft leather, and replied, "Wal, I hate to keep it. With yo-all a-fightin' them goddamn Yankees 'n' all, but…"

"I know," Johnny Cat said. "They're taxing everything they can get their hands on. Took two farms next county over. Just a week ago it was. Nothing we could do about it. Maybe this'll help keep 'em off your back one o' these days."

"I do thank ye. Ya know, it be all them freed darkies that's the real problem. Got all o' Texas ruined for us farmers. Yessuh," the farmer said, shoving the sack into his pocket. He spat a brown stream of tobacco juice for emphasis. Removing his crumpled hat, he rubbed his hands through thinning, sweaty hair and replaced it with a hard tug.

With his feelings for Aleta under control, Cordell strolled toward the three, said his "good morning," and advised Johnny Cat that the gang was ready to leave. Johnny Cat asked about his wound and Cordell said Aleta had done a good job taking care of it. The farmer bit the inside of his cheek to mask his relief at hearing the news of their pending departure. It was difficult not to keep from looking at the horizon. Regulators could show up any minute, or even a patrol of Federal troops. They often did, and they'd like nothing better than to start the day with a hanging of a Confederate-sympathetic farmer.

"Yo'all got plenty o' grain fer yurn hosses?" the farmer asked, swallowing his concern.

"Thanks, we've got plenty," Cordell answered with a cigarette in the corner of his mouth. "Now, if blue-bellies come, don't try to lie. Tell them we stole the grain from you—and took your horses. Tell 'em it was us and you were scared for your life. They'll leave you alone if you do that."

"Wal, all right, suh," the farmer replied grimly.

"Aren't you Reverend Cordell's boy?" the older woman asked. A hard life had robbed her face of its softness and her hair of its cinnamon, but her smile was warm and genuine, flooding her cheeks with wrinkles.

Cordell was embarrassed but answered politely, "Yes, ma'am. I'm Rule Cordell—but I don't think my father would be particularly happy to claim me."

"Oh, hush now. You boys is fightin' for all of us. He should be button-poppin' proud," she responded heartily. Cordell realized she was silently evaluating his physical structure.

"Rule, I have something I want to give you. Will you wait?"

"Well, of course, ma'am, but—"

172

"I'll be right back. Give them some tobacco, Frank," she said over her shoulder.

The three men and Aleta watched her retreat and disappear into the house. The farmer asked if either Johnny Cat or Cordell wanted some tobacco, as he was asked to do. Both thanked him and declined. Minutes later, the woman opened the back door and bounced across the yard. In her hand were folded clothes, topped off by a wide-brimmed black hat. She handed them to Cordell.

"These belonged to my youngest son, Daniel. I reckon he was about your fittin.'"

"But, ma'am, I can't..."

Hesitantly, she said, "My Frank 'n' me, we gave two sons...to the Cause. You remind me of our Daniel. I know he'd be happy to have you a-wearin' 'em. Ain't gonna do nobody any good sittin' in that ol' closet."

"Thank you, ma'am, that's mighty nice of you."

"Ride with God, son. We'll be praying for you," she said softly, and a tear escaped from her eye.

Cordell held the clothes and was silent.

Without wiping away the loosened moistness, the woman looked deeply into Cordell's face as if to find an answer to a question she couldn't bring herself to ask.

"Peace be with you, ma'am."

The words passed from Cordell's lips like a forgotten song. The half-smoked cigarette dropped to the ground aided by the brush of his hand. She reached for him and burst into crying, unable to hold back the anguish pushing against her soul. The clothes in his hands fell to the earth as her small arms enfolded him, and her torn-apart face burrowed into his chest. Tentatively, he wrapped his arms around her quivering body and glanced awkwardly at the other two men. The farmer nodded his understanding but made no attempt to come to his wife. Dark pain twisted his own face as he fought to hold back the same awful loss that had overcome his wife.

Embracing the sobbing woman with one arm, Cordell picked up the hat and clothes with the other. Carlson's eyes were devilish, but he said nothing. Cordell slowly guided the farmer's wife to the back-door steps, eased her into sitting, and sat down beside her. Her sobs were less frequent now, wheezing like a horseshoer's bellows over hot coals.

"There's nothing I can say to take away your pain, ma'am," Cordell said. "But I'm proud that I remind you of your son. I'll try to ride with that honor. You can count on it."

He took her hand, held it for a moment, and continued. "Ma'am, you keep right on remembering them, even when it hurts so much. They're too important to forget. They were mighty lucky to have a mother like you. Reckon they knew it, too.

"Your sons died to make things better for all of us. That's what Jesus died for, remember? Your sons are in heaven with him right now. They're without pain. They're waiting for you—and your husband. Remember that. They loved you. That's why they went to fight."

Cordell relaxed the grip on her hand and stood. Her head was down on her chest. Her breathing was smooth and even now, as if she were sleeping. Johnny Cat watched with surprise. Aleta looked at Cordell as if she had never seen him before. Creed Bledsoe walked over, trailing his horse. So did Quick Miller and Joe Lockhardt. The diminutive Miller stood with his mouth open in awe at the unexpected gentleness of Rule Cordell.

"What the hell is Cordell doing now?" Bledsoe

snapped. "Has it been that long since he had a woman? She's an old prune."

Johnny Cat grabbed him by the arm. The jaguar-skinned leader's face was purple with rage.

"Shut up, you idiot!" His words were bullets.

Aleta's rebuke was an instant behind: "Bledsoe, you are the fool of all fools."

Bledsoe's mouth opened, but nothing came out. His right fist curled, and he drew it backward. Behind him, Joe Lockhardt growled, "That'd make two mistakes, Creed."

"He's like a preacher," Miller mumbled, more to himself than the others.

Aleta said nothing, but her eyes welled with tears that wanted release. She turned away and wiped her face with her blouse sleeve. Johnny Cat nervously glanced at the farmer, but if he had heard Bledsoe's comments, his manner didn't reflect it. He was focused on his wife and Cordell. The Rebel captain walked back. Defiantly, Bledsoe crossed his thick arms, ready to resume his sarcasm, but Cordell ignored the poem-spouting outlaw as well as the jaguar-skin-outfitted leader and went directly to the grieving farmer.

"Do you have a Bible, Frank?" Cordell asked.

The farmer was surprised at the question.

"Uh, uh, yessuh, I do. Family book, ya know."

"When we're gone, you take your wife inside—and you read to her out of it. You can read, can't you?"

"Well, yessuh, some, I reckon."

"Good. You do it now. I'll be back one of these days," Cordell said, and left the threat for not reading undefined but present.

It was an hour after their having left the farm before anyone said anything to Cordell. Among the gang, conversation was muffled, as if they were in a church. Most were shocked at Cordell's gentle manner with the old woman. Bledsoe continued his chewing criticism of Cordell, but did so well out of his earshot. Finally, Johnny Cat rode up alongside the former Rebel cavalry captain, who was apparently lost in the thin white smoke of a cigarette.

"I appreciate the way you handled that back there, Rule. We're gonna need good folks to help us. They'll be singing our praises—or at least yours—for a long time," Johnny Cat said. "Only thing that would've been better would have been your leading us in singin' 'In the Sweet Bye n' Bye.'" His voice was oozing sarcasm.

Cordell blinked away his own daydream; his smile was a thin line that turned up only on one end. It was apparent he didn't want to talk. Johnny Cat continued anyway, this time speaking in a manner Cordell hadn't heard before. He wondered if Carlson was moved by what they had experienced at the small farm or was testing Cordell's own steadfastness after seeing him care for the old woman.

Chapter Twelve

While Johnny Cat Carlson's gang crisscrossed the land ahead of Regulators and Union troops, a solitary rider in a Confederate uniform arose from his night's sleep a half day's ride from Waco. The stars still controlled the sky, but his agitated stomach wouldn't let him rest any more. He was coming home! His imagination was already there. In his mind, people would recognize him when he rode in, yelling their greetings and cheering his return. Some would gather around him, bubbling with enthusiasm. Jessica Roget would run out to meet him with love in her eyes.

Old friends who also fought for the Cause should be around too; more than 2,200 men from the county had volunteered. Lieutenant Ian Taullery envied their earlier return, but it didn't matter now, he had made it—and there was much to catch up on and a whole life to plan for. Of course, the only family he had left was an aunt and uncle who lived on the south edge of town. His parents had both died of influenza and pnemonia when he was twelve. Uncle Vernel and Aunt Millie had taken him in. What if they were in town to trade for supplies this day? That would be grand, indeed. He could see their fine faces in his mind.

As he crossed the old bridge spanning the Brazos River, he realized that when he thought of family, Rule Cordell's face appeared. How could they have gotten so far apart? Why? But Taullery knew the answer. Way down inside where a man doesn't like to go, he knew. Rule Cordell was fighting a war against his father. If the South didn't win, somehow, Rule Cordell was lost. Forever. Or felt he was. It didn't sound right when put to words, but knowing Reverend Aaron Cordell made it understandable.

Taullery watched the Brazos ripple past, mostly brown water snapping at the leash of the shoreline. Some things never change. The bridge was used mostly by cattlemen trailing herds on the old Shawnee trail that headed toward Missouri. Today it was empty and seemed forelorn, like a forgotten friend. He muttered, "Hello, Brazos" as he passed. So far, the sound of the river was the closest thing to a "coming home" greeting he had experienced.

His best friend's reputation as an outlaw was known to him. How could he miss it? Tales rattled through the countryside as if they were the only part of Texas worth keeping alive. Union-controlled newspapers expounded on the gang's existence with venom. One story he saw even accused them of being involved in President Lincoln's assassination. It was like a bad dream, reading Cordell was running with a wild band led by a crazy man who dressed in jaguar skins and hated everything Yankee. The newspapers described Rule Cordell as a "desperate pistol-man and outlaw with a bent for violence."

Part of Taullery wanted to find his friend and talk him out of continuing this madness. But he was resigned to Cordell's never admitting defeat. The War had been over for nearly a year; he and Billy Ripton had waited for Whisper Jenson to recover enough to ride with them home. He had been riding southwesterly from the Red River, alone with his thoughts, since Whisper Jenson had first left for his home at the edge of the town of Dallas and Billy Ripton had cut off to go to his family's small spread north of the Waco settlement.

Crossing the magical Red River had been more spiritual than physical for the trio of riders—the first time any of them had been on Texas soil since they pledged allegiance to the Confederacy. At the moment their horses' hooves touched the mud of their homeland, only Whisper could put it to words. "Never thought I'd see heaven again." It was Billy Ripton who thought of their friend. "I hope Captun Cordell be all right. Will we see 'im agin, Ian? I sur wish he hadn't upped 'n' left us like that. Ya hear what they is a-callin him? An outlaw, that's what. They is a-callin' Captun Cordell an outlaw. Son of a bitch!"

Whisper took the responsibility of answering gratefully away from Taullery. "Billy, sometimes a man fights so long he doesn't know how to stop, even if he wants to."

The young Rebel didn't like the answer, and said, "He made 'em sit up straight fer you, Whisper. I were thar."

"No one is puttin' him down," Taullery finally said. "I hope we get to see him."

"All right, then," Billy said, nodding his head with

the conviction that he had just won some kind of argument. Whisper glanced at Taullery but lowered his eyes when Taullery looked back.

The streets were contagious with motion as Ian Taullery rode into Waco. Wagons rocked along, men on horseback darted ahead with apparent purpose, carriages eased along the dirt thoroughfare, and men and women crossed on foot, engrossed in the business of the day. Taullery's eyes darted from one side of the street to the other, and back again, trying to match reality with his mind's pictures. No one noticed his arrival; no one paused to even see who it was entering the town, leading a packhorse.

He heard the steady ping of a blacksmith and wondered if it was McLeen, the same man who was making horseshoes when he left. The tinkle of a saloon piano, the clatter of hooves, and the music of people talking reached his ears in a sweet serenade. It was Waco. It was home. He wanted to scream out, "I'm home, everybody!" but he didn't. He swallowed his disappointment and tried to savor this visual reunion with his hometown.

The tall horseman reined in at the tie bars outside a large saloon in the heart of the raw settlement. Over its door was a sign that had seen too much Texas weather, but the words "Bonner Tavern" were visible in a faded blue paint. His neat Confederate uniform belied long days on the trail; two holstered, ivory-handled guns spoke of a man who had seen his share of war and could handle more if challenged. An ostrich feather on his cocked hat appeared as fresh as the first day of conflict. His blond beard was trim, at least for someone who had shaved in the dark.

Without dismounting, Taullery guided the packhorse forward and to his right side with the lead rope until the animal was next to the reining stand. He was looking forward to a bath, some whiskey—and seeing Jessica Roget, the girl who had promised to wait for him. She was first in that litany. He assumed she would be working in the saloon. At least she was when he rode out with Rule Cordell to join up. Taullery had been lusting for her since leaving Virginia. He had held her and undressed her in his mind a hundred times.

His racking ache of lonesomeness had begun when both friends left, bursting with eagerness to get to their families. For a man who loved to talk, being alone was hard. Too hard. Ripton's family had a small cow-calf spread less than a day's ride from town. Before riding off, Ripton told his friends he expected his mother and his older sister to come running out to greet him, tears streaming down their faces. His father would grin that funny, lopsided grin of his and slap his youngest son hard on the back, wink, and ask him if he'd like a "little snort o' corn back in the shed."

Ripton's remaining older brother would be there, too, whooping and hollering and glad to see him, he said. Billy figured his brother would have returned from the War before he did, since he and Taullery had waited for Whisper. The boy's face had reddened with the telling, but both older men had assured him that his picture was wonderful and not to be ashamed of wanting it to come true.

At Billy's insistence, the three men had hugged before he rode off. The young man's face was wet, his chin thrust forward with pride; his words to the other two had rattled in Taullery's brain for miles: "Never will this h'yar boy ever be with sech great men as you two, 'n' Captun Cordell 'n' Genrul Lee. I be thankful fer yo-all lettin' me ride with ye."

Although weak from his ordeal and battered by the

181

long ride, Whisper Jenson could also barely contain his excitement about seeing his family again. His wife and children would be expecting him, he said in response to Taullery's suggestion. It was Taullery who had written the letter to them when Whisper couldn't bring himself to tell of his condition. Maybe he could start up his law practice again, he had said to Taullery. Lawyers didn't need two arms, he mused. Taullery had passed on Whisper's invitation to ride along with him to his house and stay awhile. The offer was genuine, but Taullery knew the man and his family needed to be together, without any distractions, at this time.

The Bonner Tavern was the third-largest building in Waco. There were three other saloons, plus an assortment of stores, shops, and businesses along crowded main streets. Cattle drives headed out on the old Shawnee Trail had built the settlement into a much larger town than Dallas. Homes created a full moon around this base of commerce. The nearest community of any size was a two-day ride north. As he sat on the silver-mounted saddle in the shadows of the saloon, Taullery's light blue eyes swallowed the sights that had once been his life, absorbing them in his soul forever.

The town seemed both familiar and strange at the same time. A few faces looked familiar but not welcoming. Watching the movement of men and women about the town made him feel more alone, not less. He saw a few people who looked familiar, but no one rushed to greet him. A dozen Union soldiers, outside of another saloon across the street, watched him with curious interest. Without consciously acknowledging it, he knew Waco had changed, but not as much as he had. Some buildings registered as a part of his yesterday; some were definitely built since he left. While the town had grown while he was away at war, it seemed small and eerily removed from the life he had known—or the man he had become. Suddenly he felt old.

To his left came a familiar voice. "God save us, it is another of the wretched devils who brought shame to our great land and a friend of my— Oh, I can't say it, dear God, I cannot speak the evil."

Before Taullery turned to face the voice, he knew it was his friend's father, Reverend Aaron Cordell. Walking with the minister were two men Taullery didn't know: a taller man with a full, gray-streaked beard and a sheriff's badge, and a stockily built Union major. Neither of the two seemed inclined to offer any greeting. If the preacher had changed any, it was to become even fatter than Taullery remembered. Reverend Cordell's eyes were certainly the same: beady and condescending as they searched the world for places where he could spread his singular view of righteousness.

Taullery stiffened as the minister continued, "I suppose you've been seeing my, my...son of satan."

"You got the description right, anyway. But I haven't seen Rule in a year."

"Sure, you two were inseparable, getting into devilish trouble. When you see him next, tell Rule that I pray his soul will see the light of the Almighty so he will give himself up to these righteous men," Reverend Cordell said in a singsongy whine as his eyes closed and his hands met in a prayerful stance. Taullery heard the major quietly tell the minister not to blame himself for his son's misdeeds.

"Rule doesn't need anything from you. Maybe it's your soul that needs the praying for," Taullery said through clinched teeth, trying hard to hold back his anger.

Reverend Cordell's face roared into a crimson glow, and he screamed, "You shall rue the day that you speak to a man of the cloth in this way. It is blasphemy! Blasphemy! 'Keep thy tongue from evil, and thy lips from speaking guile'—Psalm 34, verse 13."

"Reverend, if you're looking for evil, find a mirror—Taullery 1, verse 1."

Before the minister could respond, the sheriff observed, "Don't know many Rebs coming back with two horses and a pack full of goods. How you come by all that, mister?"

Taullery realized where this conversation could be headed and spoke in a slow, methodical tone. "Gentlemen, I've had a long ride from Virginia—where I fought in a long war. A war we lost. I'm home, and that's all I want to be. I rode into that war with two horses, and I'm riding back with two. You can look through that pack if you want—it's all my stuff." Both were a lie, but they wouldn't know, he had decided.

"I reckon you're carrying pardon papers," the sheriff continued, not choosing to follow up on the previous question.

"Right here. You want to see them?" Taullery said, and patted his left chest.

"No, I'll take your word for it, Reb."

Without another word, the three men walked on. Taullery watched them head down the planked sidewalk, letting himself calm down from the exchange. Happy noise inside the saloon caught his tired mind. Some sounds never change. They came like a gentle serenade to a man who had been alone too long. He swung down and wrapped the reins and the packhorse's lead rope in place around the reining bar.

Absentmindedly, he stroked the neck and withers of

the long-legged bay he'd been riding and mentally prepared to enter the saloon and shake off the encounter with the three sour men. Would Jessica be there? Would she run to him? Would she cry? His mind was absorbed with the pictures of their sweet reunion. How wonderful it would be to have such a beautiful thing fill his arms!

With a deep inhalation, he brushed off his uniform with several brisk swipes, then remembered the sack of gold coins he'd been keeping. He retrieved it from his saddlebags and shoved the sack inside his coat. After straightening his back, he yanked his coattails into place, pulled on the brim of his hat, and entered. The sun wasn't allowed to follow, except through the brief swing of the door. A tiny window did its best to bring the day inside through its opening, but shadow was ever victorious within. The smoke-laden room was filled with standing and sitting men, all cloaked in gray. Eight yellow holes from over-head lamps broke through the haze in a haphazard pattern.

"Hey, stranger, don't ya know the war's over? We whipped your sorry Rebel ass!"

The bellow came from a table of Union soldiers playing cards with a fat man in a three-piece suit. A trooper with a bulbous nose and wide sideburns was enjoying his friends' reaction to his brash welcome to the tall Confederate cavalryman. Most of the crowd turned to see what the shout meant. Through-out the room, Taullery noticed hints of former Confederate uniforms—faded butternut pants or an occasional kepi hat. No one was wearing what he wore, and none seemed inclined to acknowledge they once had. He felt heat at his collar, paused inside the doorway, and glanced over at the sol-diers' table.

"Strange, I didn't see you at any of the fighting. I take it you got the word from a newspaper," Taullery said. His voice rang across the room, triggering raucous laughter from every corner.

"What did you say?" The trooper stood, and nearly toppled the table in his cumbersome reaction to the Confederate's remark. Players grabbed for sliding chips, coins, ashtrays, bottles, and glasses.

"Sit down, Stafford. You asked for it," came the calming advice from the soldier seated next to him. The heavyset gambler was watching the Confederate cavalryman and not paying any attention to his table partner's eruption.

The bulbuous-nosed trooper swung his arms to remove the words of his friend and shouted, "Goddammit, Reb, you come back here. I'm gonna kick your ass."

Taullery's smile was tired. He didn't need this. "I thought you said the war was over, Yank."

"Sit down and play poker," another trooper advised, and shoved the cards toward the fat man. "It's your deal, Daryll. Let's get on with it."

The standing soldier looked around the room as if to seek support for his decision and saw no one was watching anymore. The tall Confederate shook his head in disgust and headed for the bar, ignoring the soldier's threat completely. His eyes roamed the gray for the woman who was waiting for him. With an exaggerated snort, the trooper sat back down and muttered, "I'll get that sonuvabitch later."

"Sure you will, Stafford. I'll open for a dollar."

At the bar, two men parted to let Taullery step in and the long-haired bartender asked for his order. Taullery reached inside his coat for the sack, opened it casually and tossed a coin on the flat, smooth surface, and replaced the leather bag.

"Whiskey. Leave the bottle. Say, there used to be a gal here, name of Jessica. Know where I can find her?"

The bartender picked up the coin and examined it closely, then handed him a bottle and a glass. He pursed his lips and answered, "Haven't seen her in, oh, two years, maybe. Last I heard, she and that farmer she married had moved south, down around the Rio Grande somewheres."

Taullery's face showed the impact of the news.

"Hard money's real scarce around here. If there's more where that came from, we got some fine girls out back—in the crib. Cheap, too," the bartender said, trying to soften the blow of his earlier comment.

"Yeah, thanks. Maybe later," Taullery answered softly, and looked at the filmy glass. "Say, let me have that a minute, will you?"

Without waiting for an answer, he reached for a dingy towel slung over the bartender's shoulder, wiped the glass vigorously, held it up toward the thick yellow light oozing from a wall lamp. He wiped it again, then returned the towel to the same position on the man's shoulder. The bartender was miffed at the action but said nothing and sauntered away. Before he could place Taullery's money into his cash drawer, a blue-uniformed officer at the bar motioned him over. The officer quietly asked to see the coin. After a quick glance, he squeezed it tightly in his fist, spun around, and walked briskly toward the door and outside.

Meanwhile, Taullery removed the cork from the bottle's lip and poured the amber liquid into the glass. He stared for a moment, mumbling to himself, and brought it to his nose for inspection. Satisfied, he swallowed the fiery whiskey. It burned his mouth and throat. He poured another and repeated the ceremony. Beside him, a lanky man with a reddish blaze of scarred skin on his right cheek watched Taullery with

187

interest. He wore a dirty coat, a stretched shirt, and a kepi hat that once had been part of a Confederate uniform. Unconsciously, the man touched the cap before he spoke.

"It's hell comin' home, ain't it?" he muttered with a guttural wheeze to his words. "If only Stonewall had made it at Chancellorsville. That woulda done it, by God."

Taullery nodded and poured himself another drink.

The stranger continued, "You know, you can't vote. Nossir. Them bluebellies over thar gonna keep any feller who fought fer the stars 'n' bars from votin'. Surprised you got any real money. Most o' us didn't have a cent comin' back."

Taullery ignored the probing statement, sipped his drink this time, and shoved the bottle in the direction of the jabbering man. With a "thank ye," the man poured himself a drink, softly said, "To the Cause," and swallowed the whiskey.

"Pardon my askin', mister, but ya are carryin' yur pardon papers, ain't ye?" Taullery's new drinking friend asked as an afterthought. Taullery mouthed "yes." The idea hurt too much to say it.

With no prompting from Taullery, the man launched into a litany about how Texans were a proud lot, used to being the winners, not the losers, how they had overcome Mexicans, Indians, weather, and everything else that got in their way. At least it was a voice. Taullery only half-listened to his tale of politicians raping the land with levies and taxes, taking cattle, horses, homes, farms, and ranches away from folks whenever they wanted and arresting them whenever they felt like it.

"Careful, Cyrus, somebody's gonna hear ya," came the admonition from a stockier man on the lanky drinker's left.

"I don't give a damn who hears me. I tell ya, them Northerners ain't gonna be happy 'til they shove us all into the ground."

"Be quiet, Cyrus. That whiskey's gonna git ya killed."

Cordell caught the friend's concerned look, nodded, and changed the subject. "Looks like the town has grown some since I was here last."

Liquor had sparked a pride driven deep within the man, and he continued, "You know, the only sons a bitches worth callin' themselves Texans is that bunch o' gunners. Ya know, Johnny Cat Carlson's bunch. Him 'n' Rule Cordell. Man, I hear tell you'd better walk wide o' Rule Cordell. He's just plain poison with a pistol. Hell, he'd rather shoot a Yankee than eat breakfast. Yessir."

Taullery's hand jumped at the sound of Cordell's name and whiskey spilled across the bar. The bartender came over and with an exaggerated motion swiped across it with the same towel. His sarcastic grin was caught midway when he remembered the tall Confederate seemed to have plenty of hard money. His expression turned into painted smile with raised eyebrows.

"Rule Cordell, you say?" Taullery managed to ask, hoping his voice showed only mild interest.

That was all the lanky man needed, and he launched, into a windy tale of how Carlson and Cordell had out-foxed the Regulators, punished Federal troops throughout the state, and run off carpetbaggers and Texas-bred turncoats.

His friend finally interrupted. "Stranger, to hear Stafford here tell it, you'd think those outlaws were ready to challenge Sheridan's entire army any day now."

"Well, by God, I think they—"

"What he didn't tell you is that the goddamn Union Army's offering four thousand dollars for either Johnny Cat or Rule Cordell dead or alive—and a thousand dollars for bringin' in any one of their gang."

"Hell, they'll never get those boys," spurted the lanky man.

"Don't be stupid—it's only a matter of time. They're running like dogs, with half the goddamn Union army a-chasin' them."

A hand touched Taullery's shoulder, and he turned toward it. The face was that of Howard Green, one of his school friends from before the War.

"Ian...Ian Taullery. It is you! I thought so when you came in, but I wasn't sure. You've changed...."

"And you haven't?! Damn, Howard, how are you?" Taullery spun around and shook the man's hand warmly.

The look on the man's face was the answer, but the words reinforced it.

"Not so good, Ian. Regulators done took our herd. Waitin' for us on the trail. Said we didn't deserve it. Shot my brother when he tried to stop 'em."

Taullery didn't know what to say; the man's face cracked into lines of agony, and he squeezed his eyes to keep back tears that wanted out. Taullery placed a hand on his shoulder and said simply, "I'm sorry, Howard."

From outside, a rush of blue uniforms filled the saloon. Moving with stiff purpose, seven Union soldiers moved directly toward Taullery. With six troopers at his side, a craggy-faced lieutenant pointed a pistol at him and announced, "You're under arrest. Hand over your weapons and raise your hands. Raise, 'em high, mister."

"What? What for? I've got my pardon papers. Here, let me—"

"Where did you get this?" The lieutenant raised his left fist and opened it to reveal Taullery's coin.

Taullery couldn't believe what he was hearing. He laughed and said, "Oh, so that's what this is all about." His mind was whirling. Should he tell them it came from a Yankee major's chest? Should he tell them he earned it? What would Rule do?

"My money came from Virginia, sir. For some horse training after the War."

"What kind of fool do you take me for, Reb?"

Taullery cocked his head, frowned, and said, "I'm telling you the truth, Lieutenant. What's wrong? I don't understand."

The Union officer snorted in reaction to his statement and replied, "Of course not. We've got an eyewitness that says you're part of the Johnny Cat Carlson-Rule Cordell gang. Now, hand over your weapons."

"Wait a minute, I'm not—"

He was a second too slow in seeing the lieutenant's pistol barrel, which slammed against the side of his head. Taullery crumpled to the floor.

"Haul him off, boys," the lieutenant ordered, holstering his pistol.

Pushing through the other soldiers was the sideburned trooper from the card table. He looked down at the unconscious Taullery and kicked him in the stomach.

"I knew this sonuvabitch was a goddamn outlaw. I knew it."

The lanky drunk grabbed the lieutenant's arm and said, "What fer? He done nuthin'." His friend grabbed the drunk to keep him from becoming the next target of arrest, but the drunk shook off the grasp and stared defiantly at the officer.

For an instant the lieutenant was going to arrest the

former Rebel as well, but he took a breath, lifted the man's hand from his arm, and answered loudly, "He's one of the Johnny Cat gang."

Outside the saloon, the soldiers carrying the unconscious Taullery passed Reverend Cordell, who said, "'Yea, verily I say unto you, the evil shall face their day.'" His leering smile made one young trooper shudder and look away.

Chapter Thirteen

Two days later, the guerrilla gang set a trap for a company of twenty-five blue-coated troopers en route to Fort Worth with a U.S. Army payroll wagon. Daryll had secured the information and the route earlier. He was becoming good at it. No one paid attention to a fat man who liked to play cards, and officers talked easily when poker and whiskey mixed.

From a mesa covered with scraggly pine, Cordell watched the approaching enclosed pay wagon with two drivers and a team of eight horses. Morning sun was struggling to take its rightful position in the gray sky. Federal cavalry rode alongside, armed with repeating rifles and Colt saddle pistols.

In place of his uniform, Cordell wore a black suit-coat and vest, tan pants, a blue shirt, and a wide-brimmed black hat. A fresh wild rose had replaced the Stuart stem, which he kept in his vest pocket. Gun-shaped holsters had replaced his flap-removed army issue for quicker access. The .44 Colts in them had the front of the trigger guards cut off for faster firing. Two additional short-barreled revolvers were carried in shoulder holsters strapped inside his coat. He no longer wore a bandolier of ammunition. One additional pistol was shoved into his belt at the buckle.

Only the cavalry long boots remained, along with his Comanche stone earring and the small medicine pouch around his neck. Johnny Cat had kidded him about wearing a rose in his lapel, but said nothing about the earring or the medicine pouch. No one else dared to make a comment about either. The wearing of a rose was seen as strange trademark, like Carlson's jaguar-skin clothes.

Cordell's field glasses caught the movement of Johnny Cat Carlson, Creed Bledsoe, and the one-eyed Roberts before they could actually be seen by the Yankees. To their right was Aleta; he would have known she was a woman without the glasses. She rode as a warrior without asking for any consideration as a woman. When she and Johnny Cat rode out for battle, they kissed from horseback. Cordell avoided watching; he told himself it was a private moment between the two lovers that should be honored. He knew it was actually seeing her kiss another man that caused his stomach to churn. Better to ignore the happening altogether.

Out from a long grove of trees they burst, yelling and firing. Johnny Cat was waving a Confederate flag tied to a long branch. Through the field glasses, Cordell thought the jaguar-skin-outfitted leader was singing "Dixie" at the top of his voice. He shook his head, amused at the man's style. Ten troopers immediately peeled away, like a piece of falling tree bark and took after them, firing as they rode. Cordell nodded. Just as they had planned.

Relaxed and confident, the rest of the Union men began talking again among themselves as they rode through the desolate country, little noting the stark rising edges of the cliff before them. Troopers eagerly exchanged tales of what they were going to do when they reached the fort and some semblance of civilization. Women and whiskey were the main topics.

They expected their comrades to rejoin them shortly, telling about the renegades not daring to stand and fight them, or reporting the annihilation of the foolish Rebels. Either way, the interruption was savored—an enjoyable break in the monotony of a long, hot, and very dull ride. No Rebel band or outlaw gang would dare to attack a force of this size, especially one armed with the best weapons the victorious North could provide.

Cordell's glasses caught one scout flanked a quarter mile to the front and west, to provide a warning system. He was certain the outrider hadn't discovered the ambush position. From the direction of the scout's head, it appeared he was watching the hillside where his comrades had disappeared in pursuit of the obnoxious renegades.

Wallace Harrelson was a few strides in front and below him, headed for a narrow break in the mesa's vertical ridge. In single file behind Harrelson came seven grim guerrillas, each carrying two sixteen-shot repeating .44 Henry carbines. He was leading them toward a lower sandstone ledge set like a balcony over the valley below. The handpicked sharpshooters would open up on the remaining guards as they passed below them, assuming they kept to the regular trail.

Cordell ordered, "Harrelson, make every man rub dust over his gun barrels. Sunlight off one would be enough to warn them. When they're right below us, I'll open the ball."

He lowered the glasses to his waist and continued, "Make sure everybody has a specific target. Once we open up, keep at 'em. Don't let them get set. As soon as Johnny Cat gets here, I'll leave with the boys below. We'll rush whatever you don't take out."

As an afterthought, he added, "Look for those ten troopers to come back in a hurry once the shooting starts. They'll be firing when they come. Got it?"

Harrelson responded by immediately walking down the line of the selected marksmen, repeating the orders. Cordell kept his glasses on the scout as the rifle team scooted on their butts down the hillside, one at a time, past a row of delicate cliff roses and into position. Even the small rocks kicked loose by the troopers' descent were beyond any discovery by the naked eye. Like a row of puppets on strings, each marksman kneeled into place and put his head down below the shallow rock wall.

Cordell would join them momentarily. His own Henry and a Sharps .56 carbine lay at his feet. Looking down, he saw another scrawny batch of cliff roses near him, took two long strides, leaned over, and plucked one. After the small blossom was securely in place on his lapel, he glanced at Harrelson's sharpshooters to reassure himself they were in position.

At the bottom of this side of the mesa, the remaining guerrillas held their waiting horses in growing shadows. Eight still wore remnants of their Confederate uniforms. He had no illusions about stopping all of the enemy without a closer assault. As soon as Johnny Cat returned from his diversion, the next move would be determined. The plan was to rush the remaining defenders, but they would be reinforced by what remained of the ten that rode after Johnny Cat and the others.

The former Confederate cavalryman tried to keep his mind focused on details of the ambush, but it kept wandering away to Aleta. He had never seen a woman as captivating as she was. Seeing her was like downing a bottle of whiskey in one gulp. He tried to get her out of his mind, and suddenly Ian Taullery appeared. It seemed like another lifetime when they were together. He wondered if Whisper was alive. What was Billy Ripton doing now? He glanced again at the waiting horsemen below and, for the first time, felt foolish to be there. The embarrassment passed through him, dragging the image of his father pointing a finger at him and laughing.

"Goddamn! Help! I'm slidin'!"

A startled curse jolted Cordell from his mental retreat. A full-bearded rifleman had slipped when a rock gave way and slid down the hillside until a V-shaped scrub bush caught his flailing descent. Only seconds passed, but it seemed like an eternity to the other riflemen. Every man froze and watched the approaching dust cloud—instead of their distressed comrade—daring not to breathe or whisper. Through his field glasses, Cordell immediately searched for signs that the Union company had seen the movement.

His urgent review noted no change. A flapping swallow-tailed company guidon was in syncopation with the squared regimental flag and swirling alkaline dust as the blue horsemen advanced. From below Cordell came the sounds of men struggling to help the shaken marksman back up the hillside.

"You all right, Yancey?" Cordell leaned forward and asked.

"Yeah, goddammit. Sorry, Captain. That damn rock jes' slipped out from under me. Didn't have a chance," Yancey responded, heavy breaths punctuating his excuse. Only two men called Cordell by his first name: Johnny Cat and Bledsoe. Everyone else called him "Captain," even the bulldog-faced Joe Lockhardt.

As the cavalry unit neared, the commander's white horse reflected the late afternoon's sun, appearing to glow like a large moving campfire. Behind the leader, rows of loping horses cut into the narrow throat of the arroyo. This was the worst time, Cordell thought, those moments before the battle. His mind raced to find any holes in his plan. Carlson's trio should be arriving at the base of the hill just after they opened fire on the Yankees.

Cordell inhaled deeply, kneeled, and exhaled slowly as he pulled the Sharps into position. His first shot would be directed at the company commander. Inside he was cold. The hammer of the heavy buffalo gun was a signal none of the guerrillas missed.

"Harrelson, I've got the commander. On the white horse," Cordell said without emotion.

Boom!

Thunder from the big-bored gun filled the silent valley a split second before the slug drove the Yankee leader from his horse. Terrified by the sudden removal, the glistening white animal bolted forward. Accurate rifle fire screamed from the hillside. Blue-coated targets crumpled. Horses reared and ran wildly, with empty stirrups flapping like strange wings. Dancing flags floated to the ground. Cordell laid down the smoking Sharps and began firing with his repeating rifle.

One wagon driver slumped in his seat while the other yelled for the team to run and slapped at the animals with his bullwhip. Three Union cavalrymen dismounted and returned fire from open prone positions. Five more raced ahead, seeking haven among the cavalrymen at the base of the mesa. Guerrilla fire smothered the area, making it impossible for the cavalrymen to shoot back without exposing themselves to sure death.

Over the farthest ridge came the dark shadows of the returning patrol, tattooed with bursts from their guns. Assessing the situation while in full gallop, they abandoned the trapped soldiers, changed direction, and headed for the lumbering paywagon. Cordell knew what had to be done; he couldn't wait for Johnny Cat to return. Maybe the three raiders had been shot.

"I'm going for the wagon!" he yelled over the deafening roar. Harrelson waved his hand without looking at him.

Cordell raced down the hill and swung onto his roan. The gentle Quick Miller was on foot, holding its reins. Cordell jammed his Henry into the saddle boot and told Miller to retrieve the big buffalo gun left on the ridge. Aleta's brother, Zetto, was already mounted on a black horse. Every man instantly swung into their saddles, except for Quick Miller and a new recruit, a young, uniformed ex-Rebel with a freckled face and red hair. The two would remain to hold the horses of the riflemen above.

"Come on!" he urged. "The wagon's getting away."

Joe Lockhardt growled, "By the blood of Dixie, we're with you, Captain. Let's take 'er!"

They cleared the mesa's north wall and spotted the wagon a hundred yards across the flattened prairie. The driver was standing and getting everything he could from the lathered team with his yelling and whipping. Eight mounted guards remained. Six riderless horses galloped with them.

Putting the reins in his teeth, Cordell drew both saddle revolvers and kicked the roan into a run. He didn't glance back to see if anyone was following. Closing the distance with the roan's great strides, he fired with both hands. Two Union guards spilled from their mounts as the others opened fire at the charging Rebel and the men behind him.

From the same place the Yankee outriders had come, three more silhouettes appeared. It was Johnny Cat, Bledsoe, and Aleta. Roberts's riderless horse was three strides behind them. Cordell tried not to stare at Aleta. Johnny Cat's shotgun was a distinctive roar above the other battle sounds. Suddenly caught in a cross fire, the remaining Union cavalrymen threw away their guns, reined their horses, and put their hands up as soon as the animals were under control. One of them yelled to the driver to stop the wagon; he looked around at the surrendering troopers, and Bledsoe shot him through the shoulder. The driver slumped down in the wagon seat and released the reins. With the lines flying, the wagon's horses exploded, but Cordell and Zetto finally brought them to a halt.

Cordell heard the crack of pistol fire and looked for its source. One of the Yankees slid from his saddle, his hands dropping from surrender to a feeble attempt to hold away the impact of the bullet.

Cordell yelled, "Those are prisoners of war, Bledsoe. Stop it."

Bledsoe's eyes were murderous when he looked at Cordell and said, "Who's gonna stop me?"

"That's a stupid way to die, Bledsoe," Cordell answered. "I won't tell you again."

Bledsoe raised his pistol toward Cordell and cocked the hammer of the Colt. Without hesitating, Cordell swung the roan toward the big man but made no attempt to arm himself.

"You trying to give me orders, Captun Cordell?" Beldsoe chanted. "I ain't one of your scared-ass soldier boys."

Cordell closed the distance between them to ten feet, then continued walking toward Bledsoe without saying a word.

With a cocked pistol in his fist, Johnny Cat yelled over at the angry Bledsoe, "Do what he says, Creed, or I'll shoot you myself."

Bledsoe's brow furrowed and released into itself through a snarling, "'Spirits and men: could none of them foresee...Not even thy wise father with his signs...And wonders, what has fall'n upon the realm?'"

The big man glanced at Carlson to make certain he got the subtle retort, then back at Cordell. His mouth showed surprise first. In Cordell's right hand was a cocked revolver aimed at Bledsoe's midsection. Turning his head to the side, Cordell said, "'Even a fool, when he holdeth his peace, is counted wise.'"

Bledsoe's brow furrowed again and he demanded, "What's that mean?"

"Damned if I know, Creed. Just something from the Bible. I was trying to match your recital," Cordell answered and smiled, but the black nose of his gun didn't move.

Tension-released laughter from the guerrilla raiders bounced off the mesa walls where gunsmoke and dust were settling. Aleta's throaty laugh hit Cordell's ears first. Bledsoe swallowed, returned the hammer to a setting position, and holstered the gun. Without another word, he headed for his horse, shoving a Yankee prisoner out of his way to retrieve the ground reins. Looking up, Bledsoe caught the attention of Joe Lockhardt tightly holding his left bloody shoulder with his other hand. The gruff outlaw was white-faced and fighting shock.

Glancing to make certain Cordell wasn't close,

Bledsoe mouthed, "I'm gonna stomp that son of a bitch into the ground." Lockhardt frowned and weakly shook his head.

Bledsoe laughed shrilly, but Lockhardt ignored him and growled proudly, "Well, this'll teach them Northern boys not to go a-celebratin' too soon. This hyar war ain't over yet." That took the rest of his energy, and he sat on the ground where he was.

From the back of the gang, someone yelled, "Long live Dixie!"

Johnny Cat grinned and repeated, "Long live Dixie!" and looked at Cordell.

Within Rule Cordell, there was a sudden sense of letdown. There was after every battle, he told himself. But this was different. This was a gurgling sense that what they were doing was meaningless. That this wasn't really war. He blinked his eyes, swallowed, and shook off the feeling. He knew they couldn't quit fighting, because no one else would stand against the North. No one else could.

Another Rebel screamed, "Long live Texas!" and it broke Cordell away from further self-inspection. He returned Johnny Cat Carlson's vibrant expression with what he hoped was a matching one and shouted, "Long live Texas! Long live Dixie!" Without his meaning to do so, his eyes sought Aleta on her sweat-covered horse. Her return glance was warm.

Johnny Cat shouted, "An' here's to the women of Texas! Worth dying for!" Laughing, he ran over to Aleta, and she leaned down from the saddle to kiss him.

With a wide smile on his face, Johnny Cat sauntered back to Cordell and said quietly, "Well, Captain Cordell, if you don't want to shoot these bastards, what do you want to do with them?"

The question hit Cordell hard. He had never thought about it before. In war, there was a place for prisoners.

Other soldiers took them away and he didn't have to worry about them anymore. He looked at the gathered Union soldiers with their arms held high; each wore a different expression, from fear to rage.

"I don't know, Johnny Cat. Let them go, I reckon. What do you think?"

"Before you made your play with Creed, I was going to have 'em shot. We sure as hell can't take them with us—and I don't want to fight them again down the road."

Cordell looked again at the surrendered troopers and back at Johnny Cat. Was the guerrilla leader kidding? No, he wasn't, Cordell realized.

"I won't let you kill them. That's murder," Cordell said firmly.

Johnny Cat's right scar-arched eyebrow rose even higher in response to his new friend's declaration. "You won't let me kill them? What does that mean, Rule?"

"Just what it says."

"You'd kill me over some damn bluebellies? I saved your life."

"Of course I wouldn't."

"Then what? If I order my men to shoot the Yankees, will you kill my men?"

Cordell hesitated and said, "No, I won't do that either. I just don't want you to murder these men, that's all. This battle is over. Let them go."

Johnny Cat lowered his eyes and put his hands on the handles of his holstered pistols. Suddenly he looked up at Cordell, and the face of the jaguar-skin-outfitted leader was hard with purpose."

"All right, you win. Take Quick and Lockhardt—an' anybody else that's shot up. Ride ahead to the camp. Daryll should be there, waiting. From town. Quick can start supper. Aleta will go with you too. She's good with bullet holes."

For the first time, Cordell noticed the gang's own casualties. A man in a butternut uniform was lying facedown near a tree. Near him was a dead horse. He saw the wounded Lockhardt sitting near his horse. The one-armed Caleb Truitt was propped against a tree; a black hole in his lower right leg oozed dark blood.

Cordell returned his gaze to Johnny Cat, smiled thinly, and asked, "What are you going to do?"

"I'll take the rest of the men and repack the payroll onto our horses. That'll take a while but I—"

"And the Yankees?"

"I'll let them go. But they'll be walking. Fair enough?"

"Fair enough," Cordell responded.

Minutes later, he rode out with Quick, Aleta, Lockhardt, and Truitt. The two wounded guerrilla fighters were white with shock and the loss of blood. After they cleared the second ridge, Aleta's horse eased alongside the right side of Cordell's roan. She straightened her back, thrusting her breasts against the hardpressed cloth of her blouse. He could smell a seductive scent of lilac and soap about her, and it went directly to his brain. Cordell glanced at her and nodded an awkward greeting.

Looking straight ahead at the prairie, she stated, "When I see you fight, Captain Rule, I see a great fire. *Si,* men run from the flames—and women seek the warmth. *El fuego.* The fire."

He could feel redness encircling his neck but said nothing.

She continued as if not expecting any response. "*Si,* the men trust you. Johnny Cat likes you. No man would challenge Bledsoe as you did. Not even Johnny Cat. You must be careful, Captain Rule. Bledsoe is a killer of men with his bare hands. I have seen it."

"Johnny Cat is a good man and a good friend," he

finally responded. "Bledsoe is a bully—and there's only one way to handle a bully. That's come right at him."

"Why are you here, Captain Rule?"

"I take orders just like—"

"No, I mean why do you ride with this gang of thieves?" Her eyes searched his face for an unspoken answer before he could respond.

"You already know why."

"*Sí*, I hear you say the words, but another reason lies there. The real reason, maybe so. I see this in your soul."

"My soul?"

"*Sí*. If one looks into the eyes, you can see the soul. *Bueno,* I believe this is so. You are carrying much sorrow inside, Captain Rule."

Cordell blushed and turned his face toward her. Her buckskin horse nipped at his roan, and she slapped it with the loose ends of her reins. He was impressed with the way she handled a horse. From the corners of his eyes, he examined her face and body. Being so close to her was making him tingle. He tried to study the land ahead as a means to clear his head. Heat waves danced weirdly on the distant plains. To his right was a hole that had once held water, but was now only hard earth cracked like a giant spider. Next to it was a second pond of sulfur, judging by its strong smell. A cow's skeleton supported that assessment.

"This is not for you, Captain Rule," she continued. "Johnny Cat is an outlaw. He was an outlaw before the war with the North. He was an outlaw during the war—and will always be an outlaw. He fights for Johnny Cat. Nothing else. No noble cause beats inside Johnny Cat like it does inside Captain Rule. We are all outlaws. The whole gang. Once, some were soldiers like you, but no more. The gold from today—and yesterday—will go into our pockets. You will see. Is this what you want, Captain Rule?"

Cordell stared at the widening prairie; he hadn't expected the Mexican woman's comments and wasn't sure how to react. After a moment, he declared, "Aleta, I came to fight for Texas. For the South. I will do what it takes. If that means becoming an outlaw, so be it."

Aleta glanced at him but did not respond. Ahead was a long draw that led to the camp. She pointed toward the familiar landmark without saying anything. The five riders eased down the rocky incline and rode in silence for a quarter mile through a flat basin, climbed over a ridge, and headed west. Cordell and Aleta continued riding side by side. A small calf wobbled across their trail in front of them.

Both Aleta and Cordell laughed at the unsteady animal's progress. He said, "Your momma's going to wonder where you are, bud. There, hear her? She's calling you, little fella. You turn around now."

They could hear a bawling cow coming through the brush and mesquite, searching for her baby. Aleta watched the Confederate cavalryman as he became concerned about the calf and its mother.

"He's over here, ma'am!" Cordell shouted. He reined his horse to keep the calf from following them. Aleta stopped, and the others did as well.

Quick Miller asked, "What are we stoppin' for? Are you lost, Captain? The country around here does look the same everywhere. The camp's straight ahead another two miles."

"Thanks, Quick. I'm just doing Mother a favor," Cordell replied, and reined his roan to cut off the precocious calf and head it back toward its mother, whose cries were growing more frantic.

Aleta watched him, smiling. Without dismounting,

Miller checked on the two wounded men. Lockhardt awoke long enough to ask for some tobacco, and Miller gave him a piece of chew. In minutes, the young animal had rejoined its mother at the ridge of the draw. Cordell took off his hat and bowed from the waist as the watchful cow accepted her offspring. The riders continued along the wide draw that kept them from being skylined.

Without being asked, she blurted, "My mother was white. A teacher. She taught me *bueno* English."

He nodded. "She did well. She must've been very beautiful too."

Her smile made him shout inside.

"Tell me about yourself, Captain Rule. I want to know more than the man with the guns," Aleta asked in a soft voice that made him forget about the others riding with them. In a few sentences, he recapped his life with his father, and his experiences with the dying Comanche shaman and in the Confederacy. He told her about leaving his friends and searching for a way to continue the fight against the North. He talked mostly about Ian Taullery.

"You miss your amigos terribly," Aleta said gently. "I can tell."

He frowned at her observation. Their horses bumped together and stayed side by side, her leg brushing against his. She switched the reins to her right hand and placed her left on his upper thigh for balance. Her fingers lightly squeezed his leg, staying there a moment longer than necessary before she removed it and switched the reins back.

"They gave up," Cordell responded, his mind more on her hand than on the conversation.

Chapter Fourteen

"I do not think you believe that, Captain Rule."

He glanced at her and tilted his head back and forth to relieve the tightness in his neck.

Without waiting for a further reply, she changed the subject. "What is the real reason you wear a rose on your coat, Captain Rule?"

They rode past a cluster of oak trees and heavy brush. A jackrabbit ran from cover as their horses walked past. A pistol jumped into Cordell's hand. His eyes followed the escaping rabbit and he shoved the weapon back into his belt.

"Guess I'm a little jumpy," he said, then explained about the rose. "General Stuart—Jeb Stuart—was my leader until he got killed. He liked to wear a rose in his lapel. I've worn one in his honor ever since... that day."

"Are you sure it is not for a woman that you wear

this, Captain Rule?" she asked. "An hombre such as you should have a fine woman waiting for him."

"No one waits for me. No woman. No family."

"But you said your father—"

"Forget my father," Cordell said with thunder in his voice, louder than he needed to speak. "Forget my father" echoed twice within the walls of the ravine.

He couldn't believe how easy it had become to talk with her. All of his reluctance was gone. He shared his sadness about Texas, the dog that had died on the battlefield because it wouldn't stay behind. He told about the fake defense he and his friends had created to stop a Union advance. She laughed out loud, and the ravine caught her laugh and repeated it. He studied her happy face and knew it was one of the prettiest sights he had ever seen. Suddenly, he became aware he was talking only about himself, and it made him feel foolish. How could he be so rude?

"How about you? Why are you here, Aleta?" he asked with a smile.

She told him about Union soldiers raiding her home along the border a few weeks before. Her brother Zetto was already with Johnny Cat. They killed her mother and father. They wanted her, but she hid until dark and escaped. She rode north and found her brother—and met Johnny Cat. A soft breeze meandered down the draw, sought her silky hair, and interrupted her explanation. Long strands danced across her face.

Pushing them back into place, Aleta resumed talking and ended with a strange promise: "Johnny Cat gives me warmth—and I, him—at a time when there is none in our lives. But he knows I will leave someday.

209

I want to marry a strong man who will give me *mucho* happy children and build me a strong home that will keep out the storms. This will not be with an hombre like Johnny Cat."

"Don't give up on John Carlson for that role," he answered without much emotion. "When the fury lets him loose, he will be that man, I would bet."

Remembering the others, she switched the reins again to her right hand and turned her head to seek Quick Miller's attention, leaning backward in the saddle toward Cordell.

"How are Caleb and Joe doing?" she asked Quick.

As she moved, her left hand took Cordell's hand resting at his side. Her fingers caressed his palm. His own fingers joined in the dance with hers. He was burning inside, trying to stay focused on their conversation, telling himself over and over that her hand was nothing more than her way of being friendly.

The little outlaw was proud to have Aleta ask for his opinion and stated authoritatively, "Caleb's tough. Gonna make it fine. Joe too." He looked over at Truitt, who rode with a permanent grimace, then at Lockhardt, who appeared to be sleeping in the saddle with the chew pushing out his cheek. After his assessment, he added, "I guess they're hurting bad, though."

Turning to the front again, Aleta looked straight ahead for a few strides and said, "Aleta is not a loose woman, Captain Rule. I do not hold a man's hand to pass the day." Their fingers were tingling each other's passion.

Cordell felt his face redden. He looked at her out of the corner of his eyes. Her playful gaze locked with his and he turned toward her to say something, when Quick Miller found his courage and kicked his horse next to Cordell on the side opposite of Aleta. Cordell's disappointment at being interrupted was evident. Aleta grinned, squeezed his hand, and released it. "*Muchos gracias,* my Captain Rule. We will talk more later."

Finally, Miller stuttered out what had been chewing on him since they left the arroyo. "You think anyone will care when we die? I mean, Joe was tellin' me about some village over in Ireland, I think it were...where a church bell done starts a-ringin' when someone dies—all by its lonesome. The bell jes' knows, I reckon. That's a nice way to be 'membered. Ain't it? You think that's true? You think anyone'll put one o' them nice marble stones with writin' on it over our graves? Will anyone come 'n' visit, ya think?"

Cordell didn't answer right away. He pulled a small bag of tobacco from his shirt pocket, rolled a cigarette, and lit it. Miller was afraid he had offended the mysterious Confederate leader. A wisp of smoke grazed Cordell's chiseled cheek. He fought to control the lust for Aleta that filled his body and drove itself into his manhood. Cordell wanted the little man to go away so he could return to Aleta. He wanted to tell her how he felt. Oh, how he wanted to tell her and touch her again!

"I heard tell that a man'll find his dawg a-waitin' fer him jes' outside o' heaven," Miller continued along the same thought, licking his lips nervously. "Ya know, when a dawg ya loved as a kid 'n' all, well, when he died, he done went to a fine place to wait— with all the other dawgs til ya git thar."

"That's a nice story, Quick. I hadn't heard that before," Cordell said, and looked away.

"C-Captain...I—I, ah, is we doin' the right thin'? I mean, are we r-really fightin' a war?"

211

"We thought so, Quick. Doesn't matter, it's too late—for me. An' Johnny. You could ride away, though. Maybe you should," Cordell answered, and inhaled the welcomed smoke.

"Wal, I reckoned, maybe, you could tell me what was true, Captain, you bein' so wise 'n' all. Will we ever git to have a family, like most folks? Will we jes' go on a-fightin'—ferever? Will we, huh?"

Cordell looked at Miller and said, "Well, you were wrong about that, Miller. I don't know the answers to a damn thing. I'm just a Confederate soldier who's stupid enough to think the South can still win. How smart is that?"

Aleta gave Cordell a look of disapproval and kicked her buckskin into a gallop toward a distant grove of trees. Miller commented, "Aleta's a nice lady, Captain. Don't judge her too hard. I don't think a lady should be ridin' with us either, fightin' and killin' 'n' all, but Aleta's gonna do what she wants—or what Johnny Cat wants, I reckon."

Cordell didn't answer. He was watching Aleta disappear within the dark shapes of the trees. Miller rambled on without encouragement from the Confederate cavalryman until they reached the campsite within a shallow canyon. A thick grove of cottonwoods held by its walls offered complete security from anyone riding past. A small spring offered water most of the year. Johnny Cat used it regularly as a hideout. Lookouts could spot incoming riders from five miles out.

By prearrangement, Jacobson Darryl waited for them in a compact surrey pulled by a black horse with one white foreleg. Smoke from a long, black cigar encircled his round, ruddy face. He greeted Aleta, the first to arrive, with an off-color remark

212

she pretended not to hear. Before the others rode in, she had curried her buckskin and hobbled it. At Cordell's order, a small, smokeless fire was built and soon a pot of coffee was laid on its glowing coals and another of hot water for cleaning the wounds. Aleta tended to Lockhardt and Truitt. Rule Cordell walked over to her and asked how it was going.

"Why do you care, Captain Rule?" she said, her dark eyes crackling with anger.

"W-what do you mean?" He was struck by her response, expecting soft words of encouragement.

"You know what I mean," Aleta stated, without looking up from the wounded men resting on saddle blankets. "You could have given poor Quick some peace, some comfort. He looks up to you. He wanted you to tell him it was going to be *bueno*—and you could not do so. You are selfish. Aleta was wrong about you. You are just a killer of men—and nothing else. Leave me alone. I do not want you near."

"How would I know if it's going to be all right? You want me to lie to him?"

"I thought you were a different hombre, Captain Rule." She stood and crossed her arms; tiny crow's-feet presented themselves around the corners of her eyes as she squinted in anger. "Go away! Adios!"

"Well, I guess you were wrong," he said. "I'm just one more man who has trouble thinking around you. Sorry. I'll try not to trouble you anymore." He stomped away.

Johnny Cat and the rest of the gang returned with a gaiety that seemed contrived to Cordell. The guerrilla leader passed around bottles of whiskey found in the payroll wagons. Aleta rushed to him and planted a long, passionate kiss on his lips.

"Aha, men! That is what we fight for! Let's cele-brate our victory—and ol' Darryl can tell us what's happening around 'n' about."

Something in Creed Bledsoe's cocky expression bothered Cordell, but he decided it was simply that he didn't like the big man. After every man had enjoyed the whiskey, Darryl briefed them on the activities in and around Waco, where he had been staying. The wide-bellied gambler was full of news and eager to share all of it, beginning with word that a Federal regiment of Negro soldiers had passed through a week back and clashed with the white townspeople. A burned building was blamed on the regiment but there was no proof. Some Northerner had won the election for mayor. Regulators turned away every white male who tried to vote, except three old men.

The gang grumbled as one man.

With his arm around Aleta, Johnny Cat took a swig from his whiskey bottle and demanded, "Forget all that crap, Darryl! What the hell is going on with that bunch of bluebellies stationed there? Are they staying around town—or are they headed our way?"

The fat gambler took out the cigar, looked at it, then returned it to his mouth. He puffed on the returned cigar and said, "We got trouble, Johnny Cat. Big trou-ble. They're sending out a company of Union regulars in one direction and a company of Regulators in another. Gonna make a big sweep—to git us trapped in the middle. Their orders are to wipe us out."

"They ain't gonna bother you none," Harrison blurted. "So what's with the 'we' crap?"

Daryll ignored the comment and continued. "Johnny Cat, I think you'd best be headin' south. Real quick-like. There was talk about them leaving soon-like. But I couldn't find out just when. I'd be betting on the day after tomorrow. Could be sooner, though. The blacksmith has been mighty busy gettin' all them Union hosses fancied up with new shoes. I reckon they'll light out as soon as the shoeing's finished."

Johnny Cat Carlson was silent; he blinked twice and looked at Cordell. "Well, preacher-man, what do you say? Do we run—or fight? Or do we fool 'em and go hit the bank in Dallas? Or should we start prayin'?"

Bledsoe laughed loudly. Too loudly. The other men chuckled nervously. One guerrilla with a Confederate uniform stepped away from Bledsoe just in case, but Cordell never looked at the big man.

Cordell pushed the brim of his hat back on his head and said, "You're the leader. It's your call. If you're asking for my advice, though, I'd take a good look around you. I count eight. Nine, with Darryl here. Two are hurt. You're up against an enemy with everything. Men. Money. Even the law. We've got to fight smart—or someone'll be prayin' over all of us."

Johnny Cat rubbed his unshaven cheek with his right hand, then pointed at the former Confederate captain and said, "You talk like a man who's giving up."

"If I decide to give up, Johnny Cat, I'll tell you right out. You won't have to guess. My thinking was about keeping the Cause alive. If robbing a bank in Dallas right now will help it, then let's ride. If making sure we can fight another day is better for Texas, let's do that instead."

For the first time, Cordell's eyes locked onto Johnny Cat's own penetrating stare. Creed Bledsoe stepped forward, making a point of easing his coat behind the handles of his holstered guns. All chatter snapped into silence. Even the trees seemed to hold their breath as the other men backed away. Jacobson Daryll's hands moved toward the carriage reins looped around the whip in its stand, then froze.

Stretched out on the ground, Joe Lockhart swallowed the tobacco he was chewing and started coughing. Lying next to him, Caleb Truitt searched with his single right hand for the pistol lying at his elbow. Daryll studied Cordell for an instant, looked down at the front of his buttoned vest, and wiped away a trail of cigar ashes.

"Hell, you're just yella, Cordell," Creed Bledsoe snapped. "Look at you, wearin' that stupid rose. You may fool the others. Johnny Cat too. But you can't fool me."

With a strange smile pasted on his face, Cordell turned toward Bledsoe. The brawler was poised to draw the guns in his trouser holsters; his arms were bent, and his fingers flickered inches from the handles.

"You can call me anything you want to, Bledsoe—but if you ever mention this rose around me again, I'll kill you," Cordell growled. "I wear it in honor of a man you wouldn't be worthy of cleaning up the crap from his horse. Do you understand?"

Bledsoe's cheeks drained, his thin eyebrows arched. Both fists clenched and reopened but stayed away from his guns. He tried to see what others might be doing. He was bothered by the style of this man who was smaller than he. Most men cowered at his bullying. Most men avoided arguments with him. He liked that. This Cordell didn't seem to understand who he was.

"I said 'Do you understand?' Answer me," Cordell repeated. A fury barely controlled flickered in his eyes.

Finally Bledose muttered, "I—I understand."

"Good," Cordell responded, and resumed the discussion. "As I was saying, it seems—"

Like the snap of a bullwhip, Bledsoe reached for a holstered pistol. As his hand settled around the butt, Cordell's Colt was staring at Bledsoe's nose ten feet away. The tree clearing grew small, no bigger than the dark hole at the barrel end of Cordell's gun.

"Bledsoe, you dumb fool!" spat Johnny Cat, his own hand lying against a jaguar-skin-holstered pistol at his hip. He looked around the gang, searching for a way to ease the tension.

"Say, Quick, how soon do we eat? I'm starved," Johnny eagerly asked as his gaze landed on the buffalo-coated outlaw working at the fire.

"Put it away, Rule," Johnny Cat advised. "Bledsoe gets his head up his ass sometimes. Let it go."

Quick Miller glanced at Cordell, hoping for a friendly response, but none came. Cordell was staring at Bledsoe, but he was aware of Johnny Cat out of his peripheral vision. Bledsoe's face was shattered yellow pastry as he moved his right hand slowly up and away from the untouched gun. Gingerly, both of his hands folded together as if he were about to pray. His eyes blinked twice and avoided Cordell's glare. The former Rebel captain holstered his gun. Joe Lockhardt's sigh of relief sounded like a rusty water handle.

Johnny Cat walked over to the nervous Quick Miller, who was rapidly laying strips of salt pork into a large frying pan. After filling it, the small outlaw took the iron handle with both hands, partly because of its weight but mostly to keep his nervousness from upsetting the pan, and placed it on the edge of the fire. As the meat began to sizzle, Miller stood over it and cut chunks of a raw potato, letting them drop into the pan. A handful of wild onions and Indian root lay near his boots to be added later. He glanced up at Johnny Cat and tried to smile. The fierce leader patted him on the back but was watching Cordell.

"Bledsoe, you just calm yourself down," Johnny Cat advised. "You aren't any match for our preacherman here. Get yourself a swig of bluebelly whiskey."

"Don't mind Bledsoe none," Yancey blurted. "He don't mean nuthin', Captain."

"Shut up!" Bledsoe snapped. "I'll decide what I mean."

Darryl glanced around the group, grunted under his breath, and announced that he should be getting back. But no one was listening. Cordell walked over to the fire and said something more to Johnny Cat. With his back to Creed Bledsoe, Cordell took a small tobacco sack and papers from his pocket and began to fix a smoke.

"I'm sorry, Rule. There's no account for me to say what I did. Ain't no man here that's fought harder'n you. I'm sorry," Johnny Cat apologized.

"That's all right. There's nothing easy about running when everything in you wants to fight," Cordell responded with a half-smile. "But all we've got is us. An' we've got to match being smart with being tough."

"Times like that make a man wonder, don't they?" Johnny Cat said, and put his hand on the Confederate cavalryman's shoulder. "You start wondering if you'll ever do anything normal again. Sleep next to a woman who's your own and not have to worry about running. You're hers and she's yours. You know, have a family. A small place of your own. Vote for a mayor, even. Go to church…"

Cordell looked over at the Rebel leader, removed the cigarette from his mouth, and caught the wild man's eyes.

"Not until today."

His voice was hard yet dull, like a man awakening from a deep sleep, like a man not caring what another man thought. Johnny Cat met his gaze for an instant and glanced at Aleta, who was checking the dressings of the wounded men.

"I'd like you to think about that bank in Dallas, though," Johnny Cat added, returning his attention to Cordell. "We could hit that rascal and be away before anybody knew what hit 'em."

"If we head south now, Johnny Cat, we could hit a bank down there just as easy. And be safer."

"Always the soldier, aren't you," Johnny Cat said with a smile. Relief rolled down his face.

"I thought you said I was a preacher."

"Aw, Rule, you know I was just kidding."

Cordell heard Bledsoe loudly proclaim, "'And the soul of the rose went into my blood...'" Cordell turned around and saw that the big man was standing ten feet away, motioning with his fists for Cordell to come toward him.

"Come on, Captain Yellow Belly. Let's see how tough you are with your fists, cavalryman. You got the guts to drop those irons?" Bledsoe snarled.

Johnny Cat's hand on Cordell's shoulder preceded his whispered words of caution: "Don't do it, Rule. I've seen him kill a man with his fists. He's just full of whiskey. Don't."

"I've got no quarrel with you, Bledsoe. Didn't you get enough fighting at the arroyo?"

"Hey, how about your precious Yankees, soldier boy? We shot 'em. Yeah, every damn one of them. They was on their knees sobbing, and we shot 'em," Bledsoe announced loudly.

Cordell's face was dark as he turned toward Johnny Cat.

His eyes widened, Johnny Cat said, "I...w-we couldn't just let them go, Rule. You know that."

Without another word, Cordell flipped the cigarette to the ground, tossed aside his hat, and unbuckled his gun belt. The ring of pistols dropped at his feet. He removed his jacket and the shoulder holsters in one motion.

Bledsoe sneered, "I'm going to take you apart, Cordell. I'm gonna piss on your sorry face. You'll wish you never saw this day."

Leering, the big man expected Cordell to answer him with some kind of banter as the Confederate captain stepped close with both hands at his sides. Instead, Cordell suddenly threw a powerful right blow that drove deep into Bledsoe's stomach. He was sawed in half by the unexpected attack, bending over desperately to remove the pain. A breath behind his opening strike, Cordell's second punch was a vicious uppercut to Bledsoe's jaw, catapulting him backward.

Inside, Cordell was cold and oblivious to anything except destroying the bigger man. Nothing mattered except this single act. He grabbed Bledsoe by his shirt, lifted him back to his feet, and slammed another punch into his torn stomach. Dazed but dangerous, Bledsoe swung wildly at him twice. Cordell slipped the first swing, but the second stung his left shoulder, making him lose his grip. Bledsoe ran at the off-balance Cordell, but he sidestepped the bull rush and hammered Bledsoe to the ground again with a wicked slam to the back of his head.

Bledsoe struggled to his feet and came at Cordell with fury and fear in his eyes. He had never fought a smaller man who knew how to handle himself with fists. He had always counted on his brute strength and the other man's intimidation to carry the day. He landed a wicked smash to Cordell's ribs and followed with a jab to his face that caught the cavalryman's chin and knocked him to the ground.

Cordell sprang back to his feet before Bledsoe could move in for further punishment. Both men stood toe to toe and exchanged heavy blows. Cordell felt nothing, saw nothing, only a need to destroy. Bledose's face turned into his father's. Cordell smashed Bledsoe's nose and split open his upper lip with a lightning-fast combination of punches. He followed with a savage strike that drove even more anguishing pain into Bledsoe's midsection.

The big man looked like a squeezed water sack. Cordell swung again for Bledsoe's head, but missed, and the big man caught Cordell's right eye with a thundering jab. Blood popped from the cut above it. Another Bledsoe blow to the stomach took Cordell's wind. Without a sign of reaction, Cordell threw a left cross, followed by a right jab that tore into Bledsoe's crimson face and dropped him to his knees. The brawler grabbed at Cordell's shirt to catch his balance as he fell. Buttons sprang free from the cloth.

Desperately, the brawler grabbed for Cordell's legs. Cordell's lifted knee slammed into Bledsoe's bloody face. Bledsoe's neck snapped backward and he crumpled to the ground. The fury within Cordell was not softened by the apparent defeat, and he yanked Bledsoe to his wobbly feet and shoved him against a tree. Holding him up with his left hand, Cordell hammered the senseless Bledsoe in the midsection with his right and drove into his raw meat face with a straight, snapping blow. The cracking of Bledsoe's nose was like a pistol shot.

"Stop, Rule, you're gonna kill him!" yelled Johnny Cat. "He's done, man. He's done. Let him go."

Realizing the state of his opponent for the first time, Cordell released Bledsoe. The limp body slid down the tree and fell facedown on the earth. Cordell staggered backward, heaving for air. His hands were cut and already swelling; blood ran down the side of his face from the cut above his eye. His body was heaving for air and his mind was whirling with fury and just beginning to register the pain of Bledsoe's blows. Johnny Cat stepped beside him and placed a hand on his shoulder. Cordell pushed it away.

"I want Bledsoe out of here as soon as he can ride. Tell him if I ever see him again, I'll kill him," Cordell said, staring down at the unmoving man. He paused, looked at Johnny Cat, and said, "And if you ever lie to me again, I'll shoot you where you stand."

Chapter Fifteen

Johnny Cat Carlson gulped and stepped back. The scarred eyebrow leaped upward. His face couldn't hide his new respect for Cordell. Standing off to the side, Aleta looked as if she had been hit in the face with a frying pan. Her face was pale and drawn. When Johnny Cat came over to comfort her, she turned and walked away. He laughed and looked for a bottle. It was Wallace Harrison who came to Cordell first.

"Captain, Bledsoe has been askin' for that for a long spell. Wish I was man 'nuff to do it myself," Harrison said. "Now, you'd better git them hands in some salt water. We're gonna need them workin' good." He smiled, and Cordell, breathing heavily, smiled thinly in return. The cavalryman touched the cut over his eye and winced.

"He got ya good thar, Captain, but you 'bout tore him apart. Never seed the like. Damn! That was some-thin'. Woulda paid good Yankee gold to see that, yessir. I woulda."

At the campfire, salt from a cloth sack was poured into a pot of hot water. Harrison asked for a rag, and Miller dipped one in the water and gave it to him, never taking his eyes off of the bloody Cordell.

"Ease your hands into h'yar, Captain," Miller said gently, lifting the pot with held gloves to keep the heat from his fingers. "It'll feel good. It's not too hot. Just right."

"I'll do this, Wallace," Aleta said. "You see about getting Bledsoe awake and away from here. You heard Captain Rule. Quick, finish with the supper. Put the pot down. Right here. *Sí.*"

Aleta took the wet rag from Harrison's hand before he had raised it to Cordell's face. Harrison nodded and walked away. Miller placed the pot where he was told and went back to cooking.

"Sit down, Captain Rule," she ordered. "No, right here. By this pot. *Sí.*"

Cordell stared at her for an instant, his mind barely removed from the fight, then obeyed and sat down. She took his right hand and placed it in the pot of hot water. He withdrew it instantly, recoiling from the heat. She looked up from the pot and smiled. Her gaze washed over him as she took his hand with both of hers and ran her fingers along his palm as she examined the skinned and bloody knuckles. Cocking her head slightly as if to obtain approval, she placed the hand again in the water. She took his other hand and repeated the process, letting it go slowly into the pot. With both of his hands soaking, she began to dab blood from Cordell's torn face.

"Your poor handsome face is hurt, Captain Rule," she said, wiping away the remains of the fight. "I am so sorry for my words earlier. *por favor,* please forgive me. I was wrong. You are the man that a woman should find and keep for herself."

He was breathing more normally now. He stared at her as she worked. Her face moved closer as she cleaned the slice above his eye. Her other hand held his chin. Her eyes touched his, and he shivered.

"Your shirt is ruined, Captain Rule. Let's take it off and I will get you another from your gear," she said, and immediately began moving her hands across his bare chest to push the torn cloth aside.

Chapter Sixteen

Under her breath, she said, "Oh, my Captain Rule, what am I going to do with you? You are like the sun. I must have your heat. Aleta was so worried. He could have killed you."

He swallowed, and it tasted like blood.

"Would it have mattered to you if he did? I would get beat up every day if it meant you would be this close," he said in a soft whisper, the words made thicker by his swelling lip.

She removed his shirt with a last tug and laid it beside them. Her fingers felt a reddened area on his mouth. He winced. Their eyes kissed and were magnets for their mouths. Less than an inch apart, Cordell and Aleta heard Johnny Cat's jovial advance.

"How is that preacher man doin', Aleta?" Johnny Cat hollered as he approached with a bottle in his hand. "Treat him nice, now. He's my friend. He is a goddamn warrior. Here, I brought him a bottle. A little whiskey will be good for him."

Aleta turned toward the leader and said, *"Sí,* Aleta will take good care of him."

"Where the hell did you learn to fight like that, Reb?" Johnny Cat said, and handed Cordell the bottle.

The tired cavalryman took a swig. The hot liquid burned his throat, but it tasted good and he drank again. When he handed the bottle back, Aleta grabbed it, drank a long swallow, and gave it to Johnny Cat. The fiery leader chuckled at Aleta's interception, patted Cordell on the shoulder, and walked over to the cooking fire. Aleta's brother, Zetto, was half a step behind Johnny Cat. He frowned at her, mouthed "Cuidado"—meaning "look out"—and turned away. Slowly she stood and went to the wagon where the men kept their extra gear and clothes. She returned with a dark red shirt, helped Cordell into it, and buttoned it for him. Her eyes moved back and forth from the buttons to his eyes. Finishing with the last button near his neck, she whispered, "I could do this for you every day, Captain Rule. You would like it."

On the other side of camp, the heavyset Darryl announced again, "I'd better be getting back to town."

Harrison blurted, "Seems to me you're mighty fond of stayin' in town—while we sleep in somebody's barn and eat cold beans. That ain't no Reb uniform you're sportin', ya know."

Again, the gang was tense. Miller glanced at Cordell. Aleta had rolled a cigarette for him and was lighting it. Her right hand cupped his face as she held the match.

Johnny Cat stepped forward before Darryl had a chance to respond and growled, "That's enough, Joe. Darryl's got a job to do. Just like the rest of us. He spends his days talking sweet to a bunch of Yankees and Yankee lovers. If they catch on to him, he'll hang before we know about it. Any one of you want the job? Just hold up your hand."

No one moved as Johnny Cat stared at each man. He stopped when he came to Cordell. Aleta was still wiping blood from his face with a rag.

Cordell grinned and said, "I don't think any of us could handle all that hot food—and whiskey—and good-smelling women—and fine clothes he has to put up with. Nossir, not for me."

Johnny Cat licked his lower lip, threw his head back, and roared in wild laughter. Everyone joined in, anxious to forget what had just happened.

As he reached for the carriage whip, Darryl paused and said, "Say, I almost forgot. The Yanks arrested some poor ranny yesterday in town. Said he was one of us. I never saw him before myself. This damn Taullery guy was wearing his Reb uniform just as sure as—"

"What did you say his name was?!" Cordell interrupted, and yanked the cigarette from his mouth. His face was dark; his eyes were black bullets aimed at the fat man. He took Aleta's hand from his face and headed toward the carriage.

Surprised by the reaction, Darryl hesitated before responding. "Uh, uh, Taullery. Leastwise, I think that's what it was. Been a lieutenant in the Confederate cavalry. Had some hard cash money. The Yanks said it was from a payroll we stole. Anyway, that's what the word was, going around town."

"Describe him," Cordell said.

"Well, let's see. Tall. Yellow hair. His uniform looked like he was just starting the war, not ending it. Handsome sort of fella, I suppose. Not like you boys," Darryl said and grinned at his closing remark.

Cordell didn't smile, so no one else did either. The

other gang members watched the strange man they called "Captain," wondering what this meant. Johnny Cat looked over at Aleta and rolled his eyes upward to signify the strangeness of Cordell's action, trying to spark a smile from her. She ignored his attempt and walked toward the string of horses.

"What's the matter, Rule?" Johnny Cat asked.

"That's a good friend of mine. Ian Taullery. Didn't know he was back in Texas. We fought together, rode with Stuart. He's from Waco. We grew up together."

Darryl curled his lower lip and said, "Word was, he had just rode in. The war in Virginia ended a long time ago."

"Anyone with him?" Cordell asked.

"Well, not that I know of."

"What have they done with him?" Cordell said, moving to the side of the carriage and putting both hands on the side railing.

"Best I know, he's in jail. They'll beat him until he tells them what he knows about us. Which ain't nothing. Then they'll hang him—or maybe they'll just shoot him in the back and say he was trying to escape. You know what they do."

Cordell took a deep breath and looked at Carlson. "Johnny Cat, this changes everything. I have to go into Waco."

The wildly dressed leader hesitated and said, "We'll go with you."

"Thanks, but this is my problem. Besides, it isn't a job for eight or nine guys. They'd see us coming and tear us apart. But one man might make it. You guys go on. I'll catch up later. I assume you're going to head for Houston and that rancher down there with the funny-looking barn."

"Naw, I want to take that bank. In Dallas. We'll head there first. Then we'll swing south."

Cordell was too agitated to argue. The fat gambler pulled the whip from its stand and cocked his arm to start the horses when a thought stopped him.

"Say, now I get it. Word was flyin' around about a preacher puttin' the finger on your friend. Didn't think much of it at the time, if you get my drift, but the preacher's name was Cordell too. Be that a relative?"

Cordell's face was strained. His teeth clinched as he answered, "Yeah, he's my father."

"I thought you said you didn't have any family 'round here?" Johnny Cat challenged.

"I don't."

"Damn," Harrison responded.

Cordell nodded in agreement.

Johnny Cat started to ask something but decided against it and ordered, "Let's eat and ride, boys. We're headin' for Dallas—and gold." He turned to Cordell, extended his hand, and the Confederate warrior took it in a warm handshake. Their eyes met with an understanding that they would never ride together again.

"It's been good riding with you, Rule," Johnny Cat said in little more than a whisper. "You've got a share of that payroll. An' the other, too. I'll get it for you."

Cordell said, "You keep it. Give it to the next family you come across that needs help. But I'll be back giving you trouble before you know it. Don't worry about me. You be careful."

"I won't try to talk you out of what you're going to do. He must be a helluva friend."

"He is. I should have never left him. We rode into this hell together; we should have left together. I'm going to tell him that."

"Well, pray for us, preacher man."

Cordell chuckled and said, "I'll do that. An' you keep these boys off the ridges and try to remember you're outnumbered."

The jaguar-skin-outfitted leader broke into a wide, toothy smile and said, 'Take one of the extra horses and some grub. Bullets if you need 'em. Think about taking some of that gold, Rule—it may come in handy."

"Thanks."

Without realizing it, Miller broke up the conversation by bringing two platefuls of hot food. Johnny Cat and Cordell accepted them gratefully and began eating where they stood. Johnny Cat watched Cordell slowly grip his swollen hand around a fork but said nothing.

Miller remained for a moment, watching them, and said quietly to Cordell, "For luck, I'm going to wear a rose—until you get back with us, Captain." His eyes were tentative, seeking approval from Cordell.

"I'd like that, Quick. Here, take mine," Cordell responded, held the tin plate and fork with his right hand, and pulled the tired rose from his coat lapel with his other. Miller accepted it as if he were receiving a trophy.

"I'll w-wear it with honor, Captain. For you—and for G-General Stuart."

"I know you will," Cordell said. "About that conversation we had coming in? I think all of us will be remembered, one way or the other. Oh, an' I think a man's dog will be waiting for him just outside of heaven."

"You do?"

"Yes, I do. You ride proud, now."

Johnny Cat ignored the exchange and sauntered over to where Harrison was cleaning up the beaten and groggy Bledsoe. Cordell finished his meal and said his good-byes to the rest of the men. He walked to the string of horses set up down by the farthest cluster of big trees. A soft ridge shielded the horses from direct sight from this direction. He was surprised to see his roan already saddled, the saddlebags filled. A bay with three white stockings stood beside his horse, also readied. It was Aleta's favorite horse. He stood, looking for the guerrilla who had prepared his departure, but saw no one.

"Well, thanks," he finally uttered loudly.

"*De nada,* you are welcome, my Captain."

Aleta walked from behind a wide-bellied cottonwood, looking as beautiful as the first time he had seen her. Her eyes were soft and hooded. She moved toward him without another word, but a tear escaped and ran down her cheek. She half stumbled and ran into his arms. They embraced. Their mouths raced for each other. Suddenly he stopped and pushed her gently away. He stared at her tear-laced face and said, "Aleta, I will never forget you."

"I am going with you. That's my horse."

"No, you can't. You must stay—with Johnny Cat. I'll be—"

"I want to be with you!" Her body was trembling.

Cordell held her tightly and said, "You'll be fine. Johnny Cat is a good man. You must keep him safe."

Aleta placed her fingers over his lips to silence him. She whispered, "I love you, Captain Rule."

Cordell's breath was torn from his lungs. He didn't think it would come back fast enough. He tried to speak but couldn't.

Her approach became one of logic. She said, "Besides, I can check out the situation in Waco a lot easier than you can. *Si,* you know this is true."

She kissed him as a punctuation mark to her assessment.

"No, Aleta. I want you with me more than anything I've ever wanted—but you can't go with me. Johnny Cat is my friend, and you are his woman. You must stay. That's the only way it can be."

He stopped before his words would have changed and he would have begged her to go with him. Holding Aleta away from him with both hands, he squeezed his eyes to hold back the emotion that was roaring through him.

"But, my darling Rule, they'll be waiting for you. They know he's your amigo. They will—"

"Those bluebellies haven't killed me yet. I'll get Ian loose before they even know I'm around. Then we'll hightail it for Billy Ripton's place. It's west of Dallas. He can hide there until they forget about him. I'll ride on."

"I won't ever see you again, my darling. I can't—"

"Oh, Aleta, don't you know how easy it would be to say 'yes' to you? So easy. I've loved you since the first time I saw you. Just being around you has made me realize the awful war is over. That all I want is a home, a family, a wife. All I want is to live."

"Then take me with you. You said it—you love me. I love you. That's all that matters, Rule."

"If you leave now, it will be the same as killing Johnny Cat. I can't that to him. He saved my life."

"What about my life? Our life together?"

"Aleta, please. You must stay. I know I'm right."

She tried to move closer, but his hands held her gently, but firmly, away. He heard her say, "Look into my eyes, my darling, and tell me that you have not dreamed of making love to me."

His mind was screaming for him to give in; his body was pulsing with the need to hold her tight.

"Of course I have. Every night. That's why you must go now. Please. Before I—"

"So it isn't enough to leave me—you have to steal my woman too!" The question was a lance into the couple's parting. Johnny Cat Carlson stood twenty feet away with a pistol in his hand pointed at Cordell.

Cordell took a step toward Johnny Cat, moving Aleta to the side. He removed his hands and spoke calmly. "I asked her to kiss me good-bye. I don't have anybody like her wondering if I'll come back—like you do. She was nice enough to oblige me. Don't read anything else into it, Johnny Cat."

"Didn't look to me like she needed any asking."

"Oh, come on, Johnny Cat. She's like a sister to every man here, including me. How could you think anything else? Remember when you told me that I wasn't being nice to her, that she thought I didn't like her? Now you're imagining love stories about us. Get serious, Johnny Cat," Cordell responded in a casual manner.

Johnny Cat's gun lowered; Cordell relaxed. Then his gun snapped back into its position, aimed at Cordell's stomach. Turning his head slightly to the side, Carlson growled, "How come her horse is saddled?"

"Oh, that. Hell, that's my fault," Cordell said with a chuckle. "I wasn't paying much attention when I threw up the leather. Not easy leaving friends, no matter the reason. Aleta's already told me in no uncertain terms that it was hers. You want to help me switch before she gets mad at me?"

Johnny Cat shook his head, grinned, and lowered the hammer of his Colt with his thumb. He reholstered the weapon and said, "I'm the fool, Rule Cordell. I should have known better. Forgive me. You are a good friend."

"It's Aleta you should ask for forgiveness, Johnny Cat, not me."

Johnny Cat stared at Aleta. Her face was washed in tears as she stood next to Cordell, unmoving. With her hands at her sides, she appeared to be a woman beaten by wind and rain. Her eyes met Johnny Cat's briefly, then looked away.

"I am sorry, Aleta. I really am," the flamboyant leader said. "I'm damn sad Rule's going, too. We all are. But he'll be back. He's got a friend to help—and…and then he'll be back. He'd be doin' the same thing if I were the one the bastards had. I know that. Sometimes I wish…"

Without finishing his sentence, he turned around and began walking back to the camp.

Cordell watched him and said, "Go with him, Aleta. Please—go now. It's the right thing to do. I know it."

She grasped his fingers in her right hand, placed her other hand on his chest, and looked into his face. In a voice that barely reached his ears, she said, "I want a memory of you, Captain Rule. I wish that was a night of love. I know this cannot be. Please—give me something. Then I will go, I promise. I will not make it harder on you. *Por favor.*"

Cordell hesitated for an instant, took off his hat, and removed the medicine pouch worn around his neck on a leather thong. He handed the tiny bag to her, then took off his stone earring and placed it in her hand as well.

"Here, these are the only possessions I have, other than guns and a horse. They kept me safe through the war. You keep them and I'll know you're safe too, wherever you are."

She guided the soft doeskin loop of the stone earring over her right ear, then held the medicine pouch with both hands and lowered it around her neck. The tiny bag disappeared between her breasts under her shirt.

Cordell smiled and said, "See how lucky it is? What a place to get to stay!"

She smiled weakly and touched the pouch beneath her shirt. Her eyes blinked twice before she kissed him lightly on the lips and whispered, "That is where you should be. I love you," then turned away. Cordell couldn't watch her leave, and he immediately began unsaddling the bay horse.

After switching to a line-back dun for his second horse, Cordell rode out, leading the second mount. He waved to his former comrades before clearing a ridge that separated them completely. Aleta was nowhere in sight. It was better this way, he thought. He knew this country well, and he eased the roan into a land-eating lope. Horses and rider passed four quiet farmhouses unseen as each family worked the land. The rope-led horse kept up the pace with no sign of fatigue.

His mind was a whirl of conflicting images: Aleta's proclamation of love; the foolishness of leaving her behind when he wanted to take her with him; the lightness of his decision to do so; his friend Ian Taullery being arrested by Union soldiers and his father being responsible for it. He tried to stay focused, but everything kept turning to her. Once, he reined in the big roan and decided he would go back. He shook his head to get the thought out of his mind and spurred the roan into a hard run toward Waco.

He galloped in and out of a mile-long string of trees lining a fat creek, passed a spongy swale of slick-wet grass, and slipped over three broken hills. A man-high, jutting pile of rocks next to a wind-bent, young tree was the prelude to a heavily wooded area, looming like a welcome sign. To his right were the remains of an old campfire. Out of habit, he reined in his big roan to listen and look back. The dun was blowing, so it was a good time to stop.

Comforting sounds of dusk were around him. An owl saluted as it flew across his path, searching for an early dinner. He was surprised to see an owl at this time of the day. It reminded him of the old shaman. He hadn't thought much about him for a long time. He touched his chest where the small medicine pouch should have been. He felt naked without it, but the connecting thought to Aleta made it good again. A cigarette would taste good, but he decided against it. Even a tiny spark could be seen by a man from a long way off. Dismounting, he wrapped the reins of the roan around a low branch of the sad tree, then untied the lead rope from his saddle horn and lashed it around another to hold the bridled dun. His hat became a container for canteen water which the horses gratefully accepted. After a swig from the canteen himself, he let the growing coolness dance across his face.

Above Cordell, a pale moon was fighting through the dying sky. The sight of the misty shape reminded him once more of the Comanche shaman who had befriended him before the War. He had been directed to come to the old man's lodge when the first sign of Mother Moon appeared. It was a moon just like this one, six years before. Without thinking about it, he felt again for the medicine pouch that was no longer there. His earring was missing too. He was uneasy. It felt as if someone or something was near him. Like heavy air. Yet not. He took a deep breath, deciding he was just tired, and the sensation became more of a push. In response, he spun around, knowing there was nothing near before he did it, but needing to challenge the feeling. He took another breath and suddenly fell to his knees. Had he been pushed? It seemed like it, but he wasn't certain. Inside, a ball of agony came hurtling upward toward his mouth.

Chapter Seventeen

His mind erupted with the sayings of the old Comanche shaman he had met six years before. His name was Moon. Cordell had dismissed his remarks as nothing more than the rambling conversation of a dying man. He had worn Moon's gifts of a stone earring and pouch until now, partly out of courtesy, partly because he liked the wild appearance it gave him, and partly from superstition.

He could smell again the shaman's lodge, tangy with sweetgrass smoke from a tiny fire in the center and the mixture of herbs kept for healing. The smell of death was there, too, and raced through his nostrils. He could see again an open bag crammed with buffalo tails, horns, bones, and horn-sucking tubes for curing illnesses. Feathers of the owl, Mother Moon's winged messenger, were stuck, like afterthoughts, in a black iron kettle. In a far corner was a fully beaded medicine pipe bag resting on a tripod covered with red cloth.

Lying on the ground next to it was a rattle, a small drum, and some dried herbs.

Cordell and Taullery had happened upon the small Comanche encampment on their way to join the War. Hunger had driven away their apprehension about riding into the village. The two young men were greeted with genuine hospitality, and Cordell had been summoned by the shaman to come to his lodge when Mother Moon was first seen in the sky.

After a suitable pipe ceremony, the old shaman had nodded with approval as the wisps of smoke were gathered into the arms of the silver moon peering through the slanted opening at the top of the tipi.

"Mother Moon watches over me tonight. She has done so for many moons. She has given me the power to see what most of the People cannot. It is my strength—and my curse. She told me of your coming."

He paused, drew again from the pipe, and watched the smoke rise before he continued. "You are to be a warrior in the *Taibos'* great battle about men with dark skins. Your road will be hard. It will be long and lonely. Men will follow you into battle but not know you. They will fear you and the death song from your iron sticks. It is so."

The old man had paused, and Cordell had thought he had died. His entire body wilted, and his head fell against his chest. The medicine pipe tumbled from his fingers. Just as Cordell reached for him, Moon straightened and said, "I have seen my next road. It is straight. The ancients are eager to have me join them. It is well, but I need your help."

Moon took a long deep breath, bringing a crackled cough that shook his entire body. When it stopped, he explained, "I am a worried old man. Mother Moon tells me the God of the *Taibos* has grown strong. I have already talked with the Comanche spirits, and they are satisfied with my coming. But my old ways may not be enough, and I have not met the *Taibo* God. He has chosen others to talk to. I would like to enter the other world with the power of your God at my side as well. Will you talk with this *Taibo* God—for me?"

He handed Cordell the medicine pipe. The young man hesitated, then drew on the pipe, imitating the shaman's presentation to the four winds, the earth, and the sky. As he smoked and gave tribute, he recited the Lord's Prayer, hoping he wouldn't forget any of the words. It was the only thing he could think of. His hands were clammy with tension.

"Aiee, Mother Moon says your talk is strong. Listen! She tells me you walked the black road when a small *tua*. The Voice tells me you are the son of a father who wraps the *Taibo* God around him but does not see this God. He is a cruel father, unworthy of your love. Ah, this is so."

Cordell was surprised that the strange old man knew something about him but guessed that Taullery had told him. Moon held up a trembling hand as if to hold off the young Texan's questions and said, "You must forgive him, your father. You must open your heart and let the pain flee from you. Not now. You are not ready, my son. You will know when it is time. You will quit running—from yourself—and be ready to let the *Taibo* God take you where he wants you to go. Moon will watch over you if the spirits are willing. And your God does not mind."

The shaman had handed Cordell a stone earring and a small pouch with a leather neck thong. "Here. These are for you. I have made them for you. The rock is a piece of Mother Moon to protect you. In this bundle is the medicine of the owl to guide you. It is well. I must go. The spirits are calling." Cordell had given the old shaman a Bible his mother had given to him; he had brought it along in his saddlebags. Moon had held it above him with both hands, letting moonlight embrace the book.

Cordell's memory released him, and he squeezed shut his eyes. He clasped his hands together so hard, his fingers ached. The prayer that followed was a wailing cry into the dusky air. The roan's ears perked up and the horse swung its head toward Cordell.

"God, forgive me. I have killed men. I have been driven by hate. I have hated my own father. I have stood against you. Please help me free my friend...."

Tears ran down his tanned cheeks and splattered on his gathered hands. His prayer rambled on, louder, then softer, repeating itself. He prayed for Taullery, for Aleta, for Billy Ripton, and for Johnny Cat Carlson. Finally he let go, lay down on the ground, and slept. An hour later, Cordell remounted. He couldn't remember feeling so clean and fresh—as if he had just had a warm, soothing bath.

Evening lay across Waco as he rode at the edge of town. He saw his father's church. Next to it was a small wood-framed house. Strings of smoke from nearby chimneys were caught in the darkening sky as if weaving the handful of first stars together. His boyhood home looked smaller than he remembered. So did the church. Candlelight and gas lamps glowed inside the stark place of worship, accented by singing. Sunday-evening vespers were nearly over, as he had assumed they would be. His father's heavy baritone led the gathered people inside. It was an unmistakable voice, slightly off-key but formidable.

His sweating horses were stopped beside a trio of tall cottonwoods leaning toward the church, as if listening to the music. Dismounting, he wrapped the reins of the roan around one low branch and the reins of the bay around another. Then he untied the lead rope from the dun's head and his saddle horn and recoiled it. He used his hat again to give the animals a drink from his canteen.

Cordell's back shivered as his mind took him where he didn't want to go, back to walking home with his mother and father after such a Sunday-evening service. He was seven. Reverend Cordell challenged his mother about smiling at a man, and he wanted to know why. His voice rose like an ax, accusing her of all manner of vile activities.

"Aaron Cordell, you are a foolish man," Rebecca Cordell chided with a warm smile. "Mister and Missus Decker held a supper in our honor a month ago. I was merely being polite and thanking him again." She continued, not noticing the reddening at the minister's white collar. "You hush, now. Young Rule doesn't need to hear such foolish things, my husband—nor do our neighbors."

The minister's response was a savage back-of-the-hand slap across her face. Dazed, she dropped to her knees, blood already draining from her mouth as the reddened force of the blow spread across her white face. Young Rule Cordell screamed, "Don't hit my mother!" and ran at his father, striking him hard at his knees and knocking his eyeglasses from his face. The minister cursed and swung his fist downward like a hammer at the back of his son's head.

The next thing Rule remembered was his mother wiping a cool cloth over his forehead as he lay in his bed. As his consciousness took hold, he saw his mother's own face, an agonizing quilt of purple and red swollen flesh. Her right eye was closed and swollen. He cried when he saw her, and she held him and whispered that it was going to be all right.

Cordell blinked away the daydream and realized it would no longer bother him. It was something he couldn't do anything about, and hadn't caused to happen.

"Amen," came the thundering voice of his father from inside the church. "Amen," answered the parishioners, and Cordell looked at the full moon above him and whispered, "Amen. Thanks, Moon. I ran from myself a long time, didn't I?"

The service was over. From the shadows, he watched the people leave and head to their homes. After he thought they had all left, Cordell walked to the window and peeked inside to make certain. Involuntarily, he shivered at the sight of his father counting the rewards from the collection plate and frowning. No one else was in the church. Rule Cordell slipped to the back door and entered quietly. Within seconds, he was standing fifteen feet from his father, who was now adding some numbers on a piece of paper but still frowning.

Sensing someone, Reverend Cordell glanced up and said, "The church is closed now. Come back Wednesday for our evening prayer service."

Rule Cordell didn't answer. Shadows wrapped his face. Intrigued, the minister stood slowly and repeated, "Perhaps you didn't hear me. I said the church was closed. Services are over for the evening. You are too late. Now, please go. I have many tasks that remain to be done as the Lord's good servant."

"I just need to borrow something, Reverend."

Reverend Cordell turned his head to the side and squinted into the shadows that surrounded him, uncertain of the message—or the messenger.

"My flock demands much of me. Please go. God bless you."

"Oh, this will be easy for you. I just need to borrow one of your robes and your glasses—so I can free Ian. Remember him? He's the one you put in jail for not doing anything, except being my friend."

His eyebrows arched in discovery, the minister snarled, "Aha! It's you, Rule. I thought it was. What has Satan in store for you this night? You and your evil buddy."

"It's good to see you, too, Father," Rule Cordell replied. "Do you still keep your robes in the closet over there?"

"My—what?"

"You heard me. Sit down and do your counting. I'll only be a minute." With a rage that rumbled through his fat frame, Reverend Cordell threw back the chair and stomped toward his son, yelling, "Get out of here, you son of Satan! You're nothing but the whelp of a sinful woman who will rot in hell!"

Rule Cordell flinched in spite of himself, but his voice was even and firm. "I said sit down and count your gold, Judas. You know Ian was completely innocent. He just rode in from the War! You also know my mother was an angel to stay around you as long as she did—or don't you look in a mirror occasionally?"

The statement brought the minister to a sudden stop. His half-smile was twitching at the uplifted corner of his mouth. He said coyly, "You wouldn't have the guts to do anything to me. I'm your father. This is a church."

"You're not certain about that, are you? Yesterday, you would have been smart not to bet on my caring whether you were my father no matter where you were. My view of a church came from my view of you. So it wouldn't be hard to figure this place is nothing but hate. I'm thankful a wise old man helped me see where I was blind. Took him six years, but he finally did it. I've forgiven you, Father. Your hate's not a part of me—anymore. I won't hurt you, but I won't let you hurt my friend, either."

Hesitantly at first, the elder Cordell returned to his

chair, sat, and crossed his arms. Cordell lashed him to it with his rope and used a kerchief to tie a gag around his mouth. He knotted the lariat's loose end to the sturdy leg of the front pew so his father couldn't waddle outside tied to the chair. Minutes later, Rule Cordell emerged from a cloak room wearing his father's robes, white collar and stiff-brimmed hat.

"Oh, if you know how to pray, I suggest you pray that I make it back here to let you loose—or that somebody cares enough to look for you before your Wednesday-night service," Rule Cordell said, reaching for the minister's eyeglasses. "I'll return these and the rest of this stuff, if I can."

Reverend Cordell shook his head back and forth wildly to avoid the removal of his glasses, until Rule's hand came to rest on the minister's shoulder. The former Confederate captain placed the spectacles on his own face and blinked at the blurriness. He pushed them farther down his nose so he could look over the frames.

"Good-bye, Father. I wish you a good life," Cordell said as as he paused at the back door. His father's eyes spat venom.

After tying the horses around the corner of the building next to the jail, Rule Cordell walked stiffly down the darkened street toward it, imitating what he remembered as his father's authoritative strut. Six Union soldiers were stationed outside the jail. He was counting on their not having had much exposure to his father's church or his father. They watched him approach out of boredom rather than attention to security. His black robe showed an ample stomach, thanks to a pillow from the church, which caused one soldier to comment, "It looks like Bible-thumpers eat mighty fine." Muffled laughter followed.

Cordell's flat-brimmed hat was pulled down over

his eyes, and he bellowed, "God bless you" as he passed them, holding a Bible chest-high with both hands. Their responses were a cacophony of "Evening, sir," "Thank you, Reverend," and "Bless you, sir." He stopped at the door of the jail and knocked with authority. Without glancing around, he waited for the tiny, barred identification space to open and a deputy's squinting eye to appear. The main window was boarded shut for the night. As it swung open, Cordell tilted his head downward to receive more help from the shadows. The deputy might be a little more religious than the troopers.

"Evening, my son," came the minister's confident greeting.

"Well, Preacher, what brings you here?" the thick-mustached deputy said through the door. His eye, staring through the opened space, blinked with surprise.

"I came to offer God's word to the Confederate soldier you are holding."

"Gosh, that's mighty fine o' you, Reverend," the deputy said, removing the bolt from the door and swinging it open. "I reckon that fella could use a little prayin' fer. He's gonna hang day after tomorrow."

Cordell stepped into the dimly lit office, closed the door behind him, and pushed the bolt back in place before the deputy thought about doing it. Cordell let his eyes adjust to the lamp-lit room. A rack of rifles was straight ahead on the wall. A single shotgun rested on the end position closest to them. To his right, a cluttered desk commanded most of the room. Four cells were visible in the back, with bars from the floor to the ceiling. Prisoners were in each confinement. He heard Taullery talking before he saw him in the far cell.

"Are you alone, my son?" Cordell asked, keeping his face away from a direct review by the deputy.

"Wal, yessuh, Reverend, I is."

"My, such a great responsibility."

"Wal, yessuh, I reckon it is," the deputy said with a smile at the compliment. "'Course, them trooper boys is ri't outside if need be. I kin handle myself, tho."

"Well, I suppose they have more soldiers on guard in the back."

"Naw. No need fer that. Shoot, thar be a whole company o' them boys across the street in the saloon. No offense, Reverend."

"None taken, my son. Before I go to see the prisoner, let me pray for your soul too, Deputy."

"Gosh, ya-all don't hafta do that. I mean, yur a busy man, Preacher."

"Shut your eyes and let us pray."

The deputy closed his eyes and bowed his head. When he reopened them after the short prayer, he was staring into Cordell's pistol with a small pillow from his father's bed tied around the barrel. It had been the extended stomach under his robe. His other hand held the Bible.

"B-b-but, I—I—I...Y-y you're not Rev—"

"No, I'm not. But I'll be praying over you again real soon if you make a sound. Don't worry about those bluebellies outside. This pillow will keep everything nice 'n' quiet if I have to blow your head against that wall. Even if they do hear, you won't know it. You'll be dead. Savvy?"

"Y-y-yes, P-P-Preache—"

"Ease your gun out and let it drop. Good. Now, get the key to Taullery's cell. Quick—or I'll do it without you."

The deputy looked down at his groin and groaned as he saw the widening wetness; he raised his head slowly and took a deep breath. He was now more worried about the stain than Cordell's threat.

"You won't tell no one, will ya?" he asked as he opened the desk drawer and removed a circle of keys. "'Bout this hyar, I mean." He nodded his head downward to indicate the wetness.

"It's our little secret."

"That's right kind o' you, Preach," the deputy said. "You're Rule Cordell, ain't ya?"

"No. He's dead."

"Oh. Yessuh. Wal, I'll show ya whar Taullery be. I reckon he'll be ri't smart glad to see ya. He's a talker, that Reb, if n I do say so myse'f."

As they approached the cell, Taullery rose from the cot and walked toward the front. His smile was full, even though his face carried the signs of a recent beating.

"What took you so long?" he said, grinning as the deputy unlocked and opened the barred door.

Cordell smiled, and they hugged.

"What's the plan?" Taullery asked.

"As soon as you get your fancy pistols, the deputy here is going to invite all those nice bluebellies to come inside."

"Hey, you look pretty good in that outfit," Taullery said.

The deputy showed Taullery where his two pistols were stored in the desk; the tall cavalryman moved stiffly in spite of trying not to show it. Taullery reloaded them and strapped on his gunbelt. Cordell laid the Bible on the desk, removed the pillow from his pistol, and tossed it there too. He took the shotgun from the rack and checked the loads. He picked up the deputy's gun, emptied the bullets, and shoved it in the nervous man's holster.

"Now, Ian, you get back in the cell and hide your guns. The deputy and I will invite the boys in to stop all the noise you're making."

"Oh, I got it. You figure I'm the one who likes to talk loud, is that it?"

"Perfect part for you, my friend."

"Be glad to oblige."

Taullery went to the cell and immediately started singing "Dixie" as loud as he could. Cordell shifted the shotgun to his left hand and pulled the pistol carried in his gunbelt under the minister's frock.

"Louder, Ian!"

"…are not forgotten. Look away, look away, Dixieland…"

With Cordell's pistol sticking in his back, the deputy opened the door and leaned around it. "Will ya boys mind comin' in hyar a minute? I got a goddamn Reb that won't shut up, no matter what I do. He's disturbing the rest o' the prisoners, yessuh. Me too, dammit all."

"Hell, yes!" "Where is that son of a bitch?" "It's my turn to go first." "Lemme at the bastard!"

Reaction to the request was eager. Cordell watched from behind the door as the six men rushed into the jail and were immediately directed by the deputy toward the cell. They wouldn't have needed the help, as Taullery was in full voice.

"…and I'll make my stand to live an' die in…"

"Make that 'die,' Johnny Reb. Give me the goddamn key, Deputy. We're gonna kick Dixie here all the way to hell," snarled the first soldier to reach Taullery's cell. A barrel-chested sergeant, he waved his fist impatiently in the lawman's direction.

The last trooper turned back to Cordell and said gently, "Reverend, you might want to go outside. You won't want to see th—" His sentence ended abruptly as Cordell swung the shotgun into full view. He held it one-handed. In his left hand appeared a revolver. The soldier froze, his eyes wide.

Inside his cell, Taullery said, "I'm sorry you don't

like my singing, Yank. Maybe you'll like these better." Two silver-plated Colts were swung from behind
him to point at the sergeant. The hammers cocking
reinforced the change in the situation.

"W-what the hell?" stammered the sergeant, and froze.

The third trooper from the cell started to raise his
uncocked rifle, but Cordell's words stopped him.

"That will be the last thing you ever do, soldier. Is it
your choice?"

Heads snapped backward to see Cordell holding a
shotgun with one hand and a pistol in the other. The
deputy stood to his right as close to the cell door as he
could. He kept looking down at his pants, and he
moved his folded hands in front of the wetness.

"Hey, Preacher, what the hell is this?"

"He ain't no preacher, Sergeant."

"What?"

Cordell smiled and said, "Drop your rifles and
unbuckle your gunbelts. Anything sudden and this
shotgun takes out you two closest to me. Oh, you
might survive a belly wound. I hear it's done. My
friend puts you away, Sarge. You other three, well,
you might have a chance. My friend will get one of
you, and maybe I'll get lucky and get one of you, too.
So which one of you will live…maybe?"

From the farthest cell came encouragement. "Shoot
all those bluebelly bastards!"

"If'n you fire them irons, the whole town'll be here
in a buckshot minute," the sergeant said.

"A shame you won't be here to know if that's true,
isn't it?" Cordell said. "I figure they'll just think it's
Sunday night and somebody's been drinking too
much, But you could be right. Dying's a mean price to
pay for the show, though."

Rifles and pistol belts thudded against the floor.
Taullery and Cordell ordered the Union soldiers into the

empty cell, along with the deputy, and locked it. As they headed for the front door, Cordell laid the shotgun on the desk, grabbed the Bible, and tossed the set of keys to a prisoner, who grabbed them and shouted gleefully, "Long live Dixie!"

"Where are we headed, Rule?" Taullery said.

"Down the street—to the left. In the alley. Second building. Our horses are waiting. But we've got to swing by the church before heading north. I tied up the reverend and took these things. Said I'd bring them back and let him loose."

"You think of everything, don't you?"

"No, that's your department, Ian."

"How is your father?"

"The same as always. You have to feel sorry for him. He's a pitiful creature."

Taullery glanced at his friend. It was the first time he had heard Cordell speak in such a way about his father. They stepped onto the planked sidewalk and saw dark shapes moving toward them from the south end of town. A bullet exploded against the jail door; a second ripped a chunk from the support post. One shot clipped a plank where they stood and ricocheted, whining into the still night air. Across the street, a terrified horse snapped its reins from the hitching rack and bolted down the street.

"There they are! Kill those devils!"

Cordell knew it was his father's voice above the noise. Someone must have come back to the church.

Chapter Eighteen

Cordell fired twice toward the sky, hoping to scare the mob into retreating. A few hesitated, but the rest spread out and ran toward them. He thought most of them were Regulators, but he wasn't certain.

"Spread out! Shoot to kill! It's Rule Cordell!"

Cordell and Taullery dove to the sidewalk and began returning fire. The Bible fell from Cordell's left hand as he thumbed back the hammer of the gun in his right fist. He saw the dark figure of his father urging others on, but he couldn't bring himself to shoot at him. He winged the man standing next to the minister. Taullery downed two more, and the mob lost its confidence and spread like water to find shelter.

A bullet ripped across the top of Cordell's right arm, leaving a crimson trail on the sleeve of his father's frock coat. He yanked off the eyeglasses to get them out of his way and fired twice at a darting shadow in the alley across the street. The shadow stopped, jerked oddly, and disappeared. A shot searched for Taullery's head, singing its misdirected way into the night.

"If we stay here, we die," Cordell said, and fired in the direction of an orange flame. He rolled over on his stomach, shoved the empty pistol into his belt, and pulled the Colts from his holsters. He crawled behind a post that had once held a wooden railing in front of the jail. Another train of bullets cut at the post, his sole protection from the scattered mob. Wood slivers scattered onto his back. He fired at another fleeing shadow, stopping it in midflight. The man tumbled onto the raised sidewalk in front of the silent saloon across the street.

"Was this in your plan?" Taullery asked, firing with both pistols.

"Had in my mind a little quieter exit."

A solitary shot searched for Taullery's head. Only a fleeting orange flame told him of the source. He fired in its direction, and a scream followed. Another shot drove into his lower leg with sickening impact. The sidewalk under his leg ran red. Taullery took a deep breath to calm himself. The pain was excruciating, yanking away what breath he had.

"Let's try to get inside the jail. There are rifles and ammunition in there," Cordell said.

"There's no back door."

"Got a better idea?"

"No, let's do it."

"Can you walk?"

"Probably not, but I can crawl. You go first. I'll cover you, then you can return the favor," Taullery said through clinched teeth.

Suddenly a horseman appeared from an alley two buildings south of the jail. The rider was loping toward them and leading two horses. From the mob came cries of discovery.

"Hey, it's a woman!" "Don't shoot, it's a woman!" "Get out of the way, lady!" "She's bringing them hosses! Shoot her!" "She's a Mex, shoot!" "I ain't shootin' no woman."

Cordell glanced at the advancing rider and realized who it was. Aleta! She was leading his roan and the dun for Taullery.

"What the hell is that woman doing?" Taullery asked.

"That lady is coming to help us. Her name is Aleta. Let's go."

"Aleta? Sounds like you've been busy doing something else besides fighting Yanks," Taullery said with a forced grin.

She rode along the sidewalk, reined the horses to a quick stop, and smiled at Cordell. Her eyes sought only his. "My Captain, please hurry. Don't be mad at me—I couldn't stay away from you."

"I love you, Aleta."

"I love you, my Captain. *Vamos!*"

"Can you make it, Ian?"

"Yeah. If you two lovers don't mind, let's get out of here." He crawled forward, coiled his body into a tight knot, and sprang upward as best he could on one leg and into the saddle.

Scattered bullets continued to challenge their flight, but the shooting was definitely diminishing. Another bullet nicked the door frame and a flying chunk of wood cut Cordell's cheek. He saw the Bible lying on the sidewalk; leaned over to pick it up, and moved toward his roan. Moonlight caught his presence full-on, highlighting the Bible and his white collar.

From somewhere across the street came a startled exclamation. "My God! That's not Rule Cordell, that's a preacher! Stop shooting, boys, something's wrong here. That's a preacher! Stop!"

Right behind the first discovery came another. "That thar's one o' our own soldier boys, too. I ain't shootin' at none o' our own. An' I blast the first o' you goddamn Regulators that tries it hisse'f."

Cordell swung into the saddle, raised the Bible toward the blackened south end of the street, and yelled, "Bless you, my sons!" The gunfire stopped.

"You crazy fools, that's no man of God. Give me a gun—I'll stop them myself!" Reverend Cordell screamed.

Cordell clicked his big horse into a full run, galloping straight for the north end of town. Taullery and Aleta were already running ahead of him.

Rifle shots rang through the night, and Cordell's body snapped in response to the bullet that drove through him. He grabbed for the saddle horn to keep from falling off as the impact shook him. He tried to say something but couldn't. They raced for the safety of the open land ahead. His strength was leaving him fast. Shock was eating into his grit, but he leaned forward and took hold of the big roan's mane with his other hand to keep his balance.

As they neared the bridge that crossed the Brazos River, Taullery turned toward Aleta to thank her and saw Cordell. "Damn, his own father shot him. The son of a bitch!"

Aleta screamed, "We've got to stop. Oh, please God, no…"

"No, Aleta, we can't. Not yet. Can you hold on, Rule? How bad is it?"

The blood-covered minister's frock served as an answer to the second question; the first was answered by Cordell waving his hand to continue. Taullery glanced behind him but could see only shadows moving in the street. He saw no gunshots.

"Hang on, Rule, it's just a little farther," he yelled.

The town was disappearing from their sight as they crossed the bridge.

On the other side, Taullery reined his horse, grabbed the reins of Cordell's roan, and brought the big animal to a halt. Aleta finally brought her agitated horse under control. She jumped down and ran to see how badly hurt Cordell was, pulling her horse behind her.

Taullery listened. No one was following. This side of the bridge was a different world. Still and quiet. In the distance, another world raged on. Swirling gray shapes of men. Shouting rose and came again in softer echo. But they were safe for now. At least for a while. No horsemen were headed their way, he was certain of it. Lightning flashed in the far distance, dancing closer by the minute. He saw the coming rain before he felt it. Thick drops splattered dents in the Texas earth.

A lightning flash lit up the town far behind them. He saw what had to be Reverend Cordell standing alone in the middle of the street. Anger driving through him, Taullery grabbed the carbine in the saddle sheath and started to pull it free. His eyes were locked onto the shadow of the evil man. It was too far for the rifle, but it didn't matter. He just wanted to shoot at the bastard.

Out of the corner of his eye, he saw Cordell lift his head. The wounded Rebel said, "No, Ian. N-no." His head lay against the roan's neck as Aleta reached him.

Taullery's deep breath preceded his release of the gun. He tried to focus on what they needed to do next. A posse could be forming; he couldn't assume it wasn't. Moonlight had been whisked away by the coming storm. He didn't dare get Cordell down from his horse to care for his wound. They might not be able to get him back into the saddle quickly if riders came. He looked up at the sky and let the rain massage his face. Silently, he said a thank-you, for it would wash away their tracks. For now they needed distance. How well could Cordell ride? Taullery watched Aleta push a tiny pouch inside Cordell's blood-soaked tunic. Her worried face was all the description Taullery needed.

"Aleta, I'm Ian Taullery. How bad is it?"

"*Sí* I know who you are. Rule talks about you *mucho*," she said, looking up from her attempt to stop the bleeding. "The bullet went through his left shoulder. He has lost much blood. Captain Rule is a tough man. He will live—to have our children."

"Is he still bleeding? We can't get him down yet. Do you understand we must keep going?"

She looked at her bloody hands as she withdrew them from Cordell's tunic. Her eyes were wet. "How could a father shoot his own son, Taullery? I do not understand."

Taullery looked at her; his shoulders rose and fell as he searched for the right words. There weren't any. "I don't know. Someday I'll get a chance to square things—even if Rule won't. I swear it."

Aleta kissed Cordell's hand and saw where another bullet had creased his arm.

"We'll head for our friend's ranch. Billy Ripton's," Taullery said, his eyes studying the town again. Reverend Cordell was gone. "We'll be safe there."

Cordell raised his head halfway. "I-I-Ian, tie my hands to t-t-the saddle. I'll be all right. A-Aleta, where are you?"

"I am right here, my Captain Rule, where I will always be." She kissed his hand again.

Lightning crashed on the neck of a long slope far ahead of them, turning the uppermost ridge golden for a heartbeat. The yellow halo exposed the three riders before the loud crack of its violence was heard. Then everything returned to darkness. Taullery took the hands of the nearly unconscious Cordell and tied them to his saddle horn with a rolled-up handkerchief. All night sounds were destroyed by the storm's roaring song. The only thing Taullery could see ahead of them was a thick wall of rain, but moving was safer than staying. The badly wounded Cordell stirred as he finished the tying.

"W-w-where are w-we? R-r-river?" Cordell stammered, disoriented, his eyelids fluttering. He didn't attempt to move his hands or appear to know they were lashed.

"Across it. We're safe for now. It's just raining hard, my friend," Taullery reassured him. "But we've got to keep moving or they'll catch up with us. After the rain. We can make it to Billy Rip's and we'll be safe there."

The wounded man took a shallow, uneven breath, fighting for the air that was held captive by the pounding rain. He was silent, as if searching for something in his mind, then he spoke with a burst of fearful energy.

"I lost the Bible."

"That's all right, Rule."

"It's my father's bullet, isn't it?"

"Yeah, the son of—"

"Promise me you won't do anything about it."

"Rule, somebody ought to—"

"Promise me, Ian."

"I promise."

Midday sun was hot on their shoulders as Ian Taullery, Aleta, and an unconscious Rule Cordell rode slowly toward the Ripton ranch house. Strings of smoke from the chimmey were caught in the blue sky that had emptied itself of rain all night. Taullery rolled his tongue across his lips; whoever was inside would have seen them by now. Wouldn't Billy Rip recognize him? What if the posse had outridden them during the night and were waiting? No. No one knew of their friendship, especially not Reverend Cordell.

Mentally, he rehearsed his actions if a shot was fired or if he spotted someone about to shoot. Everything in him wanted to grab his rifle now and hold it. But that might bring on shooting, if the house was occupied by their enemies. He tried to bend his injured leg, but it was too stiff to move. He looked down at the dark-stained pantleg and grimaced. Pulling lightly on the reins, he made his horse walk slowly toward the quiet structure. His eyes searched the house for movement or the glimmer of gunmetal. Where was everybody? A trickle of sweat skidded down his tanned face, and he looked at Aleta. She was oblivious to his concern, watching Cordell, who lay across his saddle. Should he tell her of his concern? Yes.

He took off his hat and held it in front of his face. He ran his hand through his hair to appear casual. "Aleta, something doesn't look right. They should be coming outside to greet us. If shooting starts, grab Cordell's reins and get out of here. I'll follow."

Aleta nodded her understanding as he replaced his hat and yelled toward the silent homestead, "Hello the house! Billy Rip, it's me, Ian Taullery. Rule Cordell and his lady friend, Aleta, are with me!" She looked up and smiled at his description.

The front door flew open and Billy Ripton stepped onto the porch. He was bareheaded. In his crossed arms was a rifle. "Hot damn if it ain't! Come on in, you old Johnny Reb. We'uns couldn't augur who ya be at first. Been a mite jumpy since a company of bluebellies done rode through hyar this mornin'."

"Troops? This morning?" Taullery was instantly fearful. How could they have gotten in front?

"Yeah, they was a-comin' back from a big fight. All

full o' stories and feelin' proud as punch. I reckon that's whar yo-all been."

"Where'd they go?" Taullery said, and dismounted. Pain shot through his wounded leg as soon as he put weight on it. He hopped to the other foot and let his stiffened right leg barely touch the ground. Somewhat settled, he took the reins of Aleta's horse and Cordell's.

"They was headed for Waco, they done said," Billy Ripton said.

Taullery shivered when he realized the Union company had passed them in the morning.

"Say, did yo-all say that thar was Captun Cordell with ya? Hell, I knew them Yanks was full o' it. They done tolt us they shot up the whole Johnny Cat gang a-headin' for Dallas late yesterday, it were. Kilt 'em all, yessuh, that's what they said, weren't it, Paw?"

The elder Ripton joined his son on the porch, lifting his hand to shield the sun from his sunburned face. A double-barreled shotgun was in his other hand at his side. He smiled broadly, and Taullery could see the resemblance between father and son.

"Wal, son, whar's yur manners? Tell these folks to git theirselves down 'n' come inside. Maw's afixin' dinner, an' she'll be ri't happy to have Billy's friends join us. Hell, that's all he talks 'bout is you, Ian—'n' that thar Rule Cordell. A real bad man, I hear tell. Sur did have them Northern boys a-hot-footin' this way 'n' that. Him 'n' that Johnny Cat Carlson. Hear tell he was as wild as they git. Yessuh. Had us a few more like them two, an' thar ain't no way the North'd won. No suh."

"The soldiers said they killed Rule?" Taullery asked.

"Yessuh, gave us a real talkin' about it. Real proud they was. Said he was a-wearin' a rose on his lapel jes' like always," Billy Ripton answered. "Didn't they, Paw?"

"Yessuh, that be the short o' it. But yah-all got away, huh?"

Under her breath, Aleta murmured, "Oh, poor Quick. Poor Johnny Cat." She crossed herself.

"No. We came from town. Waco," Taullery said. "The Yanks there arrested me—for being a Reb. Rule came and busted me out before they could hang me. Aleta, here, came and saved us both."

Taullery looked at Aleta and smiled. "Looks to me like you and Rule have a new start on life, little lady. They think he's dead. Reckon they'll forget about me, too, if I just stay out of their way for a while."

Dismounting, Aleta ran over to Cordell, who was struggling to come awake. He saw Billy Ripton running toward him, then Taullery smiling at him, and finally his eyes discovered Aleta as she hurried toward him. He grinned at her and tried to get down from his horse, forgetting about his tied hands. His legs gave way, and he fell into her arms with his hands awkwardly held in place.

"Grab him, Billy Rip," Taullery said. "He took a shot…when we escaped."

"I have him. Did you hear that, my Captain? The bluebellies think you are dead," she said, holding him steady and kissing him over and over. He tried to reach for her, but his whitened hands wouldn't budge. "We can go anywhere. Anywhere!"

Trying not to get in the way, Billy Ripton untied the handkerchief and Cordell's shaking hands immediately sought her face. Neither Aleta nor Cordell seemed aware of him at all. Cordell tried to stand on his own, nearly collapsed, and stepped back to regain his balance. He was pale but smiling. Aleta tried not to look at the dried blood covering his clothes.

"Does that mean we can get married?" Cordell's arms wrapped around her. She was surprised he had heard anything.

"Oh, you heard, my Captain Rule. *Sí,* my love. *Sí.*"

"Then we'll start a small church somewhere in a pretty valley. What do you think?"

"I think it's time we got a look at that bullet hole, Rule," Taullery said. "Give me a hand, will you, Billy Rip? This preacher's got wobbly legs."

"Hey, Captun Cordell, I done tolt the folks 'bout yur teachin' me how to pray 'n' all. Maw'll be ri't smart happy to have ya do it o'ver dinner. Yes suh, she will, won't she, Paw?"

"Wal, I reckon we'd better do sum prayin' for Texas," the elder Ripton said.

Taullery looked at Cordell and smiled. Rule Cordell nodded, closed his eyes for an instant, and added, "Yeah, let's do. An old friend told me Texas would be waiting for me."

Made in the USA
Lexington, KY
21 June 2019